THE COMPLETE CASES
OF CARTER COLE

THE COMPLETE CASES OF

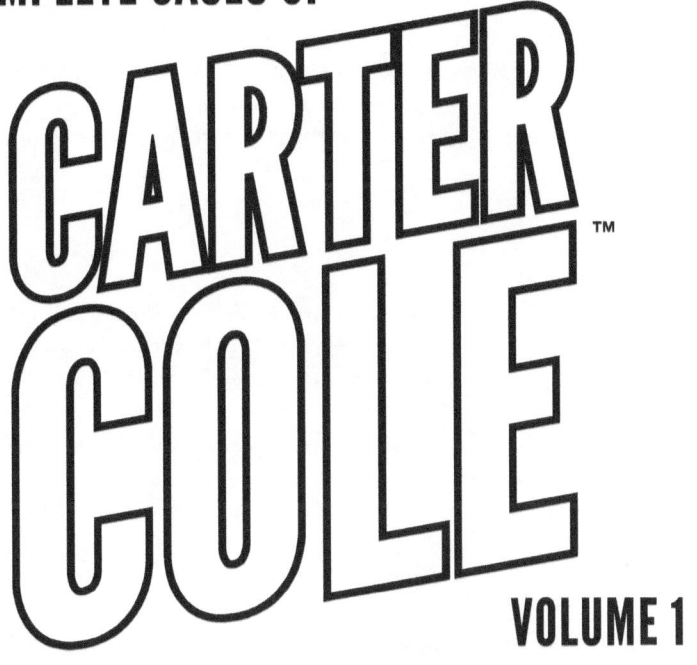

CARTER COLE ™

VOLUME 1

FREDERICK C. DAVIS

ILLUSTRATIONS BY
JOHN FLEMING GOULD

POPULAR PUBLICATIONS • 2022

TABLE OF CONTENTS

THE CASE OF THE CRIMSON CLAWS

INTO THE BENNERLY HOME HAD COME THE DEVIL'S OWN DEATH MESSENGER—A CLAWED KILLER WHOSE SLIGHTEST SCRATCH BROUGHT INSTANT DOOM. WHY WAS IT THRUST UPON THAT FEVER-RIDDEN HOUSEHOLD WHERE DISEASE WAS ALREADY REAPING ITS OWN GRIM GRAVE HARVEST?

CHAPTER ONE
THE PURRING TERROR

IT WAS a soft, throaty sound, almost inaudible, that rippled through the quiet of the gloomy room. A sound that stopped the breath of the man in the chair and brought terror into his flashing eyes.

He sat with white hands gripping the arms of the chair, with haggard gaze peering through the amber glow of the lamp. He sat this way a full minute without moving, his blood chilled in his veins, his wizened body clammy with the cold dew of unutterable fear. The blades of the mantel clock scissored upon the hour of twelve, and into the midnight silence this man listened while horror froze his heart.

There was no sound in all the house save the rippling murmur which came out of the gloom and the hot, broken breathing of the man in the chair. Now he heard it again—that soft, throaty, animal sound—and stiffly drew himself up, quaking with the uncontrollable fear that gripped him.

He heard the purr of a cat.

The sound had awakened him; he sensed the cat lurking near, but he could not see it. There were two doors in the room, one standing ajar, the other wide open and connecting with a hallway. The sound was coming from the hall. Only the soft purr of a cat, but it brought the rigidity of terrible fear to the thin body of Lewis Bennerly.

IN THE next room Bennerly's oldest son, Norton, lay ill of typhoid fever. In another room upstairs his second son lay stricken with the same dread disease. The nurse who attended them had gone to bed on the second floor, for both her patients were sleeping fitfully. Lewis Bennerly had anxiously come to doze in the chair in the library, so that he might be the first to hear if Norton cried out in the night.

But the voice he was listening to now was the soft purr of a cat, and silent padded feet were bringing the unseen animal closer along the hallway, toward the door at which Lewis Bennerly was staring in fear.

The black-garbed figure staggered back even as the cat sprang in fury.

From the darkness of the hall, two eyes peered across the sill—two eyes, bright green, shining evilly from the deepest shadow. While Bennerly stood transfixed with icy terror, the sleek black form of the cat glided soundlessly into the light. Its gleaming eyes fastened on the man standing beside the chair, and it kept on purring.

"Get out!" Bennerly choked. "Get out!"

His snarling voice stopped the purr of the cat. Its black hair bristled. Bennerly's terror communicated itself to the animal, and they stood peering warily at each other—man and cat. It was the man who moved first. He whirled to the fireplace, snatched up a pair of tongs and struck savagely at the black-furred feline.

The cat bounded and the implement hit the floor violently. The impact echoed hollowly through the house as the cat streaked to the second door that was standing ajar. The direction of its move wrung a choking cry from Bennerly's lips. He leaped after the cat and struck again. "Get away!" He thrust into the black bedroom and stood with the tongs upraised, combing the dark fearfully for a pair of shining eyes.

From the gloom came a rustle of movement and a tired voice asked: "What—what is it?"

"A cat! A cat's in here!"

Lewis Bennerly snapped a switch. A shaded table lamp threw a yellowish glow over the emaciated young man who was elbowing up on the bed. Norton Bennerly's eyes glimmered with a fear as strong as his father's. Then father and stricken son stared together at a shadow under the table—a deep black shadow with shining green eyes.

"Get out!"

The hysterical cry ended with the crash of fire-tongs on the table-legs. A swiping blow missed it in midair; it bounded to the bed where the fevered man lay. Norton Bennerly cringed, slapped at the animal and it turned on him in fury. He screamed and fell back, with red streaks marking his face where the cat's claws had furrowed.

The nearness of the cat to his beloved son aroused Lewis Bennerly to a new attack of unreasoning ferocity. He struck again, and the black cat leaped through the light to the window-sill. The tongs splintered the lower glass-pane from its frame. The cat's bared claws flashed as it reared and spat. Then the tongs crashed violently on the sill once more as it whirled through the broken window and vanished into the darkness outside.

Lewis Bennerly stood paralyzed and cold. He dropped the tongs and a convulsive shudder shook his body. He gazed in horror at the red slashes made by the claws of the cat on the face and neck of his son. Norton Bennerly's sunken eyes were closed and he was lying motionless. Now a new dread gripped the father as a young woman hurried into the room.

Efficiently, the nurse who had been sleeping upstairs and who had been awakened by the strident voices and blows of the tongs, hurried to the bed. She bent above her patient, straightened, looked at Lewis Bennerly. "You must—you must realize your son was gravely ill. It will be a shock to you, but you must—"

"The cat killed him!"

Lewis Bennerly's frantic exclamation silenced the nurse. The gleam of his widened eyes, the horror pictured on his face, the muscular tension of his quivering body frightened her. She could only stare as he blurted crazily again: "The cat killed him! The cat killed him!"

Over and over again it came from the lips of Lewis Bennerly. Regardless of the cool reassurance of the nurse, regardless of the brisk matter-of-factness of the two physicians who hurried to the house in response to her call, regardless of all their reiterations that Norton Bennerly had died of the ravages of typhoid, Bennerly declared it over and over again with a mad persistency that could not be shaken.

"The cat killed him! The cat—"

CHAPTER TWO
CARTER COLE, M.D.

WITHIN A high mesh fence, topped with glittering barbed wire, spreading gardens framed the grounds of the Cole Sanitarium. Its iron gates were always locked, for inside this institution lived a thousand or more patients suffering from every conceivable abnormality of the mind. This was a place which existed apart from the workaday world, peopled by those who lived in psychopathic retreats created within their own warped minds.

Some lived a vegetable existence; some raved. Some trimmed the hedges, tended the gardens, rolled the gravel walks. Inside the building were many long, wide hallways, polished to mirror brightness. It was indeed a maze of halls, and along them, day after day, placid-faced men and women pushed heavy wooden blocks based with thick felt. They were patients and the chore assigned them had a double value. It eased their tortured minds and burnished the floors at the same time. Into this labyrinth of shining, waxed hallways three men came on the evening of the day following the death of Norton Bennerly.

A trim, very pretty and cooly efficient nurse-secretary announced their arrival to Doctor Carter Cole. "Doctors Merrick and Walston, with a commitment, Doctor. The patient is Mr. Lewis Bennerly."

"Ask Merrick and Walston to come in first, Jane," Carter Cole said. He was brisk, keen-eyed, startlingly young for one who was director of so huge a privately owned asylum for the insane.

"Yes, Doctor. But I'm not Jane—I'm June."

Cole peered at her intently, smiling. "You're June, and not Jane. You're yourself and not your twin sister. Very well. I don't know why I don't simply call you both Miss Day and be done with it. Damned if I can tell you apart."

"Yes, Doctor."

"Not that it matters," Cole added. "Both of you are ideal secretaries. Either of you appear to be supremely capable of handling any task I can give you, without questions or bungling. But it is confusing. Suppose, after this, June, you wear a red carnation so I'll know which of the Day sisters I'm talking to."

June Day remarked crisply: "It's against the rules to wear any kind of ornament, Doctor, including flowers."

Cole chuckled. "True. Then I'll simply have to continue mistaking your sister for you and you for your sister. Show the Doctors Merrick and Walston in, June."

THE TIRELESS activities of Carter Cole, M.D., famed psychiatrist, had brought him into contact with every prominent general practitioner and specialist in the metropolis. He knew both Merrick and Walston in connection with previous mental cases, shook hands with them cordially when they entered. And he listened intently to their report on the new patient.

"The two Bennerly brothers," Doctor Merrick explained, "contracted typhoid fever some weeks ago. They neglected medical treatment in the early stages, and their cases became serious. Their father—your new patient—did not contract it and an inoculation kept him well."

"It was Norton Bennerly who died last night," Doctor Walston added to the account. He was a large man and his loose clothing made him seem even larger; he wore tortoise-shell glasses, exuded a medical odor, and was a decade older in years and practise than his colleague. "Of typhoid, of course—hyperpyrexia.* Rolph is bearing up well, even after the shock of his brother's death."

"We've brought Lewis Bennerly to you, Cole," Merrick continued, "because the death of his son, Norton last night strengthened his phobia to what is apparently a dangerous stage. His is apparently a case of paranoia.** He is suffering from persecution ideas in connection with his long-stand-ing aelurophobia."

Carter Cole nodded. "Aelurophobia, an abiding fear of cats," he mused. "Mr. Bennerly is in distinguished company. The same fear was felt in lesser degree by Calvin Coolidge. Queen Marie of Roumania is another aelurophobe, and so was King Ferdinand of Bulgaria."

---

* Typhoid fever may cause death through exhaustion, haemor-rhage of the intestines, perforation of an intestinal ulcer, hyperpy-rexia, or complications. Hyperpyrexia is excessive fever.—F.C.D.

** Schizophrenia, also termed dementia praecox, is a form of mental abnormality in which there is a splitting of the personality resulting from an individual's failure to make adjustments necessary to his well-being. The abnormality is divided into three general groups, one of which is paranoia. In paranoia there is evident either delusions of grandeur, or delusions of persecution—that is, in the latter case, the afflicted person believes he is being hounded, plot-ted against, watched by someone or something hostile and destruc-tive. Most homicidal maniacs are of this general class.—F.C.D.

"Yes," said Doctor Walston. "The strange thing in the case of Lewis Bennerly is, he is convinced beyond all reason that a cat killed his son."

"He believes," Doctor Merrick added, "that he's to remain here only a short time. His concern for his other son may make him dangerously anxious to get out again. Here is a report of the case."

"Thank you, gentlemen." Carter Cole rose. "I'll talk with Mr. Bennerly now."

Again they shook hands. Walston gazed at Cole quizzically. "You're a never ending enigma to me, Cole," he said. "You live here surrounded by a thousand lunatics, and yet you're the sanest man I know. How do you do it?"

"Perhaps it's being near so many unbalanced minds," Cole answered, "that keeps my own on an even keel." He said good-night, touched a button. A trim, very pretty and cooly efficient nurse entered in response. "Ask Mr. Bennerly to come in, June."

"Yes, Doctor," Miss Day answered. "But I'm not June. June's gone to supper. I'm Jane."

Cole gazed bewildered. "Lord, isn't there something about you two that's different? Never mind—I know there isn't. I've tried that before. Show Bennerly in, whichever you are!"

"Yes, Doctor," said Jane Day.

Cole reflected that sooner or later this thing of the Day twins might make him a patient in his own institution. Two closer-mouthed young women, two separate human beings more startlingly identical, he had never met. About them he knew nothing except that they had come from a nurses' registry in answer to his need for two secretaries. If they had a family, if they had sweethearts, if they were anything other than the best secretaries a doctor ever had, he did not know. His only certainty was that they were June and Jane Day, and he invariably called each of them by her wrong name.

MISS DAY—WHICH one Cole did not attempt to decide—returned with Lewis Bennerly. There was no suggestion of abnormality about him now; but, Cole knew, at the merest glimpse of a cat he would stare in terror, tremble with fear, even become obsessed with a savage lust to kill the animal. He made no move while Cole read the typewritten report.

"You know both Doctor Merrick and Doctor Walston very well?" Cole inquired.

"Doctor Merrick has attended my family several years," Bennerly answered. "Walston was called into consultation when my sons became dangerously ill."

"I'm very sorry to hear," Cole said gently, "that last night your son Norton died—of typhoid."

Now Bennerly's eyes widened. "He didn't die of typhoid. The cat killed him!"

"But," Cole pointed out easily, "an ordinary domesticated cat simply cannot kill an adult human being."

"The cat killed him!"

"Any wound which even a terrorized cat might inflict—a bite or a scratch—could not instantly kill a grown man."

"The cat killed him!"

"If the cat were diseased, or if infection set into the scratches, there would be a lapse of time before symptoms develop. You know that, don't you, Mr. Bennerly?"

"The cat killed him!"

"There was no lapse of time in this case. The animal struck at your son, and in a moment life was gone from him. The shock, his exhausted condition—"

"The cat killed him, I tell you!"

"Why," Cole asked intently, "are you so positive the cat killed your son?"

Bennerly's lips worked tightly. "Doctor Cole, I know my fear of cats is a kind of madness. I've studied the subject. Realizing the probable cause of it* doesn't make it less of an obsession, but even if I didn't have that fear, I'd still be certain that the cat killed my son."

Bennerly's quiet, rational statement sharpened Cole's interest.

"Last night a cat got into my house somehow. I tried to chase it out, and it leaped on Norton in the bed. It clawed Norton. At that very moment he died. That's why I say— that's why I *know*, Doctor Cole that the cat killed my son."

Cole studied Bennerly, who was breathing hotly and quickly. "How," he inquired, "did that animal get into your house?"

"I don't know! The outer doors were all closed. The windows were all shut. The cat couldn't have gotten in by itself. It was *put* into my house!" Now Bennerly was gripping the chair, staring. "It was put into the house by someone who wanted it to kill my son!"

"Why," Cole asked quietly, "should anyone want to kill your son?"

"I don't know—but it's true!" Bennerly blurted it as he jerked to his feet. "That cat was an instrument of murder

---

* The phobia of cat fear may be traced back to primitive man's dread of the big cat animals of the jungle—lions, tigers, leopards. Elemental man feared these predatory animals just as all wild animals still fear them as their mortal enemies and hastily take refuge at the sound of their voices.—F.C.D.

turned upon Norton! He didn't die of typhoid! The cat killed him!"

Cole waited for Bennerly's outburst to subside before he spoke again. Then he said, gently, firmly: "Mr. Bennerly, your intelligence is disturbed only by a hatred of feline animals. Now, if I prove, beyond all logical doubt, that no cat killed your son—will you believe it?"

"You—do you think you can do that, Doctor?"

"I am going to try. If I succeed—if I become absolutely convinced myself that a cat did not kill your son—will you believe it?"

"Yes," Bennerly said in a whisper. "Yes, then I will."

Doctor Carter Cole touched a button. When the door of the office opened, he sighed in relief. This time two trim, very pretty and coolly efficient nurses came into his office. They were absolutely identical of face and figure; their white-starched costumes were exactly the same. The Misses Day even spoke with exactly the same intonation.

"Yes, Doctor?"

"Yes, Doctor?"

"Mr. Bennerly, this is Miss Day, and this is Miss Day," Cole said gravely. "Your eyes do not deceive you—they are two separate entities. Mr. Bennerly is going to his room. See that he is made comfortable. Good-night, Mr. Bennerly."

Cole stood thoughtful while his new patient was escorted away. In a moment the Misses Day, having turned their charge over to a staff doctor, reappeared in the outer office. Cole issued crisp directions.

"You," he said, pointing at the sister on the right, "are to begin gathering all the information possible on the Bennerlys, regardless of its medical or psychopathic significance. I will want a report very soon. Before you begin, call in my good friend Brick Kelly."

"Yes, Doctor," said the indicated Day sister.

"You," Cole said, pointing to the other, "are coming with me and Brick."

"Yes, Doctor," said the second Miss Day.

"It will be very odd," Doctor Carter Cole observed thoughtfully, "if I find that the cat did kill Norton Bennerly."

CHAPTER THREE
FOUR-FOOTED PHANTOM

COLE, AT the wheel of his huge Duesenberg, set out on his mission accompanied by a taciturn Miss Day, the loquacious Brick Kelly, and a snugly arm-pit-holstered automatic whose voice might or might not raise that night as the occasion required.

"Doc," said Kelly affectionately, "you're one grand guy. You treat me like a human being instead of the mug I am. There ain't anything I wouldn't do for you. If you want anybody bumped off, just ask me. But when you start on one of these screwy cases, I can't help sayin' I wish you wouldn't."

The squat, bull-necked, rusty-haired young man had been, variously, a cowboy, a side-show spieler, a truck driver, a seaman, a marine, and a sculptor's model, until the fates had led him to the Cole Sanitarium. His official capacity there was jack-of-all-trades. He had a way with clogged drain-pipes, balky oil furnaces, recalcitrant typewriters, jittery automobile motors and, as occasion demanded it, cranky alarm-clocks. Cole's Duesenberg was his special pride; he kept it in perfect tune. Because of his ability to remain undismayed in the face of trying circumstances, Cole found comfort in his assistance when working on unusual cases.

"You know, Brick," Cole told him, "my chief concern is the cure of my patients. I want to mend their minds, to make them whole and healthy human beings, to send them back into the world capable and well balanced. That's the only reason why I sometimes stray from psychiatry into mystery-investigating. That's the only reason why I'm determined to learn for myself whether or not a cat actually killed a man."

"To me," Brick Kelly retorted, "it sounds like a nut's idea, all right!"

"If it's only that," Cole answered with a dry smile, "we'll soon find out."

He swung the massive car to the curb directly behind a light roadster. Surveying the gloom-shrouded Bennerly home, he saw that someone had apparently just left the roadster and was now at the entrance. The voices of two women, one insistent, the other cooly firm, mingled as he turned to Miss Day.

"Wait here," he said—and took a chance—"Jane."

"Yes, Doctor," Miss Day answered. "But I'm not Jane— I'm June."

"In either case," Cole sighed, "wait. You come with me, Brick."

The voices of the two women at the door sharpened as he approached. The entrance was partly opened: a nurse wearing a white cap was holding it against the thrusting hand of a younger, prettier girl who was carrying a small suitcase. She drew back at Cole's approach, eyes flashing with determination, red lips quivering with anxiety. She did not give ground, but merely quieted at Cole's approach.

Cole's professional card brought a respectful greeting from the nurse. "Good evening, Doctor—I'm Miss Carson. Miss Barbara Bennerly—Doctor Cole. She insists on coming in, Doctor, but I can't conscientiously let her do that. The place is quarantined—and Mr. Rolph Bennerly's condition is such that no one may see him."

The girl, too anguished to acknowledge the introduction, declared: "He's my brother. I didn't know he was ill until today. I'm going to see him—and my father."

Carter Cole said firmly, "In consideration of your own health, Miss Bennerly, please don't insist. If you wish to see your father, please go to my sanitarium and give Miss Day—any Miss Day you happen to find—this card." Cole scribbled on it and handed it to the distrait girl. "If you hurry—"

"Why—why is my father in a sanitarium?" Barbara Bennerly asked in sudden terror. "He's not insane!"

"Not at all, but—"

THE GIRL turned abruptly and ran along the walk, carrying her overnight case. Carter Cole watched her climb into her roadster, saw the car spurt from the curb. He knew that Barbara Bennerly would respect no speed limits on her way to the Cole Sanitarium.

"Poor child," Miss Carson said sympathetically. "She just drove down from Northampton. Mr. Bennerly hadn't told her her brothers were ill—he didn't want to worry her. She read of Norton's death in the papers today. Do you want to see the patient, Doctor Cole? He's asleep."

"I don't," Carter Cole said briskly. "I want to see you. I want to know if you, by any chance, put a cat into this house last night."

"Of course not!"

"The cat which Mr. Lewis Bennerly saw last night was not a figment of his imagination?"

"There were claw marks on the patient."

"I wish," said Carter Cole, "to come in." As the door widened he directed Kelly: "Brick, take a look around outside. Try to find some indication that a cat was put into this house last night."

Kelly said, "Sure, Doc!" and started off as Carter Cole went in. At his request, the nurse conducted Cole into the rooms on the lower floor where the cat had been seen. The deceased Norton's bed was freshly made; Cole learned that the dead man had already been cremated, with the usual dispatch in typhoid cases. Cole noted the broken pane, the dents in the sill where the fire-tongs had struck—and became alert when Miss Carson said: "There were black hairs on this bed, Doctor—cat's hairs."

Cole went upstairs. In a rear bedroom, he learned from Miss Carson, Rolph Bennerly was sleeping. Doctors Merrick and Walston had seen him an hour ago; they thought he might recover. The nurse was puzzled by Cole's interest in Lewis Bennerly's room but discreetly said nothing while he probed into drawers.

"What," he asked, lifting a small flat box from beneath a pile of shirts, "are these ampules?" *

"I don't know, Doctor."

"Someone," Cole said, inspecting the little bulbs that contained a yellowish liquid, "has carefully ripped the label

---

* An ampule (name derived from Latin *ampulla*, a religious vessel), is a small glass capsule, with long sealed neck, containing medicinal liquids for hypodermic injection. Usually each ampule contains a dose. The neck of the ampule is snapped off and the needle inserted; the liquid is then drawn into the barrel of the syringe and injected into the patient. They are usually sold in cotton-padded boxes containing a dozen.—F.C.D.

from the box. They were not prescribed for anyone in the house?"

"Not for either of my patients, Doctor."

"Lewis Bennerly was not taking injections of some kind?"

"I don't know, Doctor."

"In which case," Cole said, slipping the box into his pocket, "I'll take them along. Don't mind me, Miss Carson. For a physician, I have strange methods. I can justify them only by saying that they often get results."

His strange methods took him again into the lower rooms. He opened desk drawers in the library. In the room where Norton Bennerly had died, he probed still further in drawers, looked in a closet, examined a bookcase. Curiously, he tipped from its place a volume with worn binding, which held something between its pages.

A small paper packet lay in the crease. Cole unfolded it to find a sprinkling of white crystals. He was examining them carefully when a stealthy sound at the window surprised him. The scarred face of Brick Kelly was framed by the jagged glass; Kelly's eyes were widened, startled.

"Doc!" he whispered. "Doc, listen! There's somebody on the porch!"

"What?" Cole snapped.

"Somebody hidin' on the roof of the side porch, Doc! I saw him move and—"

A CHOKING, high-pitched cry echoed through the house. It was half shout of terror, half wild protest. Within the walls of his sanitarium Carter Cole was accustomed to the shrieks of manic depressives; there he paid them scant attention. But now a chill tingled along his nerves. Again

the strangling cry rang out, forming an almost unintelligible word.

"Cat! *Cat!*"

"My patient!" Miss Carson exclaimed.

Carter Cole snapped at Brick Kelly: "Watch that man on
the porch!" His long, swift legs carried him past the nurse.
As he bounded up the stairs he thrust the folded packet
of white crystals into his pocket. Twice more before he
gripped the knob of Rolph Bennerly's room and thrust it
wide, he heard the choking cry of terror, heard the shrieked
word *"Cat!"*

Darkness filled the room, save for faint moonshine
through the windows; and in that glow Carter Cole
glimpsed a streak of black movement. It was silent, flashless
lightning in the gloom—something that leaped from the
bed in the corner and seemed to vanish in midair. Cole's
hand found the electric switch, snapped it. He stopped
short, with the breathless nurse behind him, staring aghast
at the man on the bed.

Rolph Bennerly lay among tossed sheets, motionless.
His open eyes were staring with fear. One hand was raised
to a throat streaked with red—oozing red lines gashed
through the skin. On the sheet that covered his emaciated
body was a suggestion of black—fine hairs clinging. It was
out of the throat of this man that the cry had torn. A cry
that would never be repeated—*"Cat!"*

Carter Cole's first glance told him that Rolph Bennerly
was dead.

Somewhere in this room the creature still lurked. Cole
surmised that it was crouched under the bed; but his mind
was humming with Brick Kelly's warning. A window at the
foot of the bed was open. It gave upon the roof of a porch
at the side of the house. Cole's hand held his automatic

as he thrust his head out, and peered across the slope of shingles. He saw nothing.

"Brick!" he called. No answer came out of the darkness. "Brick!" he repeated. And again no answer.

Cole spun, left the room with the nurse staring in horror at the claw-gashed dead man on the bed. He bounded down the front stairs, thrust out the entrance, ran to the side of the house. Automatic in hand, he peered at the roof of the porch; his gaze probed into the moonlight-dappled shadows of the grounds—nothing. He started away.

"Brick!" he called.

His foot struck something light yet bulky, which rolled on the grass, and he stopped short, reached and touched cold metal. The thing he lifted into his hands was a large domed cage of bronze wire, large enough to contain a parrot. Its door was swinging open; it was empty. Carefully Cole placed it oh the porch, again searching the grounds, gun leveled.

"Brick!" he shouted.

A rustle in the grass, a chesty moan, turned Carter Cole toward the rear of the house. A shadow was moving against the white wall—a man huddled down, trying to rise. Cole gripped him by the arm and Brick Kelly tottered up, one hand spread across his eyes. "God!" he blurted.

"What happened?" Cole snapped.

BEFORE KELLY could answer, a frightened whimper carried to Cole's ears from the open window above the porch. He heard high heels tapping the floor quickly, in a run. He shifted back, peering at the window, his weapon ready. From the room in which a second man had died, his body marked by the claws of a cat, Miss Carson's voice faltered.

"Doctor Cole! There's a cat in here. Under the bed!"

Cole called up: "Get out of that room! Close the door and get out!" The click of a latch told him his order had been obeyed.

Brick Kelly was tottering at Cole's side. In the light shining down, the bleeding cut above Kelly's eye was plainly visible. "God, Doc, he jumped right down on me!" the injured man blurted. "He must've been lyin' flat—I couldn't see him and came closer—and all at once he landed on me so hard he knocked me cold. Is he gone?"

"I'm afraid he has, Brick," Cole affirmed laconically. "Did you see his face?"

"I didn't see nothin' but stars when he hit me!"

Cole shifted again, keeping the open window in sight, and saw, propped against the porch, a short ladder. Nothing was lurking on the roof but as Cole's eyes turned there was a flicker of movement.

"A cat!" Kelly gasped. "It came out of the window, Doc!"

"A cat, Brick," Cole agreed. "Now it's on the porch. If—"

Cole's 9mm spat. He had seen the cat leap across the sill and onto the shingles. It had crouched there in shadow an instant, its green eyes glimmering. As Cole spoke it had again become swift black movement in blackness. Its bound carried it off the roof; it was sailing through midair when the bullet struck.

The flat report echoed from the depths of the night and a fall fluttered the grass at the side of the porch. Cole ignored the stifled cry of consternation from the nurse in the house, took long, quick strides toward the spot. As Kelly reached out Cole snapped: "Don't touch it!"

They looked at the dead black cat. Cole briskly drew gloves from his pocket, pulled them on. He lifted the limp feline body, placed it in the bird-cage and shut the barred door on it. Placing the cage in the arms of the astounded Brick Kelly, he said, "We're going back now—" and started off.

He took the wheel of the Duesenberg and Kelly clambered in the back. As Cole started the engine, his eyes narrowed in thought, and he spoke over his shoulder. "Whatever you do, Brick, don't touch that cat." His gaze turned to the cool and efficient Miss Day who was still sitting in exactly the same spot he had left her. In admiration and amazement he asked: "Do you mean that throughout those screams and in spite of the shot, you've been sitting in this precise spot all the time?"

"Yes, Doctor," June Day answered. "Your orders were to wait right here."

CHAPTER FOUR
THE CLAWS OF THE CAT

INTO THE sprawling main building of the Cole Sanitarium, along the endless shining hallways polished by the trek of those with warped minds, Doctor Carter Cole strode with Miss Jane Day at his side, Brick Kelly following and carrying the bird-cage containing the dead cat.

He strode briskly into the biological laboratory on the top floor. There he relieved Kelly of the caged cat and said: "That's all for tonight, Brick. Get that cut dressed." To the uniformed Miss Day he directed: "Read me your report while I work."

The room was long, walled with shelves, rimmed with laboratory benches; it glittered with countless bottles of chemical reagents and analytical apparatus. Miss Day followed Cole as he moved about pulling on smock and rubber gloves, and read the typewritten report.

"The Bennerlys are a monied family. The two sons became lawyers but never practised, being spoiled playboys busy burning themselves out with night life and any excitement they could find. The daughter—she's now talking with her father, Doctor—is a junior at Smith College. The father has been exceedingly indulgent to his motherless children. When the two sons came down with typhoid at the same time, the father insisted on staying with them though he risked contracting it. Doctor Walston immunized him immediately with standard vaccine.

"Among their circle of friends the aelurophobia of the family is generally known."

"What?" Cole asked as he opened the cage and removed the dead cat. "The whole family suffer from the same phobia?"

"The father," his secretary read on, "apparently taught a fear of cats to his children. They suffer with it almost as much as he."

Carter Cole was performing a strange task. The pressure of his fingers was causing the retractile claws of the dead cat to protrude. With sharp-bladed cutters he clipped the claws off, gathered them on a circle of filter paper.

"A phobia celebrated throughout history," he murmured. "A fear of cats and an excessive love of cats—evidenced in many instances. The Egyptian cat-goddess, called Bubastis or Bastet—strangely enough, the patroness of love, of matters feminine and of fashion—was a cat-headed woman. A famous French poet once put his hatred of cats into a verse."*

Cole did not look up from his task as the laboratory door opened and the second Miss Day entered. "Miss Bennerly," she announced, "insists on seeing you, Doctor."

---

* The verse to which Cole refers was written by Pierre de Ronsard, French poet of the Sixteenth Century. The lines expressing the author's aelurophobia are:

> There is no man living anywhere
> Who hates cats with a deeper hate than I;
> I hate their eyes, their heads, the way they stare
> And when I see one come I turn and fly.

"Ask her to wait in my office." Cole went on working so intently that he did not hear the resulting argument at the door. Deftly he filed and snapped the stem of one of the ampules he had taken from Lewis Bennerly's bureau; he poured its yellowish content into a test-tube. He was sifting the white powder, which he had found hidden in the book, into another tube, when he glanced up to see Barbara Bennerly standing white-faced at his side.

"I—I've got to see you now!" she exclaimed. "It's cruel—keeping my father here. He's not insane."

Cole straightened and said: "I agree. But it's best that he rest here for a short time. Miss Bennerly, you must prepare yourself for an ugly shock. Yow second brother, Rolph, is—"

"Dead!" The girl was gazing wide-eyed. "Doctor Cole, I know—I know why my brothers are dead! I know how they contracted the disease that killed them. Only tonight—this paper I read in your office while I was waiting to see father—"

HER HANDS moving with quick nervousness, Barbara Bennerly spread the paper on the laboratory bench. Her trembling forefinger pointed to a picture of a kindly-faced woman. The headline read—*DON'T EMPLOY THIS WOMAN! IF YOU SEE HER, NOTIFY THE HEALTH AUTHORITIES!* Beneath was a name, *Annie Morrigan*. The article was enough to divert Cole completely from his engrossing work.

> Annie Morrigan, a sweet-faced domestic known to the health authorities as Typhoid Carrier No. 15, has disappeared from her home. It is feared she has again taken employment as a cook. This unfortunate woman is a spreader of typhoid fever, and contact with her, or with the food she prepares, may mean

contracting the disease. Police are searching for her.*

Among the typhoid carriers in the city, Annie Morrigan, No. 15, has given the most trouble to the health authorities. Follow-

---

*   The carrier principle of typhoid was discovered by Doctor Robert Koch many years after the insolation of *bacillus typhoidus* in 1884. News of it first reached the United States in 1904. The efforts of Doctor George A. Soper, a sanitary engineer with the Department of Health in New York City, to learn the cause of scattered outbreaks of typhoid, resulted in the identification of Mary Mallon as America's first carrier of typhoid bacilli. Typhoid Mary, as she was known, was a cook and into each kitchen she entered she carried illness and often death.

This unfortunate woman may be considered a typical case. She had never had typhoid, but her body was full of the germ. The germ breeds usually in the gall bladder of a carrier, multiplying by the billions. Any food prepared or handled by a typhoid carrier is contaminated and persons eating it are extremely likely to contract the disease.

The greatest typhoid carrier was a dairy farmer in Camden, New York, in 1909; the milk he handled spread 409 cases of typhoid and resulted in 40 deaths. There are in New York City now 344 typhoid carriers. City health departments watch all carriers and in some cases exercise their wide powers to isolate such persons as being dangerous to the public health. Only two are confined in New York City: Fred Morsch (No. 46) and Mary Mallon (No. 36). The woman was isolated because her persistency in seeking work as a cook, sometimes under false names, led to serious outbreaks of the disease. Today she lies in a ward in Riverside Hospital, paralyzed on her right side, awaiting death. Mary Mallon has persistently refused to give any information concerning herself personally in order to spare her relatives the knowledge that she is the dread symbol of pestilence who became known as Typhoid Mary.—F.C.D.

ing the last outbreak of typhoid in a home in which she worked as cook, resulting in three deaths, she was confined under her own guardianship. Her unexplained absence is believed to mean that she has broken her promise to keep herself isolated, and is again working as cook. She may be using a false name, but this recent photograph of her will enable—

"I know her!" Barbara Bennerly exclaimed. "She was cook in our home just before Norton and Rolph came down with typhoid. As soon as they became ill, she slipped away—disappeared."

Cole's eyes glittered. "Are you sure of that? You had in your home this woman who is literally a spreader of typhoid—and didn't realize it?"

"She came just as I left home at the end of Easter vacation," the dismayed girl rushed on. "My brothers must have caught typhoid from eating food she prepared. Doctor Cole, what was she doing in our house? Why was she there?"

"Did you advertise or—"

"No. Our previous cook left. We hadn't time to advertise before this woman, calling herself Molly Anderson, came to the house for the job. She said vaguely she was a friend of Agatha—the girl who left. Doctor Cole, it's strange—so strange that—"

"Unless forcibly confined," Cole pointed out, "typhoid carriers often rebel against their restrictions. Her coming to your home was a disaster, but perhaps perfectly natural."

"I don't believe that!" The girl's clear eyes were blazing. "Father told me what happened last night. There's something behind all this, Doctor Cole—something terrible, something almost inhuman. For a year, more than a year, I've felt a change at home—in Norton and Rolph—like a force that was altering them."

Cole, listening intently, returned to his work. A Bunsen burner whispered out a blue flame; he manipulated tubes and reagents deftly. The girl's eyes sought his; and she repressed a shudder each time she glanced at the cat lying dead on the table.

"Don't you understand? Norton and Rolph used to be— oh, they were reckless and wild and wasteful of father's money, but it was fun to be with them—until about a year ago. They changed so. They became quarrelsome, mean. They lost all self-respect—flaunting shady women—even their eyes changed. It was as though some force was at work, destroying them, Doctor Cole!"

Cole dribbled acid into a test-tube heating in the blue flame.

"It—it was that same force that took their lives," the girl went on in a tense whisper. "I'm sure of it. That woman— the typhoid carrier—didn't come to our home of her own accord. I know she didn't! She came because she was sent. She was sent by someone who wanted to see my brothers dead!"

Cole's hand poised holding the glittering test-tube. "You think someone deliberately infected them with typhoid?"

Barbara Bennerly's hands were closed into white fists. "Where is that woman now? Why is she hiding? Isn't it because she realizes what she's done? Doctor"—the girl's eyes shone with a clear light of strong determination—"I'm going to find her. I'm going to make her tell me who sent her into our home!"

She turned quickly and strode from the laboratory.

COLE GAZED gravely at the efficient secretary-nurse who was standing beside him. "Perhaps she's right," he said quietly. "Perhaps Annie Morrigan was sent into her home as an agent of death. But the fact is—cats killed both those men."

"Yes, doctor?"

Cole straightened. "Permit me, June, Jane, whichever you are, to say 'For God's sake!' What I've just told you means that someone *did* murder those two brothers. It means that the murderer used a devilish weapon—the claws of a cat dipped in poison. You hear that two men have been killed in a diabolical way and you say cooly, 'Yes, doctor'! Doesn't anything ever get you?"

"No, Doctor," Miss Day said cooly.

"We have a man here suffering from a fearful phobia, who keeps muttering over and over again, 'The cat killed him! The cat killed him!' and he's absolutely right. My analysis shows it. Those cats brought death to those two men because their claws were dipped in curare."

"Yes—"

"Don't say it! Get busy. Check up on every purchase of curare ampules for as long back as the records go. They would be sold to no one but a physician.* I want the name of the doctor who bought them."

---

* Medical researchers have recently revealed that some diseases may be alleviated or cured by the use of small doses of venom and other deadly poisons. Snake and spider venom have been used to free patients of hitherto incurable afflications. Curare, the powerful South American poison, has also been put to this use as a remedy. Curare is an amber jelly worth its weight in gold to South American witch-doctors. Known also as *urali*, it is concocted from the climbing *Struchnos toxifera* and other plants, to which is added black and red ants and the poison fangs of snakes. Its exact composition is unknown to any but the medicine men who prepare it. It is used to tip blow-pipe darts; and one of these darts, driving into the

Miss Day strode briskly to the door of the laboratory and said: "Yes, Doctor." The minute she went out, the door opened and she appeared to enter again. This was, Cole knew, not what his eyes told him. She was not the same Miss Day, but she was just as cool and unruffled as her twin sister as she approached him.

"Curare! On the cat's claws, taken from these ampules I found in the room of the father of the two men who died. Whatever the devil is behind all this, I'm—"

"Doctor," Miss Day broke in briskly, "excuse my interrupting, but our new patient, Mr. Bennerly, has eloped."

"Eloped!"

Carter Cole snatched up a telephone, snapped crackling orders into it. A moment later, faintly at first, then swelling to a prolonged, piercing note, a whistle on the sanitarium grounds began to whine. As its eery sound traveled over the countryside, mothers hurried from their beds and into the rooms where their children slept. Men scurried with flashlights across the sanitarium grounds and out the gates— and through the stillness of the night the blood-chilling hoot of the whistle continued as they searched.

To Carter Cole, Miss Day's message of an elopement had no flavor whatever of romance. In the parlance of the

---

body of an animal or human, means instantaneous death.

The effect of curare is instantly to paralyze the entire nervous and muscular systems. No antidote is known.

The same poison, shipped in its original gourd to modern medical laboratories, is sterilized, greatly diluted, and put into ampules. Its curative effects consist in its power to paralyze nerve-centers which have become uncontrollable by the individual. As a drug it sells for $25 an ounce.—F.C.D.

institution it meant that Lewis Bennerly, aleurophobe, had somehow, under the cover of darkness, escaped.

CHAPTER FIVE
TYPHOID ANNIE

A **SLEEPLESS** night did not subtract from Carter
Cole's usual briskness throughout the next day. He
sat at his desk directing the manifold activities of the sanitarium, reading reports brought to him by June and Jane
Day. With the coming of evening, he was still at his post,
still puzzling together the jigsaw sections of a mystery that
baffled him. He had dinner brought to his office; and when
he replaced his drained coffee cup he touched push-but-
tons.

"June—Jane," he said, when a Miss Day responded,
"there has been no further word from Barbara Bennerly?"

"No, Doctor."

"Annie Morrigan has not been located?"

"No, Doctor, but I have a report on her." Her capable
hand proffered it.

> I have checked by telephone all recent reports of typhoid in
> the metropolitan area. Following her disappearance from the
> Bennerly home, a woman answering the description of Annie
> Morrigan went to work as cook for the Huntley family, address
> below. Two children in the house soon contracted typhoid and
> are now recovering. The cook slipped away in the manner of
> Annie Morrigan. I am awaiting further information in order to
> trace her later movements through her references. She must

again be working somewhere, for she is still missing from her own home.

"Excellent!" Carter Cole exclaimed. "Ring the health department. When the next case of typhoid is reported, I want to know of it at once."

"Yes, Doctor. Mr. Kelly is here to see you," Miss Day added.

Brick Kelly entered red of face, weary of limb. He uttered a vast sigh. "Wherever Bennerly went, Doc, he's sure as hell not anywhere around here." Kelly smiled crookedly, sheepishly. "If he was hidin' anywhere near me any time, I couldn't even get a rise out of him by mewin' like a cat."

"Thanks, Brick. Better stand by."

Kelly shuffled out and one of the two Misses Day entered to announce: "Doctor Walston."

Cole's face took on grim lines as Walston came in. The big man tugged his loose coat around his ample body, adjusted his thick-rimmed spectacles, peered at Cole uncertainly. Cole's greeting was perfunctory; his attention turned on a type written report placed before him.

"I called you here to ask you important questions on the Bennerly case. First, Doctor Walston, did you buy a box of ampules a week ago—ampules of curare?"

"I?" Walston asked in surprise. "No."

"The only curare ampules bought in this city recently," Cole insisted, "are registered as purchased by Doctor Sidney Walston. What did you want with it?"

Walston cleared his throat. "I—I know that curare is a specific for encephalitis—it's used in cases of epilepsy, pyramidal disease, Parkinson's disease, but—I haven't made use of it."

"Lewis Bennerly is not suffering from any of those afflictions. There is no reason why curare should have been prescribed for him—or for the typhoid patients?"

"None whatever."

Cole's eyes sharpened. "Which one of the Bennerlys, Doctor Walston," he asked, "is addicted to cocaine?"

"What!" The big physician blinked through his horn rims. "So far as I know, none of them!"

COLE'S EYEBROWS angled down angrily. "Doctor Walston, listen to a few facts. Hidden in a book in the Bennerly home I found a paper folder containing cocaine. It was almost empty. Most had been used. There is at least one addict in the Bennerly family."

Walston stared. Cole opened the flat box on his desk and indicated the few glittering, amber-filled ampules it contained. "Also, most of the curare here has been used. I suspect that a number of ampules were emptied and the stuff evaporated down to the strength of the original jelly. It was used to commit murder."

"Did you say murder?" Walston blurted.

"You probably know, Doctor," Cole continued, "how easy it is to get scratched by a cat while simply playing with it. A terrorized cat, especially when cornered, fights. Their claws can make deep cuts in a man's skin."

"Of course."

"A cat *did* kill Norton Bennerly. Another cat killed Rolph Bennerly. The claws of both felines were covered with curare jelly. Whoever put those cats into that house of aleurophobes was as intent upon murder as though he fired a gun directly at those men's hearts."

Doctor Walston started up, eyes gleaming through his spectacles. Cole straightened to face him.

"Did you carry those cats to the Bennerly home in a large cage and release them upon men who were certain to fight and terrorize them?"

"I did not!"

"Why did you wish Norton and Rolph Bennerly to die?"

"In the name of God, I wished nothing of the kind!"

"Naturally," said Carter Cole quietly as he returned to his chair, "you would deny it, Doctor."

Walston glowered as the desk-buzzer sounded. Cole called, "Come in!" grimly, and one of the two Misses Day entered with a neatly typed note. As she withdrew Cole read lines which quickened his breath.

> Two typhoid cases just reported by Cleverson family, address below. Patients are now being hospitalized. Phone call to house answered by cook giving name of Mrs. Ross.

JJ

Cole rose. "Doctor Walston," he said tightly, "you are in a serious situation. The merest hint of this will mean the end of you professionally, if it doesn't bring you to trial for murder. I am the last man in the world to wish—if you're innocent—to bring those consequences upon you. Are you willing to submit to a drastic suggestion of mine?"

Walston bristled. "What the devil are you up to, Cole? You're a psychiatrist, not a detective. You're mixing in where you have no business. Why should I submit to you in any way?"

"Murder has been committed, and the facts must be put into the hands of the police. If you prefer them to manhandle you, very well. I agree—the murder end of this case is not quite my business. But regardless of that, I'm mixing in. If you choose, you may go."

Walston asked uncertainly: "What is your suggestion?"

"That," Cole retorted, "my secretary will handle. I have an urgent engagement."

His touch on a button brought both Misses Day into the office. To one he said: "Doctor Walston is in your charge." To the other he said: "Come with me." Without further explanation he pulled on hat and topcoat, strode from the office.

COLE'S DUESENBERG drew to a stop in the quiet street of a Long Island suburb, in front of the Cleverson home—the latest in all the metropolitan area to be visited by typhoid. He said, "With me," to whichever of the two Misses Day had accompanied him, and together they went to the door.

Cole touched the bell-button and noted that the house was dark except for windows in the rear. His ring brought no answer, though he heard faint voices. Four times he pushed the bell without winning a response before he told Miss Day: "I'm going around. Watch this door."

"Yes, Doctor," Miss Day said.

At the rear of the house, Cole looked through windows into a gleaming kitchen, saw no one. At the back entrance, he heard footfalls as of someone coming down a flight of stairs. When he knocked the footfalls quickened. A glimpse through the pane showed him a short plump woman, wearing a cheap hat and a worn coat. She was gripping a battered suitcase, running in fright toward the front of the house.

Cole thrust in. Long strides carried him across the kitchen after the woman. He gripped her arm. She tugged frantically to free herself, peered into his face in wild alarm. He drew her back and his eyes narrowed as he said with cold geniality: "Good evening, Mrs. Morrigan."

"You let me alone!" the woman blurted. "I ain't done nothin'! You let go of me!"

Cole released her, but he closed the dining-room door. Annie Morrigan retreated, glaring defiantly. He followed her and she backed off into a corner.

"I'm a doctor, Annie," Cole said. "You know you're responsible for the outbreak of typhoid tonight in this house. Why did you dare come here to cook?"

"I ain't responsible for it!" the woman snapped. "There ain't nothin' the matter with me. I can cook now and nobody'll catch it from me—the doctor said so!"

"The doctor?" Cole asked. "What doctor?"

"The doctor who come to see me at home. He come of his own accord. He told me I was all right and I could go back to work. He said I wasn't carryin' it any more."

"What," Cole asked directly, "is that doctor's name?"

"I was mighty glad he told me!" the woman rushed on. "I wasn't goin' to stay cooped up in that house all the time like a convic'. He said I was all right, and he got me a job."

"With the Bennerlys?"

"None of your business!"

Cole's hand firmly grasped the defiant woman's arm as she started away. Listening, he heard movements at the top landing of the stairs. Someone was up there eavesdropping, perhaps about to come down. Again the woman tried to tear herself free of Cole's grasp, but his fingers held tightly.

"Listen to me, Annie. You left the Bennerly home when typhoid broke out. You got yourself another job, and typhoid broke out there. Now, here, in the third home since you left isolation, you've spread typhoid again. There's only one thing to do with you—lock you up—"

"You can't do it!" the woman screeched. "I'm all right! I ain't carryin' it any more! The doctor told me so!"

"What doctor?" Cole demanded again. "What doctor told you that? What's that doctor's name?"

The woman scowled, tried to tear free, shrugged, finally mumbled: "Doctor Walston."

"Walston? Doctor Sidney Walston? You're sure of that?"

"That's who!"

"Describe that man, Annie."

"You let go of me, you—" The woman's palm slapped across Cole's face. He recoiled with the unexpectedness of the blow. At the same time a startled exclamation sounded at the head of the stairs, and heels clicked quickly on the wood.

Cole twisted, let go of the woman, hurried to the foot of the stairs. A girl was running down, eyes widened with fright. "It's you, Miss Bennerly!" Cole exclaimed. "You found her, did you? Annie—come back here!"

Mrs. Morrigan was charging at the closed dining-room door, intent on making an escape. Cole hurried after her. She gripped the knob, glared back at Cole. Suddenly her gaze shifted quickly, alarm widened her eyes. She pointed past Cole and blurted: "That's him! You ask him! That's the doctor who told me!"

Cole spun. The woman's finger was pointing to one of the rear kitchen windows. In the light outside the pane there was a face. It melted away into the darkness beyond before Cole could clearly glimpse it. Obviously the man who had been peering into the room had retreated at the woman's alarmed cry. Cole started quickly for the rear door—and stopped.

At the precise instant when Annie Morrigan's hand touched the knob of the dining-room door, a bullet splintered the window-pane.

THE SHARP spatter of broken glass mixed with a breathy gasp from Annie Morrigan. Cole peered back in consternation, saw her slumping against the door. She dropped her old suitcase and raised a shaking hand to her neck that was gushing blood. The door opened upon her and she spilled to the floor.

Cole sped to the entrance. He shouldered past Barbara Bennerly, who was standing at the base of the stairs, and out. The girl started toward the woman as he stepped into darkness gashed by the flame of a gun. A second barking report sent splinters flying from another windowpane and brought an echoing moan from the kitchen.

Cole's weapon flicked level, spat once at the spot where the gun-fire had flashed. A hedge rustled as someone leaped through into the adjoining yard. Starting a sprint around the light of the windows, Cole glanced back to see Barbara Bennerly standing with both hands flat on the table, bent forward, red drops falling from her forehead to the oilcloth. Fury crackled in the epithet he blurted as he whirled back.

He hurried through the kitchen door to see the girl on her knees, clinging to the edge of the table. He took her arms, twisted her, saw an ugly, oozing cut above her eyes. The bullet had furrowed through the skin and the shock brought unconsciousness to her even as Cole held her in his arms.

"Miss Day!" he called.

There was a click at the front entrance, then quick steps hurrying around the house. Cole lowered the limp girl and pushed out the kitchen entrance as Miss Day appeared in the light. He sped across the lawn, automatic ready, and took a flying leap through the hedge. While he sprinted across the adjoining yard he heard the snarl of a motor on the street beyond. When he reached the corner the car was speeding out of sight. Concern for the wounded girl turned Carter Cole back to the house while the murderer fled through the night.

Miss Day said, with cool matter-of-factness, when Cole hurried into the kitchen: "The woman is dead."

Cole peered intently at Mrs. Morrigan lying across the sill, blood pooled under her head—a spreader of pestilence who could no longer endanger the lives of those around her. He turned after Miss Day into the maid's room adjoining, and bent over the girl on the cot. His deft ministrations brought dim consciousness to her and he strode out again.

In the living room he found a telephone. His call to the local police was a series of clipped, terse sentences which ended with, "I'm taking Miss Bennerly home, for treatment, and you can find her there." He called the number of the Cole sanitarium, got Kelly on the wire, said crisply: "Brick, meet me in front of the Bennerly home right away—there's been an attempt to kill the girl and there may be another."

HIS FACE was grim, his eyes flecked with steely lights, when he lifted Barbara Bennerly in his arms. Miss Day opened the way for him to the car. She supported the girl as Cole took the wheel, swung into the main thoroughfare that would lead him by the most direct way to the Bennerly house.

"A very pretty and a very admirable girl," Cole remarked, ignoring a red light. "Forthright and self-reliant, with as much brains as beauty, which is considerable. I like her."

"Yes, Doctor," said Miss Day.

"And I don't like," Cole went on grimly, "this ghastly mess she's been pulled into. It's the work of a desperate man. He's guilty of three murders; he almost made the score four with her. It's my intention, Jane, to see that that human devil gets what's due him—the chair."

"I'm June, Doctor," said Miss Day.

Cole sighed. "All right, June. Lewis Bennerly was right at the beginning—the cats killed his sons. The girl was right—a typhoid carrier was deliberately sent into the Bennerly home. It's a double plot to murder, a scheme to inflict slow death with typhoid abandoned in favor of a plan to inflict swifter death with curare. The reason behind that change of death plans is the key to the whole nasty business."

"Yes, Doctor."

Cole blurted: "Lord, can't you be human, Jane—June? Are you always so damnably level-headed and efficient? Are you ever anything else but a machine? *Are* you human?"

Miss Day didn't answer. Doctor Carter Cole turned and looked at her. He saw a gleam in her bright eyes, a faint curve of her red lips, a provocative lift of her shapely chin, and knew the answer. Miss June Day could, indeed, upon occasion, be very human.

"I've been thinking," she said softly. "The curare ampules point to Doctor Walston. But their being in Lewis Bennerly's bureau point to Lewis Bennerly. Isn't it possible that Mr. Bennerly bought them under the name of Doctor Walston?"

"That's the devilish part of it. Aelurophobia is a mild form of madness, isn't it? The law will consider Lewis Bennerly a maniac capable of the irrational act of killing two sons he dearly loved. If he is brought to trial, the question of his sanity will be decided by a lay jury which knows absolutely nothing about mental aberrations."

"And any specialists called in to testify," Miss Day added, "will be coached on the one hand by the prosecution, and on the other by the defense attorneys. They'll be allowed to say only what serves the ends of the lawyers who call them—only part of the truth. Mr. Bennerly is in a tight spot."

"Exactly what the murderer anticipated!" Cole declared as the Duesenberg sped along smooth cement. "If Bennerly is brought to trial he's almost certain to be convicted. He might have planned his own son's deaths. He might have wished them dead rather than see them degenerate into amoral idiocy through drug addiction. For, June, both Norton and Rolph Bennerly were addicts."

The car turned into a street of residences as Miss Day asked: "You've made sure of that?"

"*You* have," Cole said. "No, it must have been your sister. She traced down many prescriptions on file at various drug stores. They call for cocaine. And all of them are written for Norton and Rolph Bennerly, signed with the same name that has popped up again and again—Doctor Walston."

"Forged?" asked Miss Day. "By Lewis Bennerly?"

"Forged," Cole nodded. "Whether by Lewis Bennerly is something else again, it wouldn't seem to fit with our hypothesis that he killed them rather than have them continue addicts. Whatever the answer, I shouldn't like to be in that man's shoes, wherever he is."

THE CAR was slowing along the gloomy street. The head of Barbara Bennerly still rested against the firm shoulder of June Day. Cole's hands tightened on the wheel.

"Listen!" he said. "I want you to know exactly what I think happened because it's a possibility that Doctor Carter Cole might accidentally prick himself on a pin tipped with curare. Record this in that efficient brain of yours, June.

"For a reason unknown, the murderer planned to kill the two Bennerly brothers by means of typhoid.... Why only the two Bennerly brothers?... The girl was away at college. The father was immunized immediately—by Doctor Walston. The murderer deliberately sent death into the Bennerly home in the person of Annie Morrigan."

"Yes, Doctor."

"This plan," Cole went on, "began to work, but the deaths of the two brothers was still a matter of specu-lation at the time the cats with the poisoned claws were put into the house.... Why were cats used?... Because the murderer knew of the Bennerly phobia.... Why was the plan changed?... To speed the deaths.... Why the desper-ate haste?... The answer to that is that the brothers might recover from the fever—also Annie Morrigan uncon-sciously forced haste upon him."

"How, Doctor?"

"He had induced her," Cole explained, "to break her isolation, by telling her she was no longer a carrier of typhoid. He sent her to the Bennerly home. Fearing she was responsible, she left the house immediately typhoid broke out. She did not return to her own home, as the murderer probably expected. Still stubbornly believing, because she wished to, that she was uncontaminated, she took another job."

"He must have located her by following the Bennerly girl," Miss Day said quickly, in a hushed tone. "He killed Mrs. Morrigan because her disappearance was known, she was certain to be traced and found, and once she was found she would reveal the identity of the man who had sent her to the Bennerly place."

"Exactly," Cole said, bringing the car to the curb. "That's exactly it."

He slipped out, went around and opened the rear door on the side where Barbara Bennerly was sitting weakly. "The murderer of Mrs. Morrigan killed her to silence her, but why did he try to kill this lovely girl? Why did he launch this devilish murder plan in the first place? Those, June, are questions we must answer. Go first, please."

Barbara Bennerly was in Carter Cole's arms, and Brick Kelly, who had been waiting for them, was standing ready at his side. They went together into the house. The pungency in the air meant that it had been disinfected during the day. On the second floor Cole carried the girl into her bedroom. He had no need to call for whatever medicaments the Bennerly medicine closet might hold; Miss Day brought them.

Cole felt the girl's pulse strengthening as her eyelids fluttered. Her head lolled on the pillow and she looked into his eyes. Her mind was still fogged with the shock of the bullet and the pain of her bound wound, and at first her lips formed only mumbled unintelligible whispers.

"Good girl," Cole encouraged her. "You did a fine piece of detective work. You traced Mrs. Morrigan through her references, didn't you? She told you Doctor Walston had sent her to your home."

"Ye-es." The word was an effort.

Cole said gently: "You've got to rest. Miss Day is going to stay with you until you're entirely well. A few more questions. Do you know where your father is?"

"No-o."

"Have you seen him or heard from him since last night?"

"No."

"Did Mrs. Morrigan describe to you the man who sent her into your home?"

"Ye-es."

"You know who that man is?"

The girl's lips trembled but her eyes closed and her head lolled again. She gave a profound sigh. Noting a flutter of her pulse, Cole rose. His eyes met Miss Day's.

"She does know. She knows who the murderer is, but— Good."

Miss Day had brought her case with her. Cole filled a hypodermic; its needle plunged into the girl's soft arm. She breathed deeply, with slow rhythm.

Cole turned and said: "Brick, wait in the car." Miss Day had brought a filmy blue nightgown from the closet. Carter Cole felt a singular embarrassment, unprecedented in his professional career, as he helped Miss Day prepare the girl for a stay in bed. Only gossamer lingerie covered Barbara Bennerly's exquisite body when he quietly withdrew; and he noted another bright and very human gleam in the eyes of Miss June Day.

"Phone, if anything happens," he said. "I imagine I'll be answering the questions of the police until all hours."

"Yes, Doctor."

"Ah—good-night, June."

"Good-night."

Cole stepped out and stood a moment in confused thought. He was wondering whether he'd feel this same strange glow the next time he looked at that girl's sister believing it was the Miss Day he'd just left. He went troubled down the stairs.

In the car he sat a long moment before he looked up and said: "Oh, hello, Brick."

Brick said: "Geez! I been here all the time. I tell you, Doc, you ought to keep out of these cases. You ain't goin' nuts too, are you?"

"I think," said Carter Cole, "I'm almost out of this one now."

He knew in a moment that he was wrong. It was just as he was starting away that he heard a faint, stifled cry inside the Bennerly home and a sharp rapping. He braked the car even as it left the curb, for through the stillness of the night, a frantic, far-away voice was calling: "Let me out! Let me out!"

CHAPTER SIX
CATSPAW

CARTER COLE sprinted back, Brick Kelly loping after him toward the house. Now there was silence for a moment inside. Then again that far-away voice cried, "Let me out!" and the fast rapping of knuckles on thin wood followed. Cole's left hand closed hard on the entrance knob; the other leveled his 9mm.

"Brick," he said tightly, "get around in back. Eyes peeled. If anybody tries a break, stop him. This time land the first sock."

"Leave that to me, Doc! Especially if it's the same guy!"

Cole waited tensely until fading footfalls on the turf told him Kelly was rounding the house. Then he opened the door. Now the knocking was louder, mingled with the rattling of a doorknob. His long legs scissored up the steps, three at a time. The door of Barbara Bennerly's room was standing ajar. The girl, strengthened by the injection, was rising from the bed, her young body silhouetted against the light. She groped to the door, eyes pleading with Cole's.

"Back to bed at once!" Cole ordered her.

The girl sank exhaustedly into a chair beside the door. Cole strode toward her, but stopped when the knocking again echoed through the house. He eased into the adjoining room, peered at a closed door, stepped close. He twisted the knob, found the lock fast, and saw that the key was missing.

"Let me out—please let me out!" the voice inside pled.

"I'm afraid, Miss Day," Cole said quietly, "you'll have to wait until I find the key. You're not a claustrophobe, are you?"*

The girl imprisoned within the closet became quiet. She answered through the panels: "No, Doctor."

"Good. Just what happened?"

"I came in here—this is a linen closet—to get sheets to make up my own bed. Someone locked me in."

"It couldn't have been Miss Bennerly."

"It was a man. I caught the merest glimpse of him when he shut the door. He was masked."

"Masked?"

"Yes, Doctor."

"How was he dressed?"

"He was wearing a big coat."

Cole straightened. "While you're in there, June, you're perfectly safe. Please wait—no noise. Don't be frightened."

The man who had imprisoned Miss Day in the closet was, Cole was sure, still in the house. Now Cole stepped back into Barbara Bennerly's room. She had come to her feet, was holding to the door-frame and peering at him. He said gently: "You must go back to bed. You've got to—"

A faint, creaking noise that almost vanished in the sound of Cole's own words caused him to break off. The sound might have been made by a silently moving man's weight on a board in the floor. Cole turned slowly, eyes on the stairs. The noise had come from below. His gesture

---

* Claustrophobia is a fear of being in a confining space.—F.C.D.

repeated his order to the girl before he went down them slowly. He paused at the foot, weapon leveled, peering into the darkness of the library.

His hand swept across a switch, the table-lamp glowed. The room was empty. Cole went into it slowly. It was here that Lewis Bennerly had seen the cat—the black cat which had come slinking into the house from nowhere, bringing death on its claws. He opened the connecting door and stepped into the rear bedroom where the first cat's victim had died. It too was empty.

Cole looked past the doors of the closet and the bath before he turned back to the library. He crossed slowly to the two pairs of French windows, brown-draped, which opened onto the lawn. He turned to leave the room and suddenly, as a rustle of movement warned him, whirled back.

His move was fast, but not faster than the down-stroke of the gun which clicked sharply behind his ear. Cole jabbed one wild blow as he toppled. He dove against the easy chair, rolled off, lay still. His automatic slid from his lax hand; the table-light gleamed on his closed lids. A shadow hovered over him—a man in loose topcoat, whose hat was pulled low, whose face was masked, whose black-gloved hand gripped the barrel of the automatic which had felled Carter Cole.

COLE'S WORLD was a whirling blackness filled with donging echoes, but through the far-away bedlam he heard the click of the light-switch. The darkness that was upon him became deeper. He felt his one wrist and one ankle grasped, felt himself dragged. The spinning confusion in his mind continued while something strange was done to his wrists and ankles and face. Consciousness was returning to him when he heard soft footfalls move away.

His eyes fluttered open. He felt cold tile against his hands and knew that he was in the bath of the room in which Norton Bennerly had died under the poisoned claws of a cat. When he tried to separate his hands an unyielding force bound them. He tried to take a breath, and his lips clung together. He realized then that adhesive tape was strapping his ankles and wrists, that a strip was plastered across his mouth.

Then a sound brought a chill to his heart.

It was a soft, throaty, animal sound that rippled almost inaudibly in the darkness, a sound that came like gentle waves through the stillness—the purring of a cat. It might be slinking through the doorway now. It might be creeping upon him with padded feet, with claws that carried a deadly poison. Now the soft, whirring voice grew louder in the dark and Cole dragged himself upright.

He swayed and slumped against the wall. Inching forward cautiously, so as not to frighten a cat who could scratch death into him with one stroke of its padded paw, he sought the door. He felt its jamb and shouldered against it. It swung shut with a click, blanketed away the purr of the cat.

Through the darkness a faint call came. "Doctor—where are you, Doctor?" It was Barbara Bennerly, her voice weak with pain. "Where are you, Doctor Cole?"

Cole twisted, toppled and fell. His head was still whirling. He thrust at the heel of his left shoe with the toe of his right, pushed it loose, kicked it off. Shedding his right shoe was a task that made his head buzz, but by scraping the heel, pushing with his toes, he achieved it. He rolled on his face, drew his legs up behind him, tugged and stripped his socks off. With them went the shackling adhesive tape.

Carter Cole brought himself up on bare feet, panting, head ringing.

Barbara Bennerly's voice came faintly again. "Doctor Cole. Why don't you answer me, Doctor?"

Cole knew that a masked man was lurking somewhere beyond this closed door. A death-laden cat was purring in the darkness. While the tape plastered his mouth he could shout no warning to Barbara Bennerly that she would understand. An inarticulate cry would only startle her, bring her down the stairs—into the darkness where the cat was stalking. He turned from the door, lowered his head, rubbed it against the wall.

The click of the light-switch, when his head pushed it, shocked like the crack of a shot in his brain. The glare blinded him. He went on bare feet to the cabinet above the washbowl, turned, sat on the bowl, reached far up, clicked the door of the cabinet open. He searched the shelves and his gaze brightened on a tin can. It contained a trade-marked cleansing fluid—"non-explosive type." Carbon tetrachloride Cole knew it to be. It could dissolve and loosen the adhesive binding his wrists.

"Doctor Cole!" Barbara Bennerly's voice sounded nearer now through the closed door. "Doctor Cole!"

A moan pressed to Cole's sealed lips. The girl was coming down the stairs. In a minute she would enter the rooms where the cat with lethal claws was purring its death song.

Cole struggled to draw one foot under him, then the other, as he sat ludicrously on the washbowl. At last he straightened up; his fingers groped for the can of cleanser. He brought it from the shelf, jumped down, held the can behind him. He twisted the cap free and bent forward, holding the mouth of the can close to his wrists. Chill, pungent liquid gushed over his skin, drenching the adhesive that bound his wrists.

"Doctor Cole, why don't you answer? Are you down here, Doctor Cole?"

COLE BENT again, drenched his wrists once more, tugged at them. He felt the stickiness of the dissolving adhesive, yielding slowly. He rubbed his shoulder against the wall, clicked the light out. Now he turned, twisted the knob, opened the door. Again he drenched his wrists, and stepped silently out into the darkness. Through the library he could hear the soft, slipping sound of the girl's steps, tiptoeing uncertainly over the floor.

He could not hear the purr of a cat now, but he knew it was there.

He stopped, emptied the can on his wrists, then stepped aside swiftly as a switch clicked in the library and the table-lamp glowed. Warily he stood outside the shaft of light that fanned into the bedroom where poisoned cat-claws had killed a man. He saw Barbara Bennerly, her one hand on the frame of the door, a strip of bandage across her forehead, come into the room. She was fully dressed now.

"Doctor," she said faintly. "Where are you?"

Her hand passed weakly across her white face as she took slow steps toward the room in which Cole was standing. A call was on his sealed lips—an inarticulate call which would hurry her now beyond this door which Cole could shut and bolt—but sudden movement in the library startled him. The door through which the girl had just ventured slapped shut.

She turned in fright, peering at a figure revealed in the amber glow—a man whose face was masked by a black cloth. His body was covered with a great loose coat. He was bending toward her with blazing eyes, and holding high a brass cage that contained a cat. A muffled, mute cry came from the lips of Carter Cole; but the girl did not hear. She was gazing at the cat, backing from it in fright. Now the faintness she had felt was gone, swept away in the fear that seized her—the fear of the cat. She retreated with the agonized slowness of a person fleeing from a horror in a dream; and the man holding the cage stepped toward her. His eyes glared like the eyes of the cat in the cage as he brought it nearer the girl.

Cole started for the open connecting door as the man with the cage suddenly shook it. His hands, covered with heavy leather gloves, shook the cage, and the frightened cat struck out with a forepaw and spat. It squirmed frantically to escape its prison as one gloved hand of the masked man reached to the catch that would release it.

The girl stood spellbound with horror as Carter Cole lurched through the door. Sight of him straightened the man with the cage. Cole threw himself at the masked figure even while the door of the cage flew open. He glimpsed the terrorized cat bounding out, one of the gloved hands snatching a gun up from the pocket of the loose coat. In an armless tackle he flung himself against the masked man.

A stifled scream tore from the lips of the horrified girl. The cage fell, rolled, its door still yawning. Cole's swift tackle crushed the masked man against the wall. They slid down together.

Desperately Cole flung himself on the hand that clenched the automatic. A gloved fist spat against his shoulder as he tugged frantically at the softening bonds of his wrists. The tape was tearing apart when a second blow jarred him and the masked man leaped away.

Cole squirmed up as his hands came free. His fall on the gun had numbed the hand of the man who had held it; it lay now in the light. Cole seized it, twisted as he heard the spitting of a cat. Barbara Bennerly was striking at it frantically, and the cat was striking back, claws bared and glinting yellow. Cole's sticky hand turned the automatic and one shot blasted.

The cat dropped writhing on the carpet. The girl went limp with sudden relief and melted into a chair. Now Cole turned as he heard a hoarse call outside. "Doc! I've got him, Doc!"

Carter Cole stripped the adhesive from his mouth and ran into the dew-drenched grass, toward two black figures struggling beside the hedge. "Stop that!" he commanded. "You're covered!" The sharp ring of his voice brought obedience. Brick Kelly straightened panting; the other man huddled against the hedge, head bowed.

Cole kept the automatic leveled and said crisply: "Get into the house, Brick. Get that girl back into bed. Find a key in one of the other doors to open the upstairs closet. Move, Brick!"

Cole peered at the shadow figure as Kelly ran into the house. He reached, raised the cowed man's chin. His lips tightened on a sigh as he peered at the face which shone dark-lined against the blackness of the night.

His captive was Lewis Bennerly.

CHAPTER SEVEN
DOCTOR DEATH

FIVE MEN and a girl sat in the office of the director of the Cole Sanitarium next morning. One by one the efficient Misses Day had escorted them along the shining hallways to chairs near the desk. "Doctor Cole will see you soon," they had been told.

Two of the five—Chief Wellsmore and Detective Blake—were the guiding powers of the local police organization. Two—Doctors Merrick and Walston—had been physicians to the Bennerly brothers. Side by side sat Lewis Bennerly and his daughter. They waited in silence.

A brisk step sounded in the outer office, Carter Cole opened the door. Lewis Bennerly rose in dismay when he saw that Cole was carrying a magnificent white Persian cat. Cole paid no attention to Bennerly's discomfiture, he greeted his callers with brisk affability and sat behind the desk, keeping the cat on his lap while he stroked its silky fur.

The cat purred contentedly.

"I've asked you all to come here," Cole began, "because you're all connected with the case. I have placed all the facts in the hands of Chief Wellsmore and Detective Blake, our estimable police officials. They are here to make an arrest. The murderer of Norton and Rolph Bennerly—the murderer of Annie Morrigan—the intended murderer of Miss Barbara Bennerly—is in this office now."

Cole stroked the cat, and the cat purred. The two police officials peered at the floor. The two doctors gazed at each other. Lewis Bennerly peered at the cat, and the girl gazed at Cole.

"The facts," said Cole, "are plain. Suspicion points to Lewis Bennerly because I caught him last night after the murderer escaped the house. Mr. Bennerly's statement concerning these things is simple.

"He knows nothing about the curare. He escaped the hospital merely as a protest against confinement. He went back to his home and hid outside it in the hope of seeing his daughter while afraid of being caught and returned here. He was not the masked man in the house. My good friend, Kelly, having spotted him lurking about the place, seized him and let the real murderer go. This, of course, is what Mr. Bennerly says."

Carter Cole kept stroking the cat.

"Let us examine his statement. It is not likely anyone other than a medical man would know that the deadly poison curare may be obtained in ampules for medical use. He was himself in danger of death from the poisoned claws the night the cat killed Norton Bennerly. I believe his story. This crime was committed by a man of medicine."

Doctors Walston and Merrick peered at each other again, and Carter Cole continued to stroke the cat.

"Let us consider," Cole said quietly, "the evidence pointing to Doctor Walston. The curare ampules, first of all, were bought in his name. Though he was unknown to Lewis Bennerly until called into consultation on the typhoid cases, he was known to Norton and Rolph. And second, the name of Doctor Walston was signed to many prescriptions for cocaine given to Norton and Rolph. Those prescriptions reveal the motive for the murders."

There was silence in the office while the hand of Cole smoothed the coat of the beautiful Persian.

"For a year," he continued, "the Bennerly brothers were addicts. Perhaps at first they obtained their cocaine through bootleg channels. Then they began to receive it by prescription. They preferred to obtain it in this way because criminal vendors of narcotics dilute their stuff with powdered sugar. The Bennerly brothers' demands for it were heavy. To all the prescriptions they used, the name of Doctor Walston was signed.

"Those prescriptions constituted illegal use of a doctor's privilege. Discovery that he was vending cocaine to these two men must result in professional ruin, if not prison. It was an inevitability which only murder could avert. Murder because the Bennerly brothers possessed a power which forced him to continue writing those prescriptions. What that power was I confess I do not know—but it was used relentlessly by the two men craving for the drug."

THE CAT in Cole's lap was purring musically; and the eyes of Lewis Bennerly remained fixed on it.

"That," Cole said, "is the picture of murder. Two men forcing their doctor to feed them drugs illegally. The doctor faced with the loss of his practise, the loss of his professional honor, a sentence in a federal prison if discovered. The doctor escaping that tragedy by killing the men who were forcing disaster upon him. First planning to kill them with typhoid, then using poison and attempting to brand an innocent man in the event it was seen to be murder. The evidence I have presented, of course, points directly to Doctor Walston as the murderer."

Walston adjusted his horn-rimmed eyeglasses. Doctor Merrick leaned forward tensely to exclaim: "Good God, I can't believe it!"

"Nor I," Cole said quietly. "The evidence points to Doctor Walston, but Doctor Walston is absolutely innocent."

Chief Wellsmore thrust his blunt chin at Cole. "What the devil makes you think that?"

"Last night Annie Morrigan was killed—silenced. The murderer's first plan sent her into the Bennerly home. She could identify him, brand him with murder. The man who had previously killed the Bennerly brothers killed her."

"Certainly!"

"Doctor Walston could not have killed Mrs. Morrigan last night: therefore he did not kill Norton and Rolph Bennerly. Doctor Walston could not have done it because all last night, at my suggestion—because I suspected the murder plan was not complete and I wanted to remove him from the field of action—he suffered himself to be locked in a room in this sanitarium as securely as any of my patients."

"Then—"

"Then," Cole said calmly, "I think we should hear from Doctor Merrick's own lips the explanation of what hold the Bennerly brothers had on him. Shall we have it now, Doctor Merrick?"

The compact-bodied Merrick and Lewis Bennerly jerked to their feet at the same instant. The physician stood paralyzed. Bennerly, for the first time tearing his gaze from the cat, spoke swiftly.

"A check! A raised check! Merrick raised a check Norton gave him a year ago to pay his bill! Norton told me Merrick had made it good, that the matter was ended. It wasn't ended. They were holding it over him. That's the way they forced him to—"

Merrick darted to a door at the side of the office with Chief Wellsmore close on his heels. The door slammed, barring the way. Blake thrust at it. A bolt had clicked into its socket, the way was barred. Wellsmore snugged a Colt .45 into his hand and poised it to strike at the pebbled pane.

Carter Cole, still sitting at the desk and stroking the Persian, said levelly: "There's no possible way he can get out of here, Chief."

THE BUTT of the .45 splintered the glass. Wellsmore reached through, drew the bolt. Blake charged in behind him and Cole listened to their gruff, breathy voices.

"What's happened to him?"

"He knew he was cornered!"

"Watch him—maybe he's faking!"

Cole rose. Quite calmly he handed the Persian cat to Lewis Bennerly. "Will you take him for a moment, please?" he asked, and stepped toward the door. On the sill he looked back to see Bennerly holding the cat gingerly. Bennerly's eyes blinked. "I—I've never touched a cat before!" he blurted. "It—it likes me! It's purring! It—it can't hurt me, can it?"

Cole pressed a button on his desk. A trim, very pretty and efficient nurse-secretary stepped into the room. To her he said: "Mr. Bennerly and Miss Bennerly may go now. Both of them are quite all right. Please show them to the gate."

He watched Bennerly go out the door, staring in hypnotic fascination at the purring Persian, still holding it. Barbara Bennerly turned to him impulsively; her warm hand closed on his.

"How can we ever thank you for—"

"You needn't, at all," Cole said. "The cat's name is Boots, and if you promise to keep him with you, that's all the thanks I could wish. I think," he added, "you'll like him very much."

He stepped into the adjoining office where two puzzled police officers were bending over Merrick. The doctor was sprawled against the wall, one hand extended palm down, its back marked by a single red scratch. Cole knelt, found the yellow-tipped pin the dead man had kept handy.

He rose and said quietly: "I'm rather glad he did that. He might have entered a plea of insanity, been brought here. He wouldn't have belonged. There are over a thousand lunatics in this sanitarium—but they're all nice people."

THE CASE OF THE SKINNED MEN

THROUGH THE DOORS OF THE GREAT PASTEUR FOUNDATION HOSPITAL STARK HORROR HAD COME. FOR TWICE IN ONE NIGHT SOME FIEND WITH A SURGEON'S SCALPEL HAD DEFTLY PEELED AWAY EVERY INCH OF SKIN FROM TWO SUCCESSIVE PATIENTS, LEAVING ONLY A HIDEOUS MASS OF BONE AND MUSCLE ON THE BEDS. WHO WAS THE MURDER MEDICO WHO HAD COMMITTED THE ATROCIOUS CRIMES? WAS IT POSSIBLE THE BEAUTIFUL DOCTOR MARY GRAFTON HAD GONE MAD AT LAST, STRIPPING HUMAN HIDES AS SHE STRIPPED THE LEATHER FROM THE INSTRUMENT CASES OF HER FELLOW SURGEONS?

CHAPTER ONE
THE HORROR IN 319

CARTER COLE, M.D., psychiatrist by profession and crime investigator by nature, suppressed an incredulous smile and observed gravely: "I find it difficult to believe that a lovely young woman physician literally covets your skin, Mr. Gifford."

Terror gripped the man on the hospital bed. His unruly shock of snow-white hair made his fear-mirrored eyes seem the more brilliantly black as he tensely raised on one elbow. His voice trembled uncontrollably as he spoke.

"Her eyes are strange when she looks at me. I shudder when she touches me. I dread to see her come into this room because I'm afraid of her—afraid of what she might do to me."

"Actually afraid," Carter Cole asked, "that she will strip the skin from your living body?"

"Yes!"

COLE ACCEPTED the fact that John Gifford's terror was as real as it was apparently unfounded. If Gifford had not been a friend of twelve years standing, Cole might never have responded to his urgent plea on the telephone. Had he not known that Gifford was a hard-headed, self-made businessman, Cole might have dismissed instantly the intimation that Doctor Mary Grafton—as charming a

The shadowy figure went up the stairs as Cole squirmed in an attempt to rise.

young woman as had ever put lovely fingers on a patient's quickened pulse—was obsessed by a murderous mania.

But he had responded to Gifford's frantic call by driving hastily from his famous sanitarium on Long Island to the

noted Pasteur Foundation Hospital in Manhattan. He had listened with grave patience to Gifford's fearfully earnest story. Now his keen mind weighed it as he gazed at the pale face of his hoary-headed friend.

"I know Doctor Grafton, John," he observed. "Besides being an exceedingly attractive young woman, she's highly intelligent and an authority in her field. If I were a patient I should be utterly delighted merely to see her come into my room, but you say—"

"I shrink from her!" Gifford exclaimed. "Carter, I'm not mad. God knows I'm not! But she is! From the strange things I've heard about her—her irrational acts—she shouldn't be allowed to practise. I beg you to use your influence to take her off my case. As long as I know she may—at any moment—come through that door with that uncanny look in her eyes, I can't rest. I'm afraid to sleep—because I dream—"

Gifford's eyes brightened with terror. "I can't fight it down—can't drive it out of my mind! A week ago, when I was in the solarium, I wandered about. There's an experimental laboratory on the same floor. I looked in. God—I can't forget! She was in there—Doctor Grafton. I saw her bending over a dead body on a table, She was—using a sharp knife—taking the skin off. I saw her skinning a human body!"

Cole asked calmly: "Why not? Dissection is daily routine and Doctor Grafton is doing important research in dermatology.* You're fortunate she is attending you because there is no better dermatologist in New York. What you saw was entirely commonplace."

Gifford scarcely heard. "She ordered me away. I heard her bolt the door. It haunts me—the picture of that young woman with the strange eyes stripping skin from that corpse. I'm afraid to sleep because I dream of it. I dream

---

* That branch of medical science that relates to the skin and its diseases.—F.C.D.

that she's bending over me here, while I lie in bed, powerless to help myself—peeling the skin off my body—skinning me alive!"

Cole said incisively: "Look here, John. This fear is not of your own making. It was planted in your mind. Someone put it there. Who told you of these strange acts—or whatever they are—of Doctor Grafton's? Who made you believe you are in danger?"

The white-haired man sank back on the bed; he squirmed with pain and moaned. Weakened by the surge of agony, he lay breathing fast, while Cole's head wagged sympathetically. Cole glanced at the temperature and pulse record on the clipboard, noted that his friend's case of *Herpes zoster** had entered a severe stage, and rose.

The man on the bed whispered: "It was told me in confidence, as a warning, by one who knows. I'm sure he knows. Carter, I beg of you to keep her away from me—so I can sleep—sleep."

Cole assured him quietly: "I'll do all I can, John."

He was striding toward the door labeled *Director*, trying to reconcile Gifford's haunting dread with his picture of the admirable, efficient young-woman physician he knew, when a man's voice exclaimed, "We'll settle this right now, Doctor!" from a door which opened directly at Cole's side.

The slender, lovely young woman who stumbled over the sill was Mary Grafton. She was breathless, tearful; her one arm was gripped angrily by a man whom Cole recog-

---

* *Herpes zoster* is a disease of the skin commonly called shingles. There is a superstition concerning it, that when the infection spreads around the body and meets, death results. This belief has no foundation in fact. The disease is never in itself fatal.—F.C.D.

nized as Doctor Maurice Cobin. He released her, pointing toward the director's door and commanded: "Go in now!"

The young woman's eyes were frantic as she complied. Cole gazed wonderingly while Cobin strode after her, carrying in one hand a briefcase that was slashed and ripped apart.

DOCTOR CARTER COLE'S life-work was an expert search into the profound mysteries of disordered brains. The great sanitarium on Long Island where he conducted his investigations into the labyrinths of the human mind was famous the world over, yet Cole scarcely looked the part of a psychiatrist whose authoritative books were mile-posts in the advance of psychopathology. He was astonishingly young; he had the broad-shouldered, narrow-hipped physique of an athlete; his humorously piercing eyes, contained a brain that worked like lightning.

It was working now—on the puzzle of Doctor Mary Grafton.

An elevator panel slid open as Cole approached the director's office. He stepped aside to allow Doctor Channing Grafton to enter the office first. "I'm afraid, Doctor," Cole said gravely, "that your daughter is in trouble."

Channing Grafton looked startled, stepped past quickly. Cole, following, saw him push through the inner door, and heard voices mingling in the room beyond. He recognized Mary Grafton's, frantically pleading; Cobin's angrily interrupting; that of Doctor Huston Dewey, director of the great hospital, rumbling gravely.

Cole knocked and the voices stopped. He entered and said, while the four at the desk gazed at him: "I don't mean to intrude, but this case has become important to me. May I remain?"

Doctor Channing Grafton—who, Cole knew, was the young woman's foster-father and a man whose once lucrative practise had dwindled to nothing as a result of a scandalous law-suit and its devastating publicity—rapped the desk in angry protest.

"This treatment of my daughter is an outrage. Doctor Cobin doesn't know what he's saying. Give her a fair chance to explain!"

The piercing eyes of Doctor Dewey were studying the drawn face of the girl. "She has that opportunity now. I cannot overlook Doctor Grafton's strange behavior. She must explain."

Cole saw that the girl was striving to control a rising hysteria. Doctor Cobin, gazing at the mutilated briefcase he still held, gestured in bewilderment and continued: "I'm not angry because I found Doctor Grafton cutting my case apart with a scalpel. I sincerely admire her for her excellent work, for the advances she has made in autoplasty.* But surely this—this indicates a mental condition that—I'm sorry but—" Cobin hesitated, then blurted: "I'm afraid she has become a dangerous person."

The girl murmured in anguish: "Oh, no—no!"

The stern Doctor Dewey scowled at her. "Doctor Grafton, you have my deepest sympathy, I assure you. I realize that the suicide of your fiancé was a cruel shock, coming as it did on the very eve of your marriage. We've all known that. But your actions have become such that I regret I must now ask you to resign from the staff."

"Please!" the girl protested. "You don't understand!"

---

* The repair of diseased or injured parts of the body by transplanting pieces from some other part—a specialized field of medical science which includes skin grafting.—F.C.D.

"Then perhaps you will explain."

"I—I can't explain!"

"Do you mean that you don't know the reason for your own acts? If you don't, then surely you must realize that, brilliant as your work has been, valuable as you have made yourself to us, you can't continue here. It would be sheer folly to allow one of your—your temperament to come in contact with our patients."

The girl stood stunned. Cole stepped forward. He said briskly: "I simply can't keep out of this. May I ask you, Doctor Dewey, exactly what Doctor Grafton has done?"

Dewey answered: "Doctor Cole, you're precisely the man to handle this case. I hope Doctor Grafton puts herself under your care. Her actions—"

The girl's eyes turned pleadingly upon Cole as the director of the hospital rapidly detailed her amazing history.

"Several weeks ago—immediately following the suicide of Doctor Philip Price, which we all knew shocked Doctor Grafton deeply—the first episode occurred. Doctor Bell, returning from the operating room, found his medicine case torn to pieces. Its contents had been dumped out, the lining ripped away, and the leather cut apart. He had no idea who had done it or why. Doctor Grafton did not then, or later, when various other cases were found destroyed in the same way, offer the explanation that she was responsible."

"I couldn't," the girl said in a whisper.

DOCTOR DEWEY continued his explanation. "No less than ten cases met with this strange destruction during the first week—medicine cases, briefcases, cases for instruments such as sphygmomanometers,* even spectacle cases. Each time the destruction was done in secret. The staff had noticed the continued self-absorption of Doctor Grafton, but none of them had connected her with the vandalism, and she still had not confessed it."

"I couldn't!" the girl whispered in anguish again.

"We began to suspect Doctor Grafton," Doctor Dewey went on gravely, "but not until now, with Doctor Cobin actually discovering her in the act, were we sure. This young woman, Doctor Cole, is plainly gripped by an obsession which forces her to cut apart any leather case that comes into her hands."

The distressed girl, turning pleadingly to Cole, exclaimed: "But they don't understand!"

"And she can't explain!" Doctor Dewey concluded.

"No." Mary Grafton's answer was a whisper. "No."

"You actually did this?" Cole asked quietly.

Again that strained, whispered affirmative—"Yes."

Deep lights shone in Cole's thoughtful eyes. "I have personally handled every known type of mental derangement," he observed to Doctor Dewey. "In my sanitarium there are more than a thousand patients representing the full category of psychopathology. But never in all my experience have I met anything like this."

The girl's foster-father was quick to speak in her defense. "I say this drastic action against Mary is an outrage. You admit it's due to an overwhelming emotional shock. I'm sure she'll recover after a short rest. Instead of forcing her to resign, offer her a leave of absence."

---

* An instrument for measuring blood-pressure, a commonplace but vital part of a doctor's equipment.—F.C.D.

"I did that, immediately upon Doctor Price's death, and she refused it," the director explained. "This strange obsession of hers has become steadily worse, and I doubt if a mere rest will remedy it. Do you agree with me, Doctor Cole?"

"I don't agree that there is actually an obsession at all," Cole answered. "Doctor Grafton, I'm sure, has an excellent reason for what she has done—if she will only explain it."

"Thank you, Doctor Cole—but I can't explain. I can't!" Mary Grafton reiterated.

"Because she doesn't understand her own actions," Doctor Dewey spoke up briskly. "Doctor Cole, I know something of psychiatry myself. Doctor Grafton's case may become steadily more serious, unless she submits to skilled treatment. If she doesn't bring this compulsion under control it may drive her to far more destructive acts—perhaps even to—"

Doctor Dewey did not speak the word that came to his lips, but Carter Cole could read it, hovering there. It was "murder." It chilled Cole; and the chill in him grew instantly sharper when, at the very moment the director paused, a ringing scream echoed in the corridor outside the door—a scream of terror.

Silence followed—an amazed, bewildered hush. It was broken by quick footfalls in the hall and in the outer office, by the twisting of a knob and a swiftly opened door.

The nurse who stopped short on the sill had, like her sisters in the profession, been trained to accept the ordeal of the operating room without the blink of an eye, to meet death cooly—yet now she stood pale and stricken with a terror that held her momentarily speechless.

"What is it?" Doctor Dewey snapped. "What do you mean by—"

"Mr. Pomeroy!" Nurse Lovett blurted. "Oh—my—God!"

The name sent the perturbed director striding out the door, for it was that of a patient on the same floor. Cole stepped aside as Doctor Mary Grafton hurried after him. She raced past Doctor Dewey, was the first to reach the swinging door of Room 319. She pushed it open, stepped back with a shudder of revulsion as Cole and Dewey rushed dismayed to the side of a bed on which horror lay.

It was a human body which had been stripped of its skin!

CHAPTER TWO
DOMAIN OF THE
DEMENTED

DOCTOR MARY GRAFTON stood motionless and mute, widened eyes on the ghastly sight. Carter Cole peered in chilled amazement.

On the side of the bed a scalpel glittered in the light.

The corpse lay on blood-crusted white, every muscle exposed, its face frightful, red jaw gaping. Cole was the first to move. He bent forward tensely, and saw with astonishment that the cadaver's teeth had been pulled from their sockets.

The living peered at the skinless dead for a long, nerve-tightening moment of silence. The eyes of Mary Grafton turned then upon Cole—eyes in which he saw panic. He was conscious of Doctor Dewey's quick move behind him and heard the director's husky voice punctuated by the closing of the door.

"Miss Lovett, you will telephone for the police at once!"

Cole said quietly: "The police?"

"This patient is dead, Doctor Cole."

"Dead, of course."

"Murdered." Now Dewey's eyes turned searchingly upon Mary Grafton and she recoiled from him in unutterable alarm. "This patient—Edmund Pomeroy—did not die of the ailment which brought him to the hospital. This inhuman atrocity is the work of an irrational mind. This man has been murdered."

"Yes," Carter Cole said very quietly. "Murdered."

"He was," Dewey stated huskily, "the patient of Doctor Grafton."

The girl blurted: "You can't believe—"

"Please go to my office, Doctor Grafton," Dewey's voice crackled in command. "You will wait there."

The terrified girl did not move until Cole opened the door, his sympathetic eyes urging her to go. She went with a last, unspeakably bewildered glance at the thing on the bed.

"Good God! Nothing like this—" Dewey blurted, brokenly and stopped.

Cole's eyes narrowed as he bent over the bed. Certainly an expert hand had removed the skin from this body. From head to foot the sharp blade of the scalpel had worked with a surgeon's skill, stripping away all save fragments of the skin around the mouth, the eyelids and the nails.

Cole straightened, glanced once around the room, once through the windows and across the roof of the adjoining building, then stepped out. Doctor Dewey promptly turned a key in the lock of 319.

Doctor Channing Grafton was standing in the corridor, dismayed gaze turning from Dewey's face to Cole's. He said, tight-lipped: "Nurse Lovett just told me that Mary went into Mr. Pomeroy's room an hour ago. She remained—"

"—then evidently stole in to the room across the hall— where Doctor Cobin discovered her ripping his leather case," the director completed, interrupting. "Leather— skin! Good God!"

Cole observed quietly: "That man's skin is missing."

"The better part of an hour was time enough for her to—" Doctor Dewey hesitated, revolted at the thought. "You have come into this case much too late, Doctor Cole, I'm afraid. The police are on their way now."

"They'll do the usual things," Cole observed. "Try to find fingerprints on the scalpel and the bed, question that girl until she's so hysterical she'll admit anything—all the usual things in a case in which there isn't one usual element"

"A conclusive case!" Dewey stated. "Flatly conclusive. The act of a mad woman. You saw Doctor Cobin's briefcase—the leather peeled layer from layer. And in there—a man stripped of his skin!"

Cole strode quickly to the director's office. He saw that Mary Grafton was not in the outer room; then he stepped into the inner. It, too, was empty. Dewey, following Cole, stopped short.

"Gone," said Cole.

"I ordered her to wait!"

"She chose," Cole said quietly, "not to wait to be arrested for murder."

Dewey hurried along the corridor and pressed the button of the elevator. Cole followed as the panel slid back to reveal the white-uniformed attendant, and heard the director ask: "Did you take Doctor Mary Grafton down a moment ago?"

"Yes, sir," the attendant answered.

Cole stepped in with Dewey, and the car slid down. "Mad!" the director blurted. "Stark mad!"

Cole's eyes darkened thoughtfully as he followed the director past the desk, to the doorman. His answer to

Doctor Dewey's query added to the information that the girl had fled the building.

Outside the entrance, Doctor Dewey paused and exclaimed: "This attempt to escape will only strengthen the case against her. The police are sure to find her. Good God, Cole! If we'd only known—if you'd only come into this case earlier, and somehow removed that obsession from her mind, you might have saved her from this horrible thing!"

"Perhaps," Cole observed, "it's not too late even now."

ALMOST AN hour later Cole strode into the court around which the great hospital was built. This huge, open area eliminated inside rooms, and served as a parking space for automobiles. Cole's big Duesenberg sedan was among them. He took the wheel and guided the powerful motor out into the street.

His course lay across Manhattan, and the Queensboro Bridge. As he drove, he remembered the haunting words of his old friend Gifford—"Her eyes are strange when she looks at me. I shudder when she touches me. I shrink from her."

While Cole drove swiftly over the cement highway that led to his Long Island sanitarium, he could not forget the terror shining in Gifford's eyes—and those words—"Keep her away from me so I can sleep… Her eyes are strange…" And Dewey's—"Leather peeled layer from layer—and in there a human stripped of his skin!" And Mary Grafton's—"I can't explain—I can't!"

Cole's lips curved in a cool smile when he swung into the broad gate of the sanitarium. Tonight he did not, as usual, unlock it and drive in, but instead quietly opened the rear door of the car and spoke into the darkness.

"It's quite safe here. You may come out, Doctor Grafton."

A faint flutter of movement, the almost inaudible rhythm of quick breathing in the space behind him while he drove, had told him that the girl was huddled in the car. Now he saw her white face, her frantic eyes, in the dim glow reflecting from the dash. He waited, smiling, and the girl crept out of the car slowly, her eyes searching Cole's. She turned suddenly, a sob breaking from trembling lips, and ran.

"Wait—please wait!" Cole called. But she ran on—frantically through the dark shadows fringing the broad drive. He heard her sob again, then her quick footfalls abruptly vanished in the night.

Cole touched the call-button at the gate three times, then twice more in signal, before he opened the way. The massive tires of the Duesenberg were crunching not many yards up the graveled drive when a stocky man dove out of the darkness to the running-board. Brick Kelly, onetime dock-wolloper, able-bodied seaman, truck-driver and sculptor's model, now Cole's doggedly loyal jack-of-all-trades at the sanitarium, looked in and asked breathlessly: "What's up, Doc?"

"Break out the roadster, Brick, in a hurry. Somewhere in this vicinity there's a very lovely and terrified young woman. She's desperate to keep out of the hands of the police. You're to spot her and shadow her."

"O.K., Doc!"

"Don't let her know"—the car was still crawling along the drive—"and report by phone when you have something."

Kelly squinted. "Doc," he said earnestly, "there ain't anything you can ask me that I won't do. If you want somebody sunk in the river, just leave it to me. But this sounds like you're mixing into another of these screwy cases and—"

"Exactly!" Cole said. "And I'm in this one, I promise you, until I find out if and why this beautiful young woman I mentioned, skinned a man alive."

Kelly gasped "Geez!" and left the car with a leap.

COLE DREW up before the broad steps of the sprawling building which was the domain of the insane in which he held the highest command.

To his ears came a far-away sing-song of voices praying and chanting, cursing and wailing—the constant cacophonous chorus of the demented. As he entered he passed huge wooden blocks, based with felt, which every day were pushed laboriously from end to end of these labyrinthine halls by men and women with weirdly lax faces. The task absorbed their warped minds and exercised their bodies, while at the same time it polished the floors to mirror brightness. Along one of these halls Cole now strode briskly to his offices.

A very pretty and cooly efficient secretary in nurse's uniform greeted him. "Doctor Blanchard is extremely anxious to reach you on the phone, Doctor," she said. "Shall I call him back?"

"At once, Jane," Cole said.

"Yes, Doctor. But I'm not Jane. I'm June."

Cole smiled. "I might have known. You're always the other sister. Whichever you are, get Doctor Blanchard on the wire—if he's the Blanchard who's on the board of the Pasteur Foundation Hospital."

"He is, Doctor," June Day answered.

Cole knew nothing about the twin sisters Day other than that they were the most satisfactory secretaries possible. If they had families, sweethearts, or any private lives at all, such details were hidden behind their unruffled professional—and very pleasant to behold—exteriors. He was certain of only one other fact concerning them—they were perfectly identical, and constantly he called each by her wrong name.

While waiting for June Day to get Blanchard on the wire Cole himself briskly dialed a Manhattan number. The rumbling drawl that answered was that of Doctor Peter Morse, the famous medical examiner of New York City, as eccentric as he was brilliant. At mention of Cole's name, Morse boomed: "I'm just leaving on a case made to order for you. A man—"

"—skinned alive." Cole chuckled as Morse gasped. "But I'm wondering if he really was alive when the process began. If so, it's murder. If not, it's mutilating a dead body, a much less serious crime, but serious enough. You won't let the answer to that question get by you, old-timer."

Morse grunted. "I'll give it to you as soon as I've got it. That's what you want, is it?"

"It is," Cole answered, "and I want it desperately."

He hung up as the door opened on the very pretty and cooly brisk girl in nurse's uniform. "Doctor Blanchard waiting on the wire, Doctor."

"Good! I want information from the Pasteur Foundation. Of what disease was the patient Pomeroy suffering? Are there any marks of identification left on him? Has the dead man's missing skin been found yet? That's all, June."

"Yes, Doctor," said Miss Day. "But I'm Jane."

"You girls," Cole declared grimly, "sooner or later will make me an inmate of my own institution. You're always the other one! And you're not even surprised when I ask you to learn if a dead man's skin has been found anywhere other than on his body. Doesn't anything ever get you?"

Jane Day smiled enigmatically. "It's against the rules," she said softly, and went out.

Blanchard's voice rang quick and anxious in Cole's ear. "You were at the hospital when this ghastly thing was discovered," he said after clipped preliminaries. "Dewey phoned me, but before I go over I want to talk to you. I don't believe Mary Grafton capable of such a horrible thing."

"Nor I," Cole agreed. "I'll explain why when I see you, and you can count on me to the limit. Nothing irritates me like an amateur psychiatrist, and Doctor Dewey, excellent medical man that he is, is the worst kind. You're at home?... I'm on my way."

He hurried from his desk and saw that one of the Day twins—he did not attempt to determine which—was at the telephone getting the information he wanted. "Add data desired," he said into her ear as she talked, "the dead man's missing teeth, when and where found."

He started out, but stopped abruptly. A thought froze him—Doctor Mary Grafton had spent arduous years studying the human skin. She had cut leather cases apart, peeled layer from layer of the tanned hides—that was an established fact. And if she had actually, for any reason mad or sane, stripped the skin from a hospital patient, was the same demoniacal compulsion gripping her now? Could she, even now be stealing through the night, carrying perhaps a concealed razor-edged scalpel—seeking another victim?

Cole bolted into a run.

CHAPTER THREE
SKIN-DEEP IN MURDER

THE DUESENBERG rolled to a stop behind a
taxi which stood, motor running, at the curb in front
of the brownstone home of Doctor Charles Blanchard, in
Manhattan's West Sixties. Cole climbed the stoop, touched
the call-button, and was astonished by the immediate rattle
of the knob.

The entrance opened swiftly and Cole saw, in the gloom
of the musty hallway, not the bearded face of the old
medico, but the white, drawn features of Mary Grafton.

The girl peered with haunted, haggard eyes, abruptly fled
past Cole to climb into the waiting taxi. Before he could
recover from his astonishment the cab had spurted from
the curb and headed for the corner.

Steel-plated heels tapped the pavement and a stocky
figure joined Cole. "Geez, Doc!" Brick Kelly exclaimed.
"You got here fast! I just now phoned back!"

"Keep on her trail, Brick!" Cole directed quickly. "Don't
lose her!"

The taxi was swinging around the far corner when Kelly
sent his roadster after it with a snarl of gears. Cole saw the
taxi vanish, Kelly after it, and again touched the door-but-
ton. The girl had left the entrance standing ajar and he

could look along a silent, gloomy hallway, hear the bell's hollow ring respond to his touch.

Cole easily deduced the reason for the girl's furtive visit to the home of Doctor Blanchard. They were firm friends and apparently in desperation she had turned to him. Cole rang again, insistently. The bell jangled into the musty silence of the old house—but no step answered.

"Doctor Blanchard?" Cole called, and stepped in. He passed a parlor, a reception room, a consultation office, found them all empty.

"Doctor Blanchard!"

Cole's voice echoed as he peered into the dining room, the kitchen, again as he climbed the stairs of the typically narrow house to the second floor, the third. Every room was empty; his repeated calls brought no answer. A strange dread hurried Cole's long strides back down the stairway, on down to the rooms below the street level. At the lower entrance he stopped short, breath caught.

The dim glow of the street, shining inward, shrouded a still form lying on the floor of the front room—a kindly faced man with white goatee and mustache—Doctor Charles Blanchard. Cole bent over the motionless figure and the professional alertness of his eyes gave way to cold fury, for it was plain to see. Blanchard was dead.

Cole's sharp eyes searched the lower rooms for a telephone; finding none he ran quickly up the worn stairs. In Blanchard's consultation room he spotted the instrument, thoughtfully picked it up. He saw, on the desk, a cup half filled with coffee. Raising it, he smelled of it—and his eyes glittered. For mingled with the odor of the coffee was the bitter smell of almonds, sure indication to Cole of the presence of deadly cyanide.

Quickly he opened the cabinet beside Blanchard's old desk. He peered at a glass-stoppered bottle containing brownish-yellow lumps labelled *Cyanide of Potassium, C.P.* Now his lowering gaze discovered a pair of rubber gloves in the shadow on the floor beside the desk, and Cole knew that the police experts would find no fingerprints on the bottle of poison.

Grimly he raised the telephone—and again paused. A metallic click sent echoes rattling through the old house. Cole, his hand stealing toward the 9mm Luger bolstered at his arm-pit, took slow steps along the hallway. He listened up and down—but no sound followed the click within the silent house.

Luger extended, Cole went down the stairs. His first move was to the door of the forward room and his first glance through the doorway sent a quick breath through his pinched lips. For as he peered into the patch of light on the floor he saw nothing. The body of the old medico was gone.

Cole stepped in swiftly. A noise in the street turned him to the window and he pulled the heavy drapes aside. Unheard, a car had stopped in front of the house. A man, shoulders hunched, hat pulled low, was ducking furtively to the far side when Cole glanced out. Shadows masked the man's face as he hastened to the wheel. Cole spun and ran to the door.

The spring catch of the lower entrance baffled him for a moment and the delay brought an oath to his lips. At last he opened the way and sprang up, as the gears of the strange sedan ground in three swiftly ascending notes. It was a speeding, lightless, black shadow halfway up the block when he halted at the curb.

Without stopping to fire, Cole whirled again, ducked behind the wheel of his massive Duesenberg. His thrust at the starter brought only a soft snarl that lengthened as Cole's anger grew. Now the other car swung past the corner and vanished without his having glimpsed its plates or the face of the man at the wheel. He abandoned the attempt to start the car, slid out, clicked the hood up, and muttered maledictions.

The same hands that had spirited away the body of Doctor Blanchard had torn the ignition cables from the spark-plugs of Cole's car.

His heels beat angrily as he went back through the lower entrance. He snapped switches, searched for some clue to the identity of the body-snatcher. Finding none, he climbed to Blanchard's consultation room, took up the telephone. The number he dialed was not that of the police, but of the Cole Sanitarium.

"June, Jane, whichever you are," he said as the unruffled voice of one of the Day twins answered. "Has Brick reported again?"

"Yes, Doctor. From the Pasteur Foundation. I'm June."

Cole gave crisp directions. "Please get me all the facts on the recent death of Doctor Philip Price. I'm going to the Pasteur."

He strode out, clipped the dangling cables of the Duesenberg's ignition system back into the spark-plugs. In a few short moments the green lights of Central Park West were flashing past.

AS SOON as Cole slipped from the wheel, in the parking court of the great Pasteur Hospital, Brick Kelly appeared at his side.

"Do you mean to tell me, Brick," Cole asked quickly, "that Doctor Grafton came here?"

"She sure did, Doc! Left her taxi half a block away and got to the staff entrance—plenty scared. If she ain't gone out some other way, she's still in there. I've been watching this door. My car's parked out on the street."

"Keep watching," Cole directed. "If you see her come out, signal with the horn."

He sensed, as he entered the hospital and sought Doctor Dewey's office, that the girl's daring move was a continued desperate search for help. Perhaps she was seeking Doctor Howard Arnold, another stalwart veteran of the hospital, whose esteem had inspired her to undertake her arduous researches in dermatology. Cole wished, with a sigh, as he opened the door of the director's office, that Mary Grafton had chosen a field other than the study of the skin.

Cole found Doctor Dewey with a visitor—a man with close-cropped iron-gray hair, eyes sharp and crystal-clear as camera lenses—Inspector Brackett of Centre Street and the homicide detail.

Brackett's hand crushed Cole's and he said: "I've been trying to locate you. You and that young woman—Mary Grafton."

"Not, I hope," Cole remarked, "for the same reason." He spoke urgently to the stern Dewey. "A peculiar request, Doctor, but important. Please don't attempt to explain Mary Grafton's acts to the police."

Dewey bristled. "Why not? I'm more shocked than I can say that this young woman has become a murderous maniac but—good God!—I can't avoid stating the facts."

"Because you're entirely in error, and this nonsense of yours is strengthening the case against her."

Dewey glowered. "See here, Cole—"

"Wait." Cole leaned forward tensely. " 'A little knowledge is a dangerous thing.' I'm convinced that Mary Grafton is not guilty of murder, and I can't allow your 'little knowledge' of psychiatry to drive her to the electric chair."

"Did you come here to insult me?" Dewey snapped.

"What makes you so sure she's not guilty?" Brackett queried.

Cole straightened. "If that girl is brought to trial, she'll face a lay jury—men who know nothing of psychopathology. Ignorance will send her to the chair—ignorance of valid psychiatry, such as yours, Doctor Dewey."

"Cole, I've had enough of this!" Dewey barked.

Cole's voice bit. "Stand on your professional dignity, Doctor, when an innocent girl's life is at stake. You hint that she is suffering from a psychoneurosis.* This must mean that she is the victim of a submerged mental conflict. Very well. A conflict of what against what? Can you identify any submerged mental struggle that can logically account for the horrible act of stripping a human being of his skin? Can you, Doctor Dewey?"

Dewey glared.

---

*   Carter Cole has omitted mention of all other abnormalities in the Kraepelin classification as being too obviously impossible to connect with the case of Mary Grafton. These include (a) mental abnormalities resulting from congenital defects, (b) those having a basis of organic changes in the brain, (c) those caused by toxic substances such as alcohol and drugs, (d) the other abnormalities, besides psychoneoroses, due to unknown causes which include the manic-depressive, schizophrenic, and paranoiac and (e) essential epilepsy. His conclusion, reached instantly, would be impossible for one not thoroughly familiar with the Kraepelin table.—F.C.D.

"You can't, of course. Your conception of irrationality—like that of the jury which will try that girl if she's charged with murder—is absurd. If you persist in this stupidity, you'll be responsible for Mary Grafton's going to the chair."

"Doctor Cole, I'll thank you to leave," Dewey ordered.

"In that case," Cole shot out, "you may expect the fight of your life. Just one more question. Has Mary Grafton shown any peculiarities in regard to human teeth? If not, how do you reconcile your theory with the fact that the corpse's teeth were removed? Good night, Doctor Dewey."

As Cole turned angrily, Inspector Brackett's hard-corded hand closed on his arm. Brackett's crystal eyes had been searching Cole's reddening face. Now in a nerve-rasping voice he asked wryly: "Just where, Sir Galahad, is Doctor Grafton?"

"Do you think I know?"

"Maybe." Brackett loaded the word with innuendo. "She slipped out of here last night. She dropped her purse in the court and it must have broken open, but there's one thing she probably didn't have time to locate."

Brackett removed a small blue vanity case from his vest-pocket. On its lid were the engraved initials *MG*. "I found it," he added significantly, "right at the place where your big car had been standing. It's no news to you that harboring a fugitive is a serious crime, and making yourself an accessory to a murder means the chair if—"

" 'If'," said Cole with a click, "is as far as you're going, Inspector! Good night!"

COLE'S HEELS beat rapidly through the outer office. In spite of his fury and all through his rushing tirade at Dewey, he had been listening and he had heard no signal from the Duesenberg's horn. That meant that more than likely Doctor Mary Grafton was still somewhere inside the building. He was thinking anxiously of her when a frightened, horrified whimper in the corridor stopped him short.

A nurse in starched uniform was retreating through an open door, one trembling hand pressed to her lips, her eyes staring. She whirled and ran, without seeing Cole in her anguish, into the director's office. Cole, peering at the swinging door slowly closing on the room she had left, felt a chill of sharp apprehension.

It's number was 327; it was that of his friend John Gifford.

Cole was striding through it when Dewey and Brackett crowded behind him. With their breath drained from their lungs, their faces white, the three paused because all power of movement left them in their overwhelming dismay. On the bed of 327 lay new horror.

It was a man's body, stripped of its skin from head to foot as the first had been, a ghastly figure of bared muscles, frightful face, red jaws gaping toothless.

Brackett roared: "That woman's in this building! She's here now! Doctor Grafton came back and did this!"

Shock held Carter Cole motionless. On this bed, earlier this evening, he had seen his old friend, John Gifford, lying; and here in this room he had heard the horrified words: "I'm afraid—she'll skin me alive!"

Mary Grafton, seen by Brick Kelly stealing into the hospital. Mary Grafton, hiding somewhere in the huge building now. Those haunting words, "I'm afraid—she'll skin me alive!" Three blinding flashes of damning fact in the mind of Carter Cole as he stared at the horror on the bed.

Grimly he stepped forward, scarcely conscious of the voices and movements of the other men in the room. The glitter of a scalpel on the red-crusted sheet stung his eyes. The ghastly toothlessness of the cadaver's crimson mouth was a dead smile that mocked him. He turned away, swift glances searching the room, eyes probing into the darkness of the roof beyond the window—and a new chill froze him. Out on the black roof he saw a furtive movement that vanished in the night.

Cole strode out. Brackett was in the hall now with men of the homicide squad who had responded to his crackling calls, snapping orders that the building be searched. Cole went down the stairs. Alert, lips a thin line, he hastened to the Duesenberg. Kelly was inside it, watching the staff entrance. The car's motor was running.

"Has she come out, Brick?"

"Not yet!"

COLE TOOK the wheel, sent the sedan spurting out of the court. Kelly's eyes widened with amazement when he wrenched the car from the driveway and rolled it quietly over velvet grass. With the lights out, Cole swung around the building to the rear of the garage which flanked it on one side. He stopped near the wall, slipped out, peered up.

"Watch!" he snapped.

Cole took three quick steps—from the running-board, to the spare tire, to the top of the sedan. Eyes above the level of the roof, he peered through the glow from a checkerboard of windows in the side of the hospital. Against the wall he saw a shadow huddling, perceived dimly a blanched face, horrified eyes. He called very quietly: "Please come, Doctor Grafton."

There was no answer save the terrified stare of the motionless girl. Grimly Cole pulled himself up. Quick quiet steps took him across the roof to the spot where Mary

Grafton was crouched against the wall. When he reached gently to take her arm, she sprang up with a hysterical sob and darted away. Cole bounded, caught her. She swung on him—and went limp in his arms.

He lifted her slender body and his call— "Take her, Brick!"—brought the amazed Kelly to the top of the sedan. Together they lowered the girl, put her on the rear seat. Kelly pulled down the blinds and Cole slipped to the wheel. About to mesh the gears he paused, listening, breath stopped.

It was a weird squealing sound—an inarticulate, stifled cry that came out of the darkness. Its direction was baffling, and it was not repeated.

Cole heard the noise of an opening door, and knowing that Brackett's men were following orders to search the building and grounds, he touched the accelerator. The heavy car swung sharply around the garage, back to the drive, headed for the nearest bridge across the East River. Once on the cement band which led on out past the Cole Sanitarium, the speedometer needle went to 80 and stayed there.

"She's coming around, Doc!"

At Brick's words Cole spoke over his shoulder. "Don't be alarmed, Doctor Grafton. I only want to help you. Please believe that—and trust me."

Kelly sat in mute bewilderment beside the girl who had exhaustedly brought herself to a sitting position. Now she was sobbing and Cole did not speak again until he was past the gate of the sanitarium and braking at the steps. "On your way, Brick," he directed as he reached for the girl's cold hand. She stepped out, her eyes still tear-wet, terrified, and he led her along a polished hall to his office.

To the tireless, cool secretary who followed him in he said: "Jane, this is Miss Mary Smith, a self-commitment. Please see that she's made comfortable at once. Details later."

"I'm June, Doctor," Miss Day answered. "Please come with me, Miss Smith."

A second Miss Day, identical with the first, came to his desk with neatly typewritten reports as Doctor Grafton, too bewildered to speak, was led from the office. Cole stared at the report slips without seeing them and sat in silence. His fingers drummed, drummed, until finally one of them shifted to a button. One of the Day twins appeared.

"June, Jane, whichever you are," Cole asked with a faint smile, "what about the new patient, Miss Mary Smith?"

"Doctor Grafton," his secretary answered coolly, "is resting."

Cole stared at the closing door with jaw gaping. His violent slap of the reports to his blotter stopped the girl on the sill; but she betrayed no alarm. Cool, poised, she listened as Cole spoke.

"I merely want to warn you, June or Jane, as the case may be, that you may be obliged to find new positions soon. The sanitarium may be boarded up. Doctor Carter Cole may find himself experiencing an entirely new sensation—a deadly jolt in the electric chair—if I'm wrong about that young woman!"

Miss Day said merely "Yes, Doctor," and went out as quietly as she had entered.

CHAPTER FOUR
THE MAN IN THE
PADDED CELL

COLE'S AFFABILITY had an undertone of grave anxiety when he came to his desk next morning. In the labyrinthine hallways, placid-faced men and women worked at their constant task of pushing those heavy bocks over the polished floors. Inmates were tending the lawns and gardens. From the wards sounded cries of hysterical elation and groans of tragic despair. The twin Misses Day were at their desks, bewildering yet pleasant to the eye. The machinery of the great institution hummed with smooth efficiency, to care for minds to which efficiency was utterly unknown.

"Miss Smith has not asked to see me?" Cole queried of one of the two Day sisters as he came in.

"No, Doctor."

Cole noted that his twin secretaries had added new data to their reports. He read each intently. The first—

> Doctor Morse, medical examiner, reports that the death of Edward Pomeroy was due to gas poisoning. An autopsy is to be performed on the body of John Gifford today.
>
> JD

Mystified, Cole recalled that there were no gas fixtures in the hospital rooms, though gas was used plentifully in the laboratories. He knew that death by gas poisoning may be detected not only by an unnatural pinkness of the blood, but by a pink discoloration of the skin. Though he realized that the removal of the dead man's skin had eliminated a clue, Cole knew too that this information in no way turned suspicion from Mary Grafton.

To the second report had been appended—

> The skins and the teeth of both the deceased have not been found.

"Both," Cole murmured, "vital for identification purposes—fingerprints and dental charts."

Intently he read a digest of newspaper clippings prepared by one of the Day twins.

CONCERNING THE SUICIDE OF PHILIP PRICE, FIANCÉ OF DOCTOR MARY GRAFTON.

Price, an ambitious, earnest young physician, aspired to become a member of the board of Pasteur Foundation. At the annual election recently he was not elected. Several nights later he was found in the research laboratory on the top floor of the Pasteur, dying of a deep wound in the heart made by a scalpel. He lived less than an hour. His death was judged to be suicide due to despondency over his failure to win the election.

However, Price and Doctor Mary Grafton were planning to be married that same night, in Greenwich. Their departure was delayed by the necessity for Doctor Price to make an important blood test of one of his patients. Mary Grafton planned to leave with him immediately the test was completed. When she came to the laboratory she found him dying.

Investigation discounted all hints of murder. Many people came and went in the hospital that night, but the elevators took no one else to the top floor until Doctor Grafton's arrival. Only Price's fingerprints were found on the scalpel. Following his death, Doctor Grafton insisted on continuing her work at the hospital.

Cole closely scanned the morning newspapers, read startling headlines concerning the skinned corpses at the Pasteur, but saw no mention of the death of Doctor Charles Blanchard. Cole had not reported the crime and ran the risk of serious consequences for not doing so. He noted one paragraph with interest—

Doctor Howard Arnold, a senior director of the Pasteur Foundation, left last night on a vacation in the Berkshires, according to Doctor Huston Dewey. Because of the murders at the hospital attempts have been made to reach him but so far he has not been found.

Cole's finger touched a button, and a Miss Day looked in. "Miss Smith hasn't asked to see me yet?" he asked.

"No, Doctor."

"Going to her, demanding her story," Cole mused aloud, "would only raise her defenses against me. She must break them down herself. When she calls me, Jane, I want to know of it instantly."

"Yes, Doctor," said Miss Day. "But I'm June."

"Aren't you always?" Cole sighed; and the door closed.

IT WAS not until evening, when the humming activity of the great sanitarium had quieted, that Cole, sitting at his desk, still brooding over the baffling puzzle, heard one of the Day twins announce: "Miss Smith is asking for you, Doctor. And you have a caller—Inspector Brackett."

Cole had started quickly for the door. Brackett's name stopped him, chilled his nerves. Grimly he turned back, saying: "Show Brackett in, and tell Miss Smith I'll be along presently."

The chunky, muscular detective came sauntering in with ominous deliberation. "How the hell," he asked without preliminaries, "can you stay sane, living in this nut-house? Listen to 'em—ranting, singing, moaning! Don't they ever stop?"

"Never," Cole answered. "It is a sad commentary on our gentlemen of the cloth, Inspector, that at every moment of the day and night, some inmate of this institution is preaching."

Brackett took a chair without invitation, studied Cole with his camera-lens eyes, and said nothing for a moment. Cole outwaited him and at last he broke the tense silence with: "The scalpel that was found beside Pomeroy came from the laboratory where Mary Grafton was doing her skin researches. So did the second. Her fingerprints are on them."

"Naturally," Cole replied. "But that's not proof she used them to skin two humans. She wasn't seen by anyone taking Pomeroy in and out of 319, was she? She'd have to, wouldn't she, in order to kill him with gas?"

Brackett scowled. "Never mind that, Cole. Cracking this case is my job, not yours. I've warned you that harboring a fugitive will make you an accessory to the crime of murder."

"I seem to remember that," Cole said dryly.

"She didn't have a car of her own to slip away in last night," Brackett pointed out. "She had to use somebody else's. Yours? She must have come back to the building later, and somebody must have helped her skip a second time. Why was it, Cole, you had your big Duesenberg around in back of the hospital right after the second skinned corpse was found? Why did you go beating it away from there like a bat out of hell?"

"You think," Cole asked, "I'm hiding Mary Grafton?"

"Aren't you?" Brackett asked the question bluntly, his crystal eyes gleaming. "Aren't you, Cole? She's here, isn't she—in this building?"

Cole squirmed inwardly under those searching eyes of Brackett's. His answer must, he knew, either be a confession of guilt or a lie that would make the charge against him even more serious if it were discovered. Cole chose the lie. "No."

"She's not here?"—ominously.

"No."

"I hope not," Brackett grated. He sauntered deliberately to the door, and as he went out he said again, grimly: "I hope not!"

Cole bounded from his chair once Brackett was out of the gleaming hallway. In another of those burnished corridors there was a continual chorus of sobbing and joyful babbling; he went to a door at its end. Stepping in, he gazed at the young woman sitting with hands entwined, her eyes pleading.

Doctor Mary Grafton's scrutiny of Cole's face was anxious and prolonged. He faced her, waiting for her last resistance to break; and at last she said "You're wrong, Doctor Cole. I'm afraid you're wrong. I'm afraid I am mad."

Cole smiled slowly. "Seriously insane persons never doubt their sanity. Only the sane do that. Please trust me."

"Mad—obsessed," the girl whispered. "Every day and night, all these weeks, it's grown stronger—this horrible craving to prove the man I loved did not resort to the cowardice of suicide. I know he didn't! I know Philip was murdered!"

Cole said nothing. Mary Grafton's story came from her full red lips without his urging, in a rush of words.

"It's the reason I haven't been myself. Wanting to prove it—trying constantly to find a way of proving it. If—if I tell you the truth, will you believe me?"

"I'll believe every word you utter," Cole assured her.

THE GIRL'S eyes widened upon a picture her memory brought to her. "That night I found Philip—found him dying—he said—he said when he recognized me—'Mary, I hid it in the doctor's case—it's hidden in his case—his case'."

The girl was speaking distinctly, but controlling herself with difficulty.

"After Philip died, I began to realize what he meant. There was a notebook on the floor of the laboratory and a pencil—both Philip's. He hadn't been strong enough to reach the telephone or call for help. He'd only been able to fumble the notebook and pencil out of his pocket and write something on one of the pages and tear it off."

"Yes?" Cole urged.

" 'I hid it in the doctor's case'—those were the last words he spoke—but there wasn't any case in the room. I became convinced that Philip had been killed by someone who came to the laboratory by the stairs when he was there alone. A doctor with his case—went into that room while Philip was working—and killed him."

"Why?"

"I don't know. I don't know that, Doctor Cole. But I do know that Philip wrote the truth on a page of his notebook with his last strength and hid it in this doctor's case. But there wasn't any doctor's case there. Don't you see what—what must have happened?"

The girl answered her own question, her words rushing, her eyes shining with anguish.

"Philip alone. This man coming in. Perhaps a quarrel. Philip stabbed with the scalpel. The murderer rushing out, determined not to be seen. Philip lying there, dying, using his last strength to write in his notebook—to write something terribly important. Perhaps the name of that man. It must have been that!"

Cole, his face grave, was picturing the scene depicted by the girl's breathless words.

A dying man peering with glazing eyes at a small white page while his numbed fingers wrote. A physicians' case nearby, perhaps on a chair, but in any event reachable—the case left by the murderer in his desperate rush to escape. Price's cutting a slit in the lining with the scalpel that had dealt him a mortal wound, hiding the written slip in it, against possible discovery by the man who had struck him down.

"That's what he meant by 'I hid it in the doctor's case,' Doctor Cole! Then the man who killed him must have come back. Realizing that he had left his case, knowing it would prove his guilt if it were found there, he came back to the laboratory and took it. Don't you see it must have happened, Doctor Cole? There's nothing else to think!"

"Which explains why you took to ripping doctor's cases to pieces," Cole said, a startled gleam in his eyes.

"Yes!" The girl leaned forward intently. "A hundred doctors come and go in the hospital. I had to try to find that case through a process of elimination. I had to do it secretly because, if the real murderer suspected the truth, he might discover the hidden page himself and destroy it. I could think of nothing else but finding the little piece of paper that Philip had written on while he was dying. I had to find it!"

The sharp light in Cole's eyes increased. "You didn't find it! The murderer of Philip Price, without knowing it, is still carrying that paper hidden in his case—a paper identifying him as a murderer!"

"Yes! Now—now I can never find it, never! If they arrest me, if I'm forced to tell this to the police, they won't believe me. It will get into the papers, or it will come out at the trial, and the man who killed Philip will learn of it. He'll find that piece of paper himself, and destroy it!

"In that hospital there are only two men, I can absolutely trust. I told them this—Doctor Howard Arnold, and Doctor Charles Blanchard. They began, too, to follow down the theory that some doctor connected with the hospital killed him. They suspect someone definitely, I know, but they won't tell me until they're sure. When this horrible thing happened, there was no one else I could turn to.

"But Doctor Arnold left early last night on his vacation. I went to Doctor Blanchard's home. He wasn't there, and I tried to find him by going to the hospital. But—"

COLE LISTENED intently to Mary Grafton's account of her actions after she had stolen in the staff door of the Pasteur Foundation. It was obvious she wasn't even aware of Blanchard's murder, for unseen, she had hurried by the stairs to an empty room on the third floor where the offices of the directors were located. Finding Doctor Blanchard's office empty she had, on the telephone, attempted vainly to reach him elsewhere in the hospital. Hiding there in the dark room, she had heard, to her unspeakable dismay, the excitement in the corridor which told her that another skinned corpse had been found in the room of a second of her special patients.

"I was terrified—I couldn't think for I knew that they thought I was guilty. I knew they were searching the hospital. I had to get away somehow—so I crawled out the window, and onto the roof, where you found me, Doctor Cole." The girl's entwined fingers whitened. "What can I do?"

Cole said promptly: "There's one gamble we've got to chance—that the murderer is still, without knowing it, carrying that slip of paper hidden in his case which identifies him as the murderer of Philip Price. Somehow we've got to find it before he does. How? I've been thinking of a way. But more important than that—you've got to be kept out of the hands of the police."

"They'll find me!" Mary Grafton blurted.

Cole nodded gravely. "Inspector Brackett," he agreed, "already suspects you're here. I didn't convince him you're not and he may come back with a search warrant. There's only one move to make—to take advantage of the red tape of extradition. You're going with me tonight across the state line into Connecticut."

"But you're taking a frightful risk—"

"Taking it willingly," Cole declared as he rose. "We can't waste time. Ready?"

"Yes," the girl said in a whisper.

"Come with me."

She hurried at Cole's side as he grimly strode along the shining hallway and went down the stairs. He uttered crisp orders as he entered his office, and the Misses Day began to execute them—with quick efficiency. "My car," was Cole's first demand. "Brick Kelly in it" the second. "If I'm called for any reason, I'm attending a critical case." He pulled into his topcoat. "I'll be back later tonight."

From the Day twins came a quiet chorus of, "Yes, Doctor."

His hand firm on Mary Grafton's arm, Cole led her out the entrance of the sanitarium. At the steps Brick Kelly was waiting in the front seat of the Duesenberg. Cole helped the girl into the rear, pulled the blinds, cautioned her to stay out of sight, and slipped beneath the wheel. "You're here," he told the red-headed handy-man grimly, "in case of an emergency."

"Just show me one!" Kelly said.

Cole swung the massive car to the locked gate. Kelly, slipping out, quickly opened the way. Rolling through, Cole tautened and his foot slapped the brake pedal. In the shine of his headlights a chunky, bright-eyed man had appeared. Cole moaned with dismay as he heard a ringing: "Hold on! This is as far as you're going!"

Inspector Brackett came quickly to the side of the car, glaring. Cole heard Brick Kelly easing up from the rear, caught a stifled moan of dismay from the girl sheltered in the darkness of the rear seat. He left the wheel quickly as Brackett's hard hand pulled open a door.

Leaning in, Brackett snarled: "I thought so! Doctor Grafton, I have a warrant for your arrest." He turned back, smiling wryly. "As for you, Cole, I warned you. You're going to get the works!"

Cole snapped: "You have no jurisdiction here, Brackett, you're out of bounds."

"I'll take care of that!" Brackett retorted. "I'm taking this girl to headquarters with me, and what I'm going to do to you, Cole, you won't like!"

Cole sighed. His hand slipped quickly in and out of his coat. As his Luger came level he heard a blurted protest from the girl. "Geez!" whispered Kelly, and cold, grim fury flashed in the eyes of Brackett. Cole reached swiftly, then took a step backward with Brackett's police positive in his left hand.

"Brick," he said grimly, "here's the emergency you asked for. We have here a new patient who is the victim of a dangerous delusion. Handle him in the usual manner!"

"What the hell're you trying to get away with, Cole?" Brackett blurted wrathfully. "This'll make it plenty tough for you!"

Cole smiled grimly. "Pay no attention to his rantings, Brick," he went on. "It's the effusion of a fantastically disordered mind. Brackett, we are sometimes obliged to take strenuous measures to control our more difficult patients. I trust you won't make them necessary. Please about-face and march straight up those steps."

"Damned if I'll—"

"March!"

BRICK KELLY promptly and swiftly executed a maneuver which he had found of frequent aid in subduing violent maniacs. His arms hooked around Brackett's and bent them stiffly upward and backward. Brackett exploded with profanity as Kelly thrust him along the graveled drive. Cole looked into the dark interior of the car, said: "This forces me to change our plans, but don't be alarmed." He followed the fuming Brackett and the smiling Kelly into the entrance and along a glistening hallway.

"June, Jane," he said when his two secretaries came hurrying, "the usual procedure for a violent case."

He stepped into his office while Kelly forced the roaring Brackett up the stairs. At his desk he sat tense, thoughtful. A few moments later he heard the clicking of a typewriter in the outer office and knew that one of the Day sisters was coolly typing a card identifying Brackett as a self-commitment to the institution. He smiled tightly, made a lightning decision, and spoke over the telephone to the second Miss Day.

"The Pasteur Foundation, and Doctor Dewey, at once!"

His fingers drummed until Dewey answered. Then his voice crackled. "Doctor Dewey, on the staff of your hospital there is a murderer—not Mary Grafton. I ask you to cooperate with me to prevent an innocent girl's being tried for murder—for if she's tried she'll certainly be convicted. Are you willing to take drastic action for her sake?"

"Just what is it you want, Doctor Cole?" Dewey countered.

"I want you to get in touch immediately with all doctors connected with your hospital. Every member of the staff, every physician who makes a practise of sending his patients to the Pasteur, every one who might have been in the hospital on the night of Philip Price's alleged suicide. Call them to the hospital immediately, with all the urgency that an emergency case demands. Gather them in a suitable room, and stipulate that they all bring their cases—every type they own."

"What the devil are you driving at, Cole?" Doctor Dewey demanded.

"The apprehension of a murderer," Carter Cole retorted. "These directions are absolutely vital. Please have all the doctors leave their cases in an adjoining room. You'll need two of your most reliable nurses for the job of tagging each case with the name of its owner as it is deposited. They are to keep count of the total number brought. Doctor Dewey, I implore you to cooperate with me and see that this is done with the utmost speed."

"Are you absolutely convinced that Mary Grafton is innocent and that one of these men might have—"

"Absolutely convinced! If we're fortunate, Doctor Dewey, we'll have our hands on the real murderer tonight."

"Very well," Dewey answered stiffly. "I'll do it."

"I think," Cole said briskly, "you'll be heartily glad that you did."

As he strode through the outer office he called: "Jane and June, both of you this time. You're coming with me." He ran up the stairs and found Brick Kelly facing a door which was jarring in its frame, while a heavy fist pounded it on the inside. Cole smiled grimly, knowing that between the locked door and the heavily barred window resided the inspector and a mattress, nothing more. Brackett's voice had aroused a caterwauling from other confined patients, but his roaring demand to be released was loudest.

"Geez!" Brick Kelly exclaimed. "You're right, Doc. He's sure dangerous!"

"You're to camp right here, Brick, to handle him in case he breaks down the door. While you're doing it, you might pray for your boss."

Kelly moaned, "I told you you ought to keep out of these screwy cases!" as Cole bounded down the stairs. Near the entrance he found the Misses Day, garbed in neat polo coats and pert felt hats, alertly waiting. They hurried with him to the Duesenberg and climbed into the rear seat. Cole locked the gate, took the wheel, and smiled back into the dismayed eyes of Doctor Mary Grafton.

"Brackett probably told headquarters he was coming here after you. When he doesn't report back, they'll know something's wrong. That means we're desperately pressed for time. Our destination is not Connecticut now, but the Pasteur. If you're spotted again, I won't be able to keep you out of the hands of the police—but are you willing to risk that?"

"Yes—anything!"

Cole's reply was to prod power from the Duesenberg that sent it whizzing toward Manhattan and the hospital where the two skinned cadavers had been found.

CHAPTER FIVE
THE LEATHER CASE

COLE PARKED the Duesenberg in the court of the hospital. "Please stay here," he directed Mary Grafton. "Chin up—and hope!" His twin secretaries followed him briskly to the office of Doctor Huston Dewey. At the door he met the director and Doctor Channing Grafton.

"Cole!" The lean face of Channing Grafton pictured ashy anxiety. "Have they found Mary? In God's name, can't you testify that she is irrational? The chair, Cole— good God!" The words were a frantic rush. "Anything— an asylum the rest of her life—is better than her going to the—"

"Mary Grafton," Cole interrupted patiently, "is safe. Don't worry. Doctor Dewey—"

"Don't worry!" Channing Grafton echoed bitterly. "When you insist that her last defense—insanity—is false!"

"Most of the staff is already here, and the others are coming," Dewey interrupted. "They're waiting on the tenth floor, and their bags are being taken care of. There are only two men I haven't reached—Doctors Arnold and Blanchard. We'd better get along up there now."

In the corridor on the tenth floor scores of physicians were grouped, sleepy-eyed, wondering, their conversation a buzz. Cole noted as he stepped from the elevator that others were in the huge operating room, that two nurses were busy at nearby swinging doors. He looked past them. The supply room was walled with sinks and shelves bearing huge bottles of antiseptics, soap solutions, pans and pitchers. On every table and on the floor sat scores of leather cases, of all kinds, each tagged. Cole gave crisp directions to the Day twins to take charge of them.

He strode into the operating room, and found the interne checking a list at the door. He told Cole that only a few more men were waiting. Dewey and Channing Grafton stayed at his side; other physicians, members of the hospital board, clustered around him.

Dewey, frowning, said: "You owe us an explanation of all this, Doctor Cole. Surely you can confide in the members of the board. Certainly you should relieve Doctor Channing Grafton's anxiety."

Cole hesitated. "I explain," he said, "under protest. I'm trying to find a bit of paper, hidden in a doctor's case by Philip Price before he died—a slip identifying his murderer. Details later—but I assure you that the slip, if found, will explain much. I can't say more—you must keep this confidential."

Cole waited impatiently while more doctors crowded into the glittering room. His nerves burned with impatience until the interne with the check-list approached to say: "Everyone present, sir, except Doctors Arnold and Blanchard."

"Good!" Cole exclaimed, and to Dewey, "Please make it your responsibility to see that everyone stays." He rushed out, then, into the room which contained the scores of leather cases where he found one of the Day twins looking perplexed and startled.

"Doctor Cole! We just came in, with the last cases, and saw someone going out!" She pointed to swinging doors on one side of the room, duplicating another pair on the opposite wall. "I know he didn't take a case out with him, but he ran!"

Cole quickly opened the doors and peered down a flight of cement stairs, then turned back to ask: "What about the total? Does it check?"

Jane Day's pencil darted over her figures. June rapidly counted the cases, grouped in units of ten. Cole's fingers snapped impatiently until Jane's answer came: "It doesn't check, Doctor! One case is missing!"

June Day exclaimed: "But the man I saw didn't take a case out with him. I'm sure of it!"

"Nevertheless," Jane insisted, "one case is missing!"

Swiftly Cole's gaze circled the room. He strode over to an iron leaf set in the wall. It opened downward and Cole peered into a black shaft. "The linen chute!" he exclaimed. "He dropped it down the linen chute!" The Day twins gazed after him in wide-eyed alarm as he pushed out into the corridor.

COLE'S FRANTIC tapping of the elevator call-button brought a car in a moment. "Basement!" he snapped. "Top speed!" As the floor levels flicked past he cursed himself for revealing the secret of his purpose. One of the men he had told, or someone standing near who had overheard, had stolen into the supply room and, in desperation dropped his bag down the chute, was even now hurrying after it.

When the elevator slid to a stop, Cole stepped into a cement corridor, and crossed to a gray door, noting that the stairs angled down near it. No one was on them. He eased his Luger into his hand, twisted the knob, opened the door a crack and peered into the dark cellar room in which the linen chute terminated.

Cole snapped the switch at the door as he went down the iron steps. In the room there were only a few castered basket-trucks of soiled linen waiting to be rolled into the adjoining laundry. He peered up through a window as he crossed to the base of the chute, and saw that his Duesenberg was parked near it. He glimpsed the white face of Mary Grafton; it vanished at once. Grimly he opened the chute door.

A black medicine case lay on a ruffle of soiled white. Cole lifted it out. A string looped around the handle, from which a fragment of torn cardboard dangled, told him that the owner of the case had ripped the name-tag off before dropping it. He opened it, dumped its contents on the floor. Kneeling, he fingered inside—and felt a cut in the lining.

Cole's fingers gripped an edge of paper. His eyes gleamed when he slipped it out. It was the leaf of a notebook, its ring holes ripped; it had been folded once by the hand of a man now dead. Cole glimpsed a loose scrawl on one side—

—stabbed me

Philip Price.

At the instant Cole turned the slip to read the name of the murderer the lights snapped out! Blinding darkness closed upon Cole as he whirled. He had put down his Luger and now, as he groped for it, he heard swift, grating steps on the cement floor. As his other hand closed hard on the slip, maniacal fury hit him.

Cole was driven backward violently; his head cracked against the sharp edge of the open chute door. As he struck, a fist drove into his face. He grappled with a man he could not see; and while he strove desperately to escape the savage fury of the attack, another brutal blow jarred his head. He gasped, sagged back, went limp. And darkness deeper than the gloom of the chute room enveloped his brain.

Cole was conscious of a light gleaming redly, of hands probing into pocket after pocket of his clothing. He was rolled aside; then he heard linen rustling, and the lining of the case rip as it was torn out. Shuffling steps sounded around him as someone searched—a startled gasp followed, quick steps. Suddenly the light went out, and Cole squirmed in an attempt to rise.

An eon of donging sounds and flickering lights passed before he was able to bring himself to his knees. A sliding noise turned his bleared gaze upward. He saw a window opening, vague dark movements outside it. In a baffling confusion of semi-consciousness, he saw, faintly, the wan face of Mary Grafton.

She rolled limply across the sill and fell to the top of a full truck of linen. The dark figure of a man quickly crawled after her. She lay motionless on the mound of white as Cole dizzily pulled himself up, to see savage eyes gleaming at him. A second ferocious attack hit him. Desperately he attempted to fight free as a terrific blow smashed between his eyes. He dropped heavily and as he clawed to rise, his head exploded. The staggering concussion in his brain thrust Cole once again off the brink of consciousness.

COLE BECAME aware, after a timeless interval, of a rhythmic throbbing that filled all the vague darkness. Something was pressing over his mouth; something was pinioning his ankles and wrists. He attempted to tear free, and lay panting, his brain still drumming with that rapid beat in the air, his lungs filled with a burning pungency.

The faint glow from the window showed Cole that one of the soiled sheets had been ripped to strips, that tight knots were binding him. Mary Grafton was lying beside the basket-truck; she was also bound and gagged. Consciousness had returned to her, and her eyes frantically wide, she was trying to cry out. But Cole heard only a low, inarticulate squeal, choked, stifled, like those strange sounds he had heard behind the garage when, the night before he had carried Mary Grafton down from the roof.

The rhythmic pulsations in the air continued and Cole, peering up, saw that the window was now closed, within an inch. Protruding inward was a short length of black hose. Cole saw cloudy fumes gushing from it. Beyond the window, dimly, he heard the motor of an automobile humming. He looked grimly at the black, round end of the drooping hose—and knew that through it death was pouring into the chute room.

The other end of it, Carter Cole realized, was thrust into the exhaust pipe of the singing automobile; deadly carbon monoxide was streaming into the air which he and Mary Grafton were being forced to breathe.

Cole strove strenuously to tear his wrists free; the effort drained his strength and quickened his breathing. The sharp acridity of the atmosphere brought tears to his eyes; half blinded, he saw Mary Grafton was writhing in agony, striving helplessly to escape her bonds. And even while he lay with lungs burned by the poison thickening in the air, his scientifically trained mind recalled, grimly, the fact that the breathing of only fifteen parts of carbon monoxide in ten thousand parts of air for one hour was fatal.

One hour…? Cole did not know how long he had remained unconscious after the hose had started pouring poison into the air. The stupefying effects were already making themselves felt; death would not wait long. He struggled dizzily to his knees, braced against the wall, stared up and realized that the hose was beyond his reach—that he could not thrust it out and stop the inpouring of poison.

Staggering upright, he took quick short jumps across the room. Desperately retaining his balance, he hobbled to the iron stairs and worked his way up. He sagged against the wall, eyes bleared, stinging lungs beating like a bellows. When he turned and gripped the knob behind him, tried to open the way, he found that the door was locked.

He saw Mary Grafton lying with eyes closed now, saw her drifting into the unconsciousness that preluded death.

Frantically Cole attempted to call through the door. But all he could manage was a muffled stifled cry. He braced himself again, hopped down the steps, struggled across the chute room. The world was a crazy, whirling gloom around him as he went hop by hop over the cement floor in the darkness.

He twisted desperately to the open door of the linen chute, quickly rubbed the strips that bound his wrists against its edge. He realized Mary Grafton's breathing was slowing, that in a few moments he must himself drop unconscious, while the hose puffed on its stifling death into the air. He worked his wrists up and down with delirious intent—and felt the cotton strip rip.

Now he snagged the sharp corner of the door on the cloth, pulled, heard another rip. With frantic speed he tore bit by bit through the twisted material. As he worked the blackness swirled around him and his head drummed dully. When the strands parted at last, Cole toppled heavily to the floor among the spilled contents of the murderer's medicine case. Now, with unsteady fingers, he fumbled among the scattered articles, found a pair of bandage scissors. He squeezed the blades on the strips binding his ankles, cut them free. Staggering up, he climbed onto the laundry truck, thrust the window wide, hurled the puffing hose away. It curled from the exhaust pipe of one of the hospital ambulances.

He drew long, deep breaths of clear outside air, for only a moment, then turned back to struggle with the limp form of Mary Grafton in his arms. She was an almost insupportable burden as he lifted her through the window. He crawled out, staggering with the weakness induced by the poison; blindly he carried her to the entrance of the hospital.

COLE DID not know whether Mary Grafton was alive or dead as he stumbled past startled nurses in the lobby, into the waiting room. "Methylene blue!" * he gasped, as he lowered the girl.

He sagged against the wall; steadying himself, he bent over Mary Grafton, found her pulse—slow, irregular. Turning, he fumbled with the hypodermic syringe brought him by a nurse, its barrel filled with bright blue liquid. He plunged the needle into the girl's arm, made sure the point

---

*   Carbon monoxide, a product of combustion, combines with the haemoglobin of the blood, for which it has 200 times as great an affinity as oxygen. Death from breathing this gas results from a failure of oxygen supply to the body. Methylene blue, a coal tar dye, is a remarkable antidote for both carbon monoxide and cyanide poisoning, because it restores the ability of the haemoglobin to absorb oxygen from the lungs. Its action is astonishingly swift. The usual antidotal dose is 50 C.C. of a one percent aqueous solution given as an intravenous injection.—F.C.D.

had entered her vein, and slowly discharged the contents while his brain spun.

He collapsed into a chair as blackness flooded over him. Dimly he felt the prick of a needle, the dull ache of an injection entering his own body. He sat still in dull agony, until the antidotal action of the methylene blue came like balm into his body. His breathing slowed; the throbbing ache in his lungs vanished. Though still stunned, he brought himself to his feet.

Mary Grafton was lying with eyes closed, breathing deeply and regularly.

"She'll be quite all right, soon, Doctor," the nurse said cooly.

"Thanks—we needed that!" Cole murmured.

Grimly he turned to the doorway—and stopped, to stare at the grim features of Inspector Brackett, crystal eyes glittering. Cole saw over Brackett's shoulders the forlorn face of Brick Kelly, saw that Kelly's wrists were pinioned with handcuffs. And there was another man whom Cole recognized dreamily as Sergeant Hough, also of the homicide squad.

"Did you think I went to your place alone, for God's sake, Cole?" Brackett snapped. He laughed gratingly. "Your goose is cooked. I've got plenty of jurisdiction here. The girl's going to headquarters—and so are you!"

"Geez, boss!" Brick Kelly blurted. "Brackett's side-kick rushed me when Brackett was tryin' to break down the door. I couldn't stand him off!"

"Never mind, Brick," Cole said. "Brackett, before I go down to headquarters, I'm going to find out the reason for certain choking sounds behind this hospital."

"You're going to stay here!" Brackett snarled.

But Cole didn't. He thrust Brackett aside, strode out the entrance. His strength mounted as he rounded to the rear of the hospital, with the dogged Brackett and the hand-cuffed Kelly following. In the gloom behind the garage he paused, peering.

Silence.

"Living so long in that asylum, you've gone nuts your-self," Brackett broke in. "No sane man would get himself into this jam. What do you mean, choking noises?"

"I heard 'em, too, Doc, last night!" Kelly blurted.

Cole exclaimed "That's it!" and strode to a circle of blackness two feet in diameter in the green of the grass. He stooped over the iron cover of a manhole, gripped into its fingerholes and heaved aside. "Get a light!" he exclaimed as he peered into the depths. "This must be—"

The beam of Brackett's flash probed deep. Far down, leaden telephone cables passed through conduits. Between the gray tubes, two figures lay. One huddled with eyes closed; the other stared up wildly. Adhesive tape bound the hands and wrists and gagged both men. One Cole had never seen before; the other, the one with the shock of unruly white hair, was John Gifford.

"Holy Smoke!" Brackett blurted.

Cole smiled tightly. "I'll leave you the job of getting them out, Brackett. There are the men you charged Mary Grafton with murdering—both alive!"

He strode away swiftly, still haunted by things that had not been cleared up. Two dead men, stripped of their skins, had been found in the Pasteur Foundation. And Mary Grafton, alleged maniac, was a prisoner of the law.

CHAPTER SIX
MURDER MEDICO

GRIM-EYED, THIN-LIPPED, Cole pushed open the doors of the operating room on the tenth floor. He found the crowd of physicians moving about restlessly, angrily. They coalesced into groups as Dewey and Channing Grafton hurried to Cole, turned with him as he took a position in the center of the floor.

"Quiet, gentlemen!" he called ringingly. "Quiet, please!" The room grew silent. "I am obliged, gentlemen, to undertake the task of discovering which one of you is three times a murderer."

The physicians stared incredulously. Cole peered from face to face as Doctor Dewey stepped close to say: "Cole, I don't understand this—but we've just received a startling piece of information from Doctor Morse, the medical examiner. He declares that John Gifford died of—"

"Cyanide!" Cole supplied. "But John Gifford is not dead. Neither is Edmund Pomeroy. The two skinned corpses, much as I regret to report it, are Doctors Arnold and Blanchard."

"What!" Dewey gasped.

Cole stared at him. "Step back, please. Face me, all of you. Every man here is under suspicion of murder. I want to know which one of you slipped out of this room and back again while I was out."

No answer. In the hush the swinging corridor doors opened. Doctor Mary Grafton came in slowly, followed by Sergeant Hough. She was pale, her eyes pleading with Cole. And all but Cole's eyes turned to her as she said: "I—I wanted to come to you!"

Cole searched the dismayed and puzzled faces of the doctors. "Very well, gentlemen, there is a much better way to prove the guilt of one of you. My explanation will be brief because the man to whom I'm speaking does not need it at all.

"Doctor Arnold never lived to begin his vacation. He was killed by carbon monoxide piped into his room, no doubt in this building, from the exhaust of an automobile. The means of murder was effective because his hearing was poor. Doctor Blanchard was poisoned last night in his home by cyanide dropped into his coffee while his back was turned. Both were killed, gentlemen, because the murderer feared both of them. He knew they suspected him of having killed Doctor Philip Price.

"He wished to eliminate the possibility that his later crimes would be connected with his first murder. And he wished to make the deaths of Doctors Arnold and Blanchard seem to be not murders at all, but disappearances. Follow me closely, gentlemen, while I trace a murderer's desperate moves.

"First with Arnold, then with Blanchard, he silenced his victims with death. He stripped them of their skins not only to direct suspicion toward Mary Grafton, because of her supposed mania, but in order to remove the most obvious identification marks—for his plan was to make these skinned bodies appear to belong to other men.

"He was able to do this without being seen, because each time he took the skinned body to the roof of the garage by climbing on his car. He emptied the beds of his chosen rooms no doubt by knocking the patients unconscious or by using ether. In each case, he removed the living man and substituted the skinned body. He did not risk carrying away the patients; he hid them in the telephone pit behind the hospital. Doubtless, he believed they would not be found until they were dead and unidentifiable.

"You were summoned here tonight, gentlemen, and directed to bring your cases, because in one of those cases a statement was hidden, written by Philip Price, identifying the man who stabbed him to death. I found that case and that paper. I had no chance to read the name of the murderer on it, for I was knocked unconscious, down in the laundry cellar, by a man who was desperate to get hold of that paper and tried to kill me because he thought I read his name and could accuse him—but he did not find the paper."

"Doctor Mary Grafton," Cole asked gently, "did you see the face of the man in the cellar while he searched for it?"

She answered breathlessly. "No. He kept too close to the wall. I saw you lying there, Doctor Cole—and he must have seen me. Then the lights went out. I was leaving the car when he came at me and struck me. I—I have you to thank for my life."

COLE SMILED as he faced the doctors again. "Gentlemen, for weeks the murderer of Philip Price carried with him, without knowing it, evidence sufficient to convict him. He still has it on his person. When he rushed at me, I knew he wanted that paper. I was forced to decide swiftly on a subterfuge to outwit him, a place to hide it where he would not find it. I hope my move has succeeded. If it has, the man I want is now carrying that incriminating paper in the breast pocket of his coat—where I thrust it during the fight! Don't move your hands!"

Tight silence followed Cole's command. A number of the doctors looked at their breast pockets. Some had raised their hands, but each gesture stopped short of completion. Cole's smile grew grimmer.

"Watch each other, gentlemen. The lift of any hand at this moment is a gesture inviting suspicion. Stand without moving."

Cole stepped quietly to the front group of physicians. He thrust his fingers into the breast pockets of one coat after another in quick succession. He shifted from group to group, not glancing at any face as he probed, eyes alert only for that damning piece of paper. From pocket to pocket his hand darted until abruptly it paused.

Cole felt a crackle between his fingertips. Before he could raise his eyes, a swift blow caught him in the face. He tottered back—but the paper was in his hand. Cole saw a man plunging toward the rear of the room, other men crushing around him. The weight of ten, springing after the one who fled, shoved him against the wall. Cole stood still, the paper in his hand, as Mary Grafton hurried to his side. From the doctors crowding around the captive came breathless exclamations. "We've got him!" "Hold him!" "Keep his hands down!"

Cole smoothed the wrinkled bit of paper.

He felt cold satisfaction, strong compassion for Mary Grafton, as he read scrawled words that promised to put a period to the case of the skinned corpses.

Channing Grafton stabbed me.
Philip Price.

IN THE director's office the voice of Channing Grafton monotonously droned. Carter Cole watched his waxy face. Inspector Brackett leaned, peering, following each word. Doctor Dewey sat erect, cold. Mary Grafton, at Cole's side, her face white, turned pleading eyes again and again to his. During the sing-song confessional a pencil in the hand of Jane Day made stenographic lightning.

"It was the wish of my wife to adopt a daughter. I opposed the idea but it was done. After she died there was only a perfunctory relationship left between Mary and me. But the scandal of the law suit which cost me my practise, forced me to rely on her for money. Without her I would have starved.

"I resisted the match between her and Philip Price because Mary was purchasing a substantial annuity, besides carrying a large sum in life insurance, and her husband would automatically displace me as beneficiary. When she told me she was going to be married I tried to argue Price out of it, tried to stop him—and I did—in the heat of anger—with the scalpel."

Mary Grafton's eyes closed.

The monotonous voice continued. "I knew better than anyone else how deeply Mary was affected by the shock of Price's death. I suspected before anyone else that she was destroying the cases. I thought she was going mad. I was afraid it would mean losing her position—starvation for me. Then I learned—because they questioned me— that Doctor Arnold and Doctor Blanchard suspected me of killing Price. In desperation—I planned to make it seem that Mary was mad beyond all doubt—planned to remove Arnold and Blanchard. If Mary were confined in an asylum, it would provide me with an income because of the disability benefits in her insurance policies. It would have meant a steady supply of money and I thought that Mary was really going mad.

"I confess to the three murders. I will plead guilty. I'm glad—it's over—and I'm sorry for the anguish I've caused Mary."

With unsteady fingers Channing Grafton signed the notes of the confession.

"Transcribe it at once," Cole said quietly, and rose. He stepped into the outer office with Mary Grafton; Brackett and Dewey followed. Brick Kelly was waiting there; he got up, grinning slowly, wrists freed of handcuffs. A nurse, who was also waiting, said to Dewey before she withdrew: "Mr. Pomeroy and Mr. Gifford are both resting, Doctor."

"May we go, Inspector?" Cole asked Brackett. "Since Doctor Mary Grafton is quite guiltless, Mr. Kelly and I can't be held for conniving to defeat justice."

"You know damned well you can go," Brackett growled. "You cracked yourself a case, Cole. But"—he glowered—"don't ever lock me up in that nut-house of yours again. Don't ever do that!"

Doctor Dewey cleared his throat officiously. "Doctor Grafton, I—ah—owe you an apology. My attitude toward you was—er—shamefully mistaken. Of course your place here is assured. You may continue your researches here and we shall be—ah—proud to have you with us."

"A bit too late, Doctor Dewey," Cole said tightly. "Doctor Grafton's treatment at the hands of sane people has been, shall we say, rather unfortunate. Her address in the future will be the Cole Sanitarium. Not as a patient, of course. As my assistant."

Cole smiled and turned away, the hand of Mary Grafton firm on his arm.

THE CASE OF THE CRAZY WITNESS

WHEN LINDA BARCLAY SWORE
HER AUNT'S MURDERER HAD
WORN A POLKA-DOT DERBY, A
BRIGHT RED SHIRT, A GREEN
SUIT AND SHOES TO MATCH
THE HAT, EVEN CARTER COLE,
EMINENT PSYCHIATRIST AND
INVESTIGATOR OF CRIME,
THOUGHT SHE WAS CRAZY. BUT
HER TESTIMONY COULDN'T BE
SHAKEN—SO IT WAS UP TO COLE
TO FIND THE KILLER OR ELSE
SEND HER TO A PADDED CELL.

CHAPTER ONE
SIX MILES TO MURDER

DOCTOR CARTER COLE, psychiatrist and director of the famed Cole Sanitarium, turned his massive Duesenberg off Long Island's Rainbow Parkway just as the dash clock indicated two A.M. The winding drive of the Gerard estate led him to an enormous house, the windows of which shafted curtained light across elaborately landscaped grounds. Accompanied by his pretty and efficient nurse-secretary, he went up to the entrance and knocked.

Waiting, he remarked: "A summons from Julia Gerard—one of the richest women in the country, and one of the most eccentric—is almost a royal command. She wears whalebone collars, severe black dresses harking back to the Nineties, and knots her white hair on the top of her head. Her violent temper is legend. Time means nothing to her. She expects to be implicitly obeyed at any hour of the day or night, and woe betide anyone who delays—so here we are. An amazing character, Jane."

"Yes, Doctor," said Miss Day. "But I'm June."

"You always are." Cole smiled as he lifted the knocker again. "You're invariably your twin sister, and she is invariably you. Long ago I despaired of ever being able to tell you apart." He frowned impatiently. "For one who tele-

She cowered there against the table.

phoned so imperatively, Mrs. Gerard is uncommonly slow in having us admitted."

"Yes, Doctor."

COLE OBSERVED his companion with renewed wonder. He knew nothing concerning the girl and her twin sister except that they were perfect secretaries, perfect duplicates of each other, and invariably composed in the face of any emergency. In response to the Gerard command to appear at this house at once, he had summoned one of them from bed, not knowing which twin she might be, and hustled her away without explanation. Now, calm, quite undisturbed by the bizarre situation, she listened attentively as Cole went on.

"An amazing character, and an amazing request. I am here, June, to examine the lady mentally—at two in the morning! I am to test her sanity, and furnish her with a sworn statement that she is completely rational. The matter is connected with a new will she is drawing up, and she wants to make certain it will not be contested, after her death, on the ground she didn't know what she was about. Fact is, I'm willing right now, on the strength of a slight personal acquaintance, to swear the Gerard mind knows absolutely what it's doing. Still, her precaution is as wise as it is strange, considering the vast fortune involved."

"Yes, Doctor," once again was the only comment June Day offered.

Cole's hand touched the knocker once more—but he did not rap, for at that moment a scream issued from the house. It began as a moan of despair, shrilled up to a pitch of stark terror, ended in a sob of anguish. Cole stood, hand poised, as a girl's voice screamed, "Willard, Willard!" Somewhere inside a door slammed. Then the cry came again and Cole gripped the knob, turned it.

"Go in, June!" he snapped and whirled to peer across the dark grounds. Someone was running across the grass at the side of the big house. Cole sprang to the corner, but saw no one. His hand eased to his 9mm Luger, holstered under his left arm, as he looked back to see Miss Day thrusting into the house. Suddenly he sprinted. He had glimpsed a shadowy figure scurrying along the hedge.

His run carried him past gardens, out the gate at the entrance of the drive. As he went along an angle of it, the hedge fluttered somewhere beyond the corner of the grounds. Long springy strides took Cole around the curve of the broad cement highway. Seeing nothing stirring in the gloom, he turned back, only to stop abruptly again. This time he saw a face.

Limned vaguely, it appeared, then vanished. Cole's photographic mind registered it with the speed of a clicking shutter. It was a man's face, tapering to a pointed chin, the eyes widened, the upper lip bearing a dark, dainty mustache. Its resemblance to a rabbit's struck Cole as he peered into the shadows where it had been. He strode to the spot, parted the hedge, looked through, but saw nothing.

"Hello? Who are you?" he called to the darkness. And the answer was silence.

Another cry from the house hurried him to the door. He strode along a tapestried hall, stepped into a luxurious library, stopped short. Miss June Day, with the firm assurance of a trained nurse, was tightening her arms around a young girl who was struggling in terror to free herself. Linda Barclay—Cole recognized her as the granddaughter of the woman who had called him to the house—ceased her efforts when Cole appeared and gazed at him in speechless entreaty. He strode at once to the third woman in the room—Julia Gerard.

The white-haired lady—clad, as Cole knew she would be, in a severe black dress with a whalebone collar, and with a pair of rimless eyeglasses pinched to her thin nose—was lying on the floor beside the table. His expert fingers sought her pulse, raised an eyelid. She was dead.

"Willard killed her!" the girl blurted. "Willard! I saw him kill her!"

COLE'S KEEN eyes detected no signs of violence on the corpse, but he sensed an unusual pungency in the air as he turned to a perfume atomizer on the table. While he covered his hand with a handkerchief and took it up,

Linda Barclay frantically resumed her attempts to break away from June Day.

Her voice rose almost to a scream. "Don't touch it! That's what he used to kill her! I saw Willard kill her with that!"

Cole looked at her in amazement. He saw nothing dangerous in the little atomizer, with its decorated bulb and sparkling liquid content, but he could not doubt the sincerity of the girl's warning. Eminent psychiatrist that he was, he knew that to defy her terror by examining the device now might, in her hysterical condition, momentarily unbalance her mind.

Replacing the atomizer, he said firmly: "Miss Barclay's all right, June. You may release her. Telephone Chief Wellsmore at once."

Linda Barclay stood trembling, backed against the wall, staring at the dead woman on the floor, as June Day went coolly to the telephone to call the local police. Cole, studying her with his humorously piercing eyes, his large head bent forward, waited for the girl to regain control of herself. Her fists clenched with the effort, but she repeated with terrified vehemence: "Willard killed her! I saw him kill her!"

Cole went to the girl quietly. "You are speaking of your uncle, Willard Gerard? You are accusing him of murdering his mother. You realize it's a gravely serious charge. Are you quite sure—"

"I saw him do it!"

Cole turned to the telephone as June Day put it down. She said, "Chief Wellsmore is coming, Doctor," as he thumbed through the local directory. The number he called was that of the home of Willard Gerard, the dead woman's son, which he knew was located a few miles farther along the Rainbow Parkway. "Mr. Gerard?" he inquired when a man's voice answered.

"No, my name's Mackler. Mr. Gerard's in the dark-room, developing some films, and can't come out. Is there any message?"

"Yes," succinctly. "Doctor Cole is going to pay Mr. Gerard a visit in a very few minutes." He turned from the telephone to direct Miss Day. "Take Miss Barclay into the next room, June."

As the door closed, he took up the costly atomizer and admired the design of its Lalique glass. Disturbed by the girl's charge, he chanced a slight squeeze of the bulb. Very cautiously, he drew a slow breath—and smiled. "Lovely," he breathed into the rich, flowery fragrance.

Again he intently examined the dead woman, and baffled, scanned the library for any indication of what might have caused her death. A folded paper lying on the desk attracted him. One clipped page was thrown back as though the dead woman had been interrupted while reading it. He saw, printed on the first sheet, *RELIANCE DETECTIVE AGENCY* and, under this heading, *Report.* The signature on the last page widened Cole's eyes—*Louis Mackler.*

Cole skimmed through the paper. Louis Mackler's report to Mrs. Julia Gerard, on behalf of the Reliance Detective Agency, was of no benefit to Willard Gerard's reputation. It mentioned several women, times and places. It spoke of heavy betting at Belmont Track and considerable sums lost in floating crap-games. The old lady's son was painted as irresponsible and undeserving. "We trust," the report ended ironically, "this information is satisfactory to you. Please rest assured our continued investigation will disclose further pertinent facts."

COLE WAS striding down the front hall when a rap sounded at the door. His tug on the knob transformed the shadow on the curtained pane into a man standing uneasily beyond the sill. Cole's breath stopped as he gazed at a pointed face. The sharp-chinned caller, obviously trying to control a grueling anxiety, smoothed his dainty mustache and attempted a smile.

"This is Doctor Cole? Mrs. Gerard told me on the telephone she was calling you tonight, too. It's an odd time to go about such a matter, don't you think, but—we expect unconventional actions of the good lady. I got out of bed to—"

"Haven't we," Cole asked, "met somewhere before—recently?"

The rabbit-faced man in the doorway paled. "I—I don't recall. My name is Leon Fendrick. I'm Mrs. Gerard's attorney, you know. This is unusual, isn't it? It's something about disinheriting her son, bequeathing his share of her fortune to charity. Perhaps I shouldn't divulge that, but I feel an explanation is due you—this hour of the night and all that. Is the good lady—"

"You will find the good lady in the library, Mr. Fendrick," Cole said tartly. "Dead."

Fendrick emitted a strangled exclamation as, ghost-faced, he stared at Cole. Cole had deliberately flung the information at the attorney, without warning, in order to observe the reaction. Now, abruptly, he strode past with no word of explanation, leaving Fendrick staring after him in palsied torment as he slipped behind the wheel of his Duesenberg.

Carter Cole watched the odometer as he sped along the smooth, straight cement lane. It stretched empty before him in the shafts of the headlamps. The sixth mile was clicking off when he turned into another driveway. Willard Gerard's home, though much less pretentious than his mother's, had cost a small fortune. Cole's knock brought a smallish, sharp-eyed man to the door.

When Cole introduced himself, the little man said: "My name's Mackler. Mr. Gerard's still in the dark-room. Step in." He was chewing with relish on something as he led Cole along a hall, into the kitchen. There he took up the remains of a sandwich and gestured to a closed door. "He's coming right out."

'It does my heart good," Cole said cryptically, "to see a private detective bear so little malice toward a man he's investigating unfavorably."

Mackler stared, amazed as an opening door disclosed Willard Gerard. He stepped into the kitchen smiling, stripping a pair of rubber gloves from his hands—a massive man, blunt-chinned, endowed with an almost offensive degree of natural charm. Cole saw, behind him, a room with black-painted walls, shelves loaded with photographic paraphernalia, an enlarging projector, a discolored sink, and a tank in which negatives were being washed. The pungency from an acid fixing-bath followed Gerard into the room but it was not, Cole noted, the same acridity he had observed hovering in the air about the dead woman.

Gerard, greeting Cole with a chuckle, said: "I've heard of you, of course, Doctor. Are you here on behalf of my mother, perhaps to prove I'm out of my mind and, being insane, can't hold property? She's determined to cut me off with the proverbial shilling, you know—even less. I shall regret that, very much."

"You need worry no longer," Carter Cole said dryly. "You have a good many more shillings at the moment than you've ever had before. Only a few minutes ago Mrs.

Gerard died. You shan't keep the money long, though, if Miss Linda Barclay's charge is true—that you murdered the old lady." Then abruptly, intently studying Willard Gerard's staring eyes, "How did the pictures come out?"

Without answering Willard Gerard flung the rubber gloves into the darkroom. While Louis Mackler stood with a bite of sandwich half swallowed, Cole followed Gerard into the next room. He stood by while Gerard snapped a number into the receiver, spoke to a Doctor Hildreth, and begged: "Please get to my mother's place as fast as you can!" He stared at Cole again and asked breathlessly: "Are you quite sure she's dead?"

"Quite. My car," Cole suggested quietly, "is at your disposal."

He went out and sat, fingers drumming the wheel, while Gerard got into a topcoat and hat. He was remembering Linda Barclay's anguished accusation, the vehement certainty behind her charge, when Gerard and Mackler climbed in. Again, as he drove without speaking, he noted the slow revolving of the odometer. It registered a distance of exactly six miles between the two dwellings. Cole's watch told him he had made it in nine minutes when he turned into the drive.

CHAPTER TWO
THE POLKA-DOT DERBY

GERARD RUSHED into the house, Mackler loping at his side. Cole noted another car near the gate. It told him June Day's call to the local police had brought quick results. Chief Wellsmore, speaking gravely, was confronting Linda Barclay when Cole quietly went into the room adjoining that in which the dead woman lay. He signaled his secretary into the hallway.

"June, I'm enmeshed in a very peculiar situation. Gerard is sure to use me as an alibi witness in case the girl sticks to her charge. Certain things about this matter are making me cautious. Phone the sanitarium at once."

"Yes, Doctor."

"Ask your twin sister to get all pertinent information possible on the Gerard family. I want, also, information concerning Leon Fendrick, the old lady's attorney. Then ask Brick Kelly to get over here in a hurry."

"Yes, Doctor."

Cole reentered the living-room. Gerard and Mackler were standing at one side, apparently stunned by the unexpected situation they faced. Leon Fendrick, nervously fingering his well kept mustache, jerked guilty eyes from Cole's scrutiny.

Cole watched Linda Barclay's wan face as Chief Wellsmore asked her: "Now tell us exactly what you saw happen."

The girl hesitated anxiously. Her eyes turned imploringly to Cole and she said, in a vibrant whisper: "You—you'll think I'm crazy."

"Don't be afraid," Wellsmore urged her. "Tell us just what you saw."

Linda Barclay's fingers twined together. "I was in my studio, painting. I came downstairs to say good-night to Demmy—Mrs. Gerard. I stopped on the landing in the library, just staring—because it was so strange."

"Yes?"

"They were standing near the table—Demmy and Willard. His back was turned—neither of them noticed me. He was opening a box, and taking out a little atomizer. He said, 'Don't be angry, Julia—it's a peace offering.' She answered, 'You're no longer a son of mine, Willard.' He laughed and said, 'Oh, come, now, Julia. The perfume is very appropriate—it's called Night Sin. Take just one little whiff.' And he laughed again, and shot a bit of spray into her face."

"Yes?"

"She dropped dead."

Chief Wellsmore blinked at the girl. She looked beseechingly again at Cole, as though begging him, if no one else would, to believe her. She nodded frantically, fighting back her tears, as Chief Wellsmore asked incredulously: "You saw Willard Gerard squeeze this atomizer in Mrs. Gerard's face, and she instantly fell to the floor, dead?"

"I swear it's exactly what happened! I saw it just as I'm telling you. I can hardly believe it myself, but—oh, don't!"

Chief Wellsmore had taken up the atomizer. He smelled of it then, in spite of the girl's frantic gesture, squeezed the bulb. There was uneasy silence in the room while the scent dissipated through the air—rich, sweet, obviously harmless. The pleading in the girl's eyes was even stronger when Wellsmore asked: "And what else did you see?"

"Willard stood by the table, his back still turned to me, a moment after Demmy fell. Then, suddenly, he ran out of the room. I saw his face clearly, and he saw me. I can't be mistaken! It's all so strange—the way he was dressed—but I—"

"The way he was dressed?"

The girl forced out each word. "He was wearing a derby hat—a blue derby hat, with large yellow polka-dots." She paused as Chief Wellsmore straightened incredulously, as every person in the room stared—including Carter Cole. Defying their disbelief, she rushed on. "He had on a bright red shirt. His tie was green with yellow stripes. The suit was a bright orange. And his shoes were blue, with yellow polka-dots, to match his hat."

WELLSMORE LOOKED around as though doubting his ears. Willard Gerard wagged his head in sympathetic dismay. June Day, having come quietly into the room, looked quickly, with professional understanding, at Carter Cole. Cole, drawn by the girl's pleading eyes, went quietly toward her.

"Will you repeat that?" he asked softly. "Will you tell us again exactly what you saw Willard Gerard wearing?"

She rushed it out. "A blue derby with yellow dots. A red shirt. A green-and-yellow-striped tie. A bright orange suit. Blue, yellow-dotted shoes to match the derby. I did see it! I tell you I did!"

There was a hush as every eye turned to Willard Gerard. Mackler, at his side, had half raised his hand, as though to speak, but he swallowed inarticulately. Carter Cole, with the quiet firmness June Day had so often seen him use toward violent inmates of his sanitarium, asked the girl: "Will you please describe the clothing Willard Gerard is wearing now?"

Scorn flashed in the girl's eyes. "Of course. He has on a white shirt, a plain blue tie, a grey herringbone suit, and black oxfords. That doesn't matter. I saw him here—I know I saw him—and he was wearing exactly what I said!"

The accused man murmured: "That's obviously impossible. I'm afraid you're overwrought, Linda."

The girl shook her head in protest and sank into a chair. Cole watched her intently as a knock sounded on the door. A man wearing tortoise-shell glasses, smelling faintly of medicaments, ventured into the room. Willard Gerard greeted him as Doctor Hildreth—Cole knew him to be the family physician. With Chief Wellsmore's permission he withdrew to examine the dead woman. As he went out, muttering his regrets, Linda Barclay sobbed quietly.

Perplexed, Chief Wellsmore ventured: "I think you'd better rest before we ask you any more questions. The shock has been too much for you. Tomorrow, perhaps—

"I'm quite all right." The girl's eyes were a shining defiance. "Do you think I'm mad? No matter how impossible you think it is, I—I saw what I saw." Then, incongruously, "I've telephoned Mother. She's coming, and—I'll be all right."

Shrugging at Gerard, Chief Wellsmore asked: "As a matter of routine, I've got to ask you if what your niece says is true."

"Hardly," Gerard answered.

"But it is!" Linda Barclay insisted. "I tell you it is! Why should I lie? I know it's impossible—I know it couldn't have happened. But I didn't imagine it. It's true—every word is true!"

June Day took the girl in her comforting arms. Carter Cole looked speculatively at Louis Mackler. "You've been trying to say something. What is it?" he asked.

"Sure. If Mr. Gerard needs an alibi, I can give it to him. I know he couldn't have done it."

"Preliminary to that," Cole suggested wryly, "perhaps you'd better explain why you happen to be so friendly with Mr. Gerard—considering that his mother hired you to investigate his actions."

"Sure." Mackler blinked. "I was watching him for Mrs. Gerard, all right. I've been on the job for a week. I learned plenty, and he knows it. Tonight I turned the latest report in to Mrs. Gerard, and then went to his place to watch him some more."

"Your report," Cole deduced, "prompted Mrs. Gerard to telephone me and Mr. Fendrick at this unholy hour, for the purpose of attesting her sanity and drawing up a new will."

"I don't know anything about that," Mackler answered. "Well, I'm there, on Mr. Gerard's place, watching the house. First thing I know, he comes right out to where I'm standing beside the garage. He says, 'Rather uncomfortable out here, isn't it? Why not come in and have some sandwiches and coffee?' That's what he says. It's the first time any man I was trailing treated me like that. All I could think of was the boss would give me hell."

WILLARD GERARD explained. "You see, it was no secret Julia was having me watched. She told me herself. I thought it was amusing to invite Mackler in and treat him like a guest."

"Sure," Mackler resumed. "So I go in. We talk a while, then Mr. Gerard steps into the dark-room to develop some films. He says things to me through the door every once in a while. I remember, pretty soon he asks, 'What time is it, Mackler?' and I say, 'It's eight minutes of two.'"

Cole remarked: "You develop films by the factorial method, I suppose, Mr. Gerard—but you didn't have a watch or a clock in the dark-room?"

"A special clock for timing paper and film," Gerard answered, "with a large hand making one complete revolution of the dial per minute—but no regular clock."

Mackler continued eagerly: "Sure. I say, 'It's eight minutes of two,' and go on eating, and reading the evening paper. Pretty soon he asks me again, 'What time is it, Mackler?' and this time I say, 'It's just eleven minutes after two.' That's by my watch, and it's always right. He's there all the time. Sure."

Chief Wellsmore asked: "It isn't possible Mr. Gerard could have left the darkroom and gone back without your having seen him, Mackler?"

Gerard answered for the private detective. "There's only one door, and Mackler, I believe, was sitting in plain sight of it. Even to have opened the door would have fogged the negatives. You may see them if you wish."

"When Mr. Gerard went into the darkroom, and when he came out, he was wearing the same clothing he's wearing now?"

Mackler said: "Sure."

To Wellsmore, Cole observed: "I arrived at the front door of this house at perhaps one minute past two. I heard Miss Barclay scream approximately one minute later. That, of course, marks the moment when she saw her grandmother fall dead to the floor."

"Two minutes past two, until eleven past—nine minutes," Wellsmore calculated. "Even if Mr. Gerard had been here, he couldn't have gotten from this house to his in that time unless he drove very rapidly."

"The distance, Cole said, "is exactly six miles. No automobile left these grounds after I heard the scream, Chief, nor any spot nearby. I'm absolutely certain of it. That, added to what Mackler says about the time element, appears to provide Mr. Gerard with an iron-clad alibi. But"—and Cole's humorously piercing eyes grew keener—"I'm curious to know why he happened to ask Mackler the time just when he did."

Gerard smiled. "I'd promised to telephone a lady who is busy in the floor show of a night club until shortly after two."

Wellsmore shrugged. "We've got to believe Miss Barclay didn't see what she says she saw. She's evidently suffering from delusions, brought on by the shock of her grandmother's death. Under the circumstances—"

The official paused, and Cole turned, as Doctor Hildreth reappeared in the doorway. The physician said quietly: "It's very sad, but it was bound to come sooner or later. Any unusual excitement would have done it. High blood-pressure, heart complications, angina particularly—I expected it. With her temper it's a wonder she lived as long as she did."

"Your opinion is that Mrs. Gerard's death was due to cardiac failure?" Cole asked.

Doctor Hildreth looked surprised. "Of course," he said, as though any other conclusion were untenable. "Of course."

"Could Miss Barclay have imagined it all? Here is one tangible detail of what she tells us—something we can't doubt—the atomizer." Cole turned to Gerard. "You didn't present this to your mother, as she says?"

"I did," Gerard admitted. "The conversation between my mother and me, which Linda has reported, actually took place—but about twelve hours sooner than she believes. I gave the atomizer to Julia, in Linda's presence, at about two o'clock this afternoon."

"Perhaps," Cole said, "an aberration of memory, under violent emotional shock—not at all unusual."

"Under the circumstances," Chief Wellsmore went on, "we must disregard Miss Barclay's charge. First of all, Mr. Gerard couldn't possibly have killed the old lady and, second, it's not murder after all, but natural death. I shall probably ask Doctor Morse's advice, but under the circumstances I am satisfied there is nothing further to be done by the police."

Linda Barclay had remained silent. Her face had become even paler, the frantic light in her eyes stronger. Suddenly she twisted out of June Day's arms and went to the door, one arm outstretched, as though groping through darkness. Her face pictured fear when she glanced back—fear, Cole knew, that she had lost her sanity. Then, quickly, she ran up the stairs, out of sight.

Cole said quietly: "Come, June."

AS CARTER COLE crossed the porch with his secretary, the headlamps of a car swept across the rolling grounds. A coupé stopped quickly near the porch, and a woman alighted, her face anxious. She was, Cole knew, Mrs. Barclay, the girl's mother. She hurried into the house as Cole went on to a roadster standing near the Duesenberg.

"Brick," he said.

"O.K., Doc," came eagerly from the car.

The stocky, bull-necked, rusty-haired young man at the wheel was Cole's versatile assistant. He had been variously a dock-walloper, an able-bodied seaman, a truck driver, a sculptor's model. His winning way with balky drains, recalcitrant typewriters, cranky alarm clocks and mulish automobile motors made him invaluable at the Cole Sanitarium; his special pride was keeping the Duesenberg in perfect tune. June Day's telephone call had brought him uncomplainingly out of bed to do Carter Cole service.

"A special job of watching, Brick. Willard Gerard is the man, and the house is just six miles down the road. Bear two things in mind. I want Gerard to know you're watching him—but, in case he invites you in for coffee and sandwiches, you're to refuse. Also, pay special attention to the chimneys of the house and if you see smoke, flash me an alarm."

Brick Kelly's eyes widened. "Listen, Doc," he said earnestly. "All you have to do is ask me. Anything you say goes. If there's anybody you want knocked on the skull, I'm the guy who'll do it for you. But if you keep mixing into these screwy cases—"

"I want Gerard to know you're watching him," Cole cut in, "so he won't attempt to get away with anything that might otherwise go unobserved. Smoke from the chimneys may mean he's burning up a polka-dot derby and an orange suit, besides other weird garments. That's all, Brick."

Kelly stared, said "Geez!" and started off, head wagging, as Cole went with June Day to the Duesenberg. He swung it onto the parkway, but instead of turning to the left, in which direction lay the Cole Sanitarium, he swung right. Six miles later he wove for the second time that night into the driveway of Willard Gerard's home.

His finger beckoned June Day as he stepped into the garage, where a sedan stood in its place. Cole pressed his hand to the radiator and murmured, "Cold." Turning, he observed a strange device made of tin, standing in one rear corner. It was shaped like the prow of a small boat, and contained an inset, rectangular section of glass and had two stout braces affixed inside. On his way out Cole observed a bicycle equipped with variable gear and low-slung handle-bars leaning against the wall.

He returned thoughtfully to the Duesenberg with the Day twin. The alert look on June's face told him that in a moment she would say something pertinent. She did.

"Linda Barclay may be deranged, Doctor, but she's right about one thing. It was Night Sin."

"It was more than that, June," Cole observed laconically as he started off. "It was murder."

CHAPTER THREE
DOCTOR'S DILEMMA

THE COLE SANITARIUM sat behind a high spiked fence with a formidable locked gate. It was a retreat housing more than a thousand patients suffering from every conceivable mental abnormality. Within this kingdom, set apart from the workaday world, Carter Cole wielded over staff and inmates the power of a monarch.

Day and night its walls resounded with the woeful lamentations and joyful hysterics of manic-depressives. Cole considered it a sad commentary on the clergy that many of his charges were constantly preaching. Others attended the gardens and rolled the walks. The sprawling buildings were a maze of halls in which placid-faced men and women pushed huge wooden blocks based with felt, the task easing their tortured minds while it polished the floors to mirror brightness. Deep among the labyrinthine corridors, in the remotest wing, were the offices of Carter Cole.

At his desk this morning, fresh and alert, he dispatched the routine affairs of the institution with easy briskness—but his mind was haunted by the strange circumstances surrounding the death of Mrs. Gerard. He read terse reports left on his blotter by the efficient Misses Day, added notes of his own. He was absorbed and troubled when one of his twin secretaries appeared with more neatly typed slips to announce: "Mrs. Clara Barclay to see you, Doctor, with Miss Linda Barclay."

"I rather expected the call. Has Brick phoned, June?"

"Yes, Doctor. A moment ago, to say he's still watching Mr. Gerard's place. He reports no smoke and nothing suspicious—but I'm Jane."

Cole sighed. "Sooner or later, you and your sister are going to make me an inmate in my own institution. You're always the other one! Ask my callers to please wait a few minutes. I will want to see Mrs. Barclay alone first."

"Yes, Doctor."

Intently Cole re-read the reports. The first—

Concerning the Gerards:

The alienation of Willard Gerard from his mother, Julia Gerard, began six months ago. The old lady had become extremely fond of the admirable girl her son married. Their divorce, obtained by the daughter-in-law on the only grounds possible in New York State, turned Julia Gerard against her son. He continued to occupy the house on Rainbow Parkway and, in spite of his mother's warnings, became more of a profligate than ever. His only occupation, besides unbridled pleasure-seeking, is to bicycle about the country with his camera. His efforts in creative photography are apparently wasted due to lack of artistic talent.

Miss Linda Barclay, on the contrary, is said to possess genuine ability as an artist. Her grandmother provided her with a studio in the big Gerard house, where she spends most of her time in serious artistic endeavor. She has yet to make a name for herself, but she is extremely ambitious, and her career is promising.

Miss Barclay, her mother, and Willard Gerard, besides Willard's former wife, are all beneficiaries under Julia Gerard's present will. The fortune is estimated at several millions.

JD

The second report—

I have been unable to reach Mr. Leon Fendrick. His office reports they do not expect him in today. His manservant says he has many engagements in New York and will not return to his home until after midnight.

Fendrick is a reputable lawyer, though not clever enough to establish himself as an outstanding one. Almost his only client was Julia Gerard. Her retaining him for the past ten years is an example of her eccentricity, the reason probably being that she could dominate him completely. She obliged him to live near her and called on him at all hours. Her fees maintain Fendrick handsomely. He is not mentioned in the Gerard will.

JD

"Reasonable to conclude," Cole murmured, "that Fendrick is scrambling for new clients, now the old lady has paid him her last fee."

COLE'S TOUCH on a button brought a Miss Day into the office—which one he did not attempt to determine—followed by Mrs. Barclay. Linda Barclay's mother was a comely woman betrayed by a tendency to avoirdupois. She took a chair facing Cole, fingering her handbag, her lips nervously pursed.

"It—it hurts me to bring Linda here," she blurted, "but there's nothing else I can do, Doctor Cole, in all fairness to her—to everyone. Her accusing Willard is so—fantastic. Her own career is at stake. Will you help her? Will you do everything possible to—to clear her mind?"

"You believe, too, her mind is clouded?" Cole asked.

"What else can I believe?" It was a tearful question. "I've been worried about Linda since last summer—an unfortunate infatuation at Provincetown. Then her failing to have any of her pictures accepted by the National Academy. It was a terrific disappointment—she brooded. We tried to cheer her up, but—please do all you can to help her!"

"I am not yet ready to believe Miss Barclay's mind is affected," Cole murmured.

The girl's mother dismissed that as routine reassurance. "Perhaps I can explain last night. Undoubtedly Linda overheard Julia telephoning you and Mr. Fendrick. In her disturbed state she may have thought she was going to be examined mentally and confined. Being so sensitive—overwrought—perhaps she pled with her grandmother—argued desperately, and it was too much for them both. The strain overtaxed Julia's heart and something snapped in Linda's brain. Do you think that's it, Doctor Cole?"

"In all my experience," Cole said gravely, "I have never yet discovered anything in anyone's mind that can snap. Perhaps, I'd best talk to Linda alone. I'll telephone you my report."

Mrs. Barclay wiped her eyes, sobbed a sincere, "Thank you so much!" and left the office hurriedly. Cole waited thoughtfully, watching the door. It opened, after a moment, quietly. Linda Barclay, her eyes clear in a face white as alabaster, came to the chair beside Cole's desk. She sat erect, studied him as intently as he scrutinized her, finally spoke first, with disarming directness.

"Do you think I'm mad?"

"No." Cole smiled. "Not in the slightest. You never 'saw things' before last night, did you? You haven't 'seen things' since, I'm sure. I hesitate to believe that in one particular instance, and not in a million others, you had a grotesque delusion. The very fact that you're so sure of what you saw leads me to believe you saw it."

The girl asked breathlessly: "Incredible, impossible as it is?"

"Why not?" Cole's smile grew. "Eyewitnesses are unreliable agents, young lady. A belief has grown in the lay mind that eye-witnesses present the most conclusive testimony from the witness stand. Exactly the opposite is true. Scientific research, conducted by Binet, Gross, Stein, Lysmann, Gorphe, Locard, Dupre and others, all prove how defective eyewitnesses are in perception, observation and mind fixation.* I might question you in the light of their findings,

---

* Modern witness psychology has proved again and again that the most reliable witnesses are extremely apt to make serious errors of perception in good faith. An instance is a test made by Dauber in 1913. He showed to a group of school children a picture of a small boy with brown hair, wearing blue trousers and brown coat. The subjects were asked, a few minutes later, after the removal of the picture, to identify the colors, with the following amazing results: Only fifteen reported the blue trousers as blue, while 72 named another color. Not one recalled the coat as brown, but 151 gave it other colors. Concerning the brown hair, 47 recalled it as black and four called it "light". Further, eighteen described the brown shoes in the picture as black, and a number declared the boy was barefoot! Research shows that the average person, describing an individual from memory, over-estimates the height by about five inches and the age by more than eight years. Eighty-three per cent are totally wrong concerning the color of the hair. The description of the shape of the face generally is very misleading. Indeed, the appalling fallibility of eye-witnesses discovered by these experiments leads criminologists to believe circumstantial evidence is far more trustworthy.—F.C.D.

but not otherwise. Suppose you tell me again exactly what happened last night."

"Of course." The girl spoke clearly. "I came down the stairs, from the studio, to the landing. Demmy and Willard were by the table, but neither noticed me. He opened a box and took out the atomizer. He said, 'Don't be angry, Julia—it's a peace offering'. Demmy answered, 'You're no longer a son of mine, Willard.' He said, laughing, 'Oh, come now, Julia. The perfume is very appropriate—it's called Night Sin. Just take one whiff.' No—he said, 'one *little* whiff.' Then he shot the spray into Demmy's face and—she dropped."

STEADYING HER voice, the girl went on: "Willard was strangely dressed. His derby hat was blue, with large yellow dots. His shirt bright red. The tie was green-and-yellow-striped. His suit was bright orange, and his shoes matched his hat—blue, with yellow polka-dots. I'm so sure of it, because in my painting I feel color more than line. To me the whole world is completely color."

"One important question," Cole asked. "Your grandmother, confronted by this man in the weird garb, didn't mention it or apparently notice it?"

"She didn't at all," Linda Barclay answered. "I could strengthen my own story by saying she did, Doctor Cole, but she didn't. Demmy was a strange woman, generous and warm-hearted, though she pretended to be so cold. She often deliberately disregarded things because she knew she was expected to notice them. Frequently she came to my studio to see a painting I'd just finished—bright colors that thrilled me—but she'd only glance at it and say, 'It looks very much like the others,' or something like that—and go out. Perhaps she ignored Willard's strange dress because she thought he'd worn it to make her comment on it."

Cole's eyes sharpened. "There's got to be a better reason than that for Mrs. Gerard's saying nothing about that weird get-up! Assuming you saw someone wearing an orange suit, how could it have been Willard Gerard?"

The girl insisted firmly: "It was Willard."

"Mackler said Gerard was in the darkroom all the time. He asked Mackler the time at eight minutes of two, then again at eleven after. Your grandmother died at two minutes past two, about midway in that period. How *could* it have been Willard Gerard?"

Again, flatly—"It was Willard."

Cole persisted. "You say you recognized him immediately, in spite of his strange dress, though his back was turned."

"I recognized him at once." Linda Barclay's voice was now faint; she had yielded to the strain of nervous shock and a sleepless night. "I know Willard killed Demmy—by squirting the perfume in her face—I know it!"

Cole rose, touched a button. "Look here—is there anything else—no matter how unbelievable—that has any bearing whatever on the death of your grandmother?"

"I've tried to think—tried so hard. There's only one thing. Some time ago—a week perhaps—I missed certain tubes from my paint box. They were yellow, green and blue."

Cole's eyes glittered as the door opened. The young woman who entered was poised, lithely slender, strikingly pretty, obviously of high intelligence. Doctor Mary Grafton, brilliant young woman physician, now Cole's first assistant, could look upon Linda Barclay and remember herself in a similar desperate plight. Only a short while past she had been within the shadow of the electric chair, saved from it only by the astuteness of Carter Cole.* She came at once, warmly sympathetic, to the girl.

"Mary, Miss Barclay is to have every comfort," Cole instructed. "She will be subjected to no restraint whatever. Please provide her with artists' materials." And to the girl, "Please don't worry. You're absolutely all right—and I'm going to prove it."

He touched another button as Doctor Grafton escorted the girl away. When one of his twin secretaries appeared, he continued as though she knew the whole story: "I've got to prove it, Jane, because if I don't, that estimable young woman will spend the rest of her life in an asylum for the insane. In my experience I've found very little difference between sanity and insanity. Proving one or the other is a ticklish job, but that girl's entire life depends on it. Do you understand me, Jane?"

"Yes, Doctor," Miss Day said. "But I'm June."

"Of course you are! Get busy, June. Locate the late Mrs. Gerard's eye-specialist. I want to know of any peculiarity, however slight, in the old lady's eyesight."

"Yes, Doctor," said June Day as she hurried from the office. Almost immediately she appeared to return. This was Jane Day, however, answering Cole's touch on another button. She remained as unperturbed as her sister had been while Cole rushed on.

"I've got to prove that that girl actually saw a man wearing a polka-dot derby and an orange suit and all the rest. I've got to establish, beyond all doubt, that she saw a man in one house when all sane reason and logic says he was in

---

*   "The Case of the Skinned Men," taken from the case book of Carter Cole, M.D., relates the amazing story of Doctor Mary Grafton.—F.C.D.

another house six miles away. I've got to show that Julia Gerard died of having an expensive, delightful perfume, called Night Sin, squirted in her face. I tell you, Linda Barclay's happiness, her career, her fortune, her whole future rests upon that."

"Yes, Doctor," said Jane Day. "Mr. Kelly has just reported again that Mr. Gerard is still in the house. No smoke—nothing suspicious. Is there something else?"

"If I become violent," Cole said grimly, "your instructions are to throw me into a padded room—because I believe implicitly every incredible thing that girl has said!"

"Yes, Doctor."

CARTER COLE sank thoughtfully into his chair. Unaware of the passing time, he remained almost immobile while he tried to make the impossible true and the fantastic credible. Darkness flooded his office before he realized it. He looked up, startled when light shafted over him from an opened door, silhouetting the trim figure of a Day twin.

"We are still trying to locate Mrs. Gerard's eye-specialist," she announced, "and Mr. Kelly is on the phone."

Brick Kelly sounded mournful. "Doc, you're welcome to kick me in the pants. You owe me a sock on the jaw. I've been watching Gerard's place ever since dark, but he's flown the coop, Doc—and I didn't know it until now. Geez, how he got out—"

"O.K., Brick," Cole snapped. "Next best to keeping an eye on him is a chance to search that house. Get into it somehow, and wait for me. I'm on my way. I'll be very happy if, by the time I've arrived, you've found a polka-dot derby."

Breaking the connection, Cole started for the door. He was getting into his topcoat when one of the Day twins proffered another telephone and said: "Doctor Morse calling."

The famed medical examiner of New York City chuckled in Cole's ear. "You'll be glad Chief Wellsmore asked me to drop over for a look at the old lady, Cole. Interesting news. It's not heart failure at all, old boy. The traces are very faint, but Schonbein's test says it's hydrocyanic acid."

"You please me immensely!" Cole said. "A squirt of hydrocyanic acid in the face would drop the old lady instantly, wouldn't it? What's more, hydrocyanic acid can be made easily by one who knows how, from potassium cyanide—and potassium cyanide is used frequently in compounding photographic toning baths!"*

"Right," Morse chuckled. "But that doesn't give you a murderer, does it? Not unless you can prove a man was where he couldn't possibly have been."

Cole hung up and left the office. He was striding rapidly along a polished hallway when quick, light foot-

---

*   Hydrocyanic acid and its alkali salts, sodium and potassium cyanide, are used extensively in the arts. Free hydrocyanic acid is liberated by the action of strong acids on the alkali salts. It takes third or fourth place in the frequency with which death is caused by poisons. It volatilizes quite rapidly and for that reason, when death is due to inhaling the vapor, is sometimes impossible to identify. Hunt and Gettler, authorities on toxicology, have declared: "There have been undoubted cases of poisoning with hydrocyanic acid where competent chemists have been unable to detect the substance a few hours after use." Its lethal action is extremely rapid.—F.C.D.

falls sounded behind him. A Miss Day—which, he did not know—caught his arm breathlessly, stopped him.

She said, immediately recovering her cool aplomb: "We have just reached Doctor Jacoby, Mrs. Gerard's occulist. He says, although the old lady tried to conceal it, and not even her children knew of it, she was color-blind. He—"

"Color blind!" Cole's teeth clicked. "That explains why she would make no comment on a polka-dot derby and an orange suit—the whole rig would look gray! It explains her vague comments on Linda Barclay's paintings. Jane, our witness isn't crazy, but the case certainly is!"

Miss Day said, unperturbed, "I'm June, Doctor"—but Cole was already slamming out the door.

CHAPTER FOUR

CARTER COLE—
SAFE ROBBER

COLE ROLLED the Duesenberg past the Willard Gerard place, slid off the pavement, clicked off headlamps and ignition before he walked back. The house was silent, but lights were burning beyond the drawn window drapes. Cole circled to the rear door, found it unfastened, stepped into the kitchen. His call brought Brick Kelly stealthily down the stairs.

"Am I wrong, Doc," the handy man asked anxiously, "or is this breakin' the law?"

"You're not wrong, Brick. We could both get several years for this. Did you find the polka-dot derby?"

Compassion shone in Kelly's eyes. "No polka-dot derby here, Doc."

"No orange suit?"

"Geez, Doc!" Kelly gasped. "I hate to see this happen to you!"

Cole opened the dark-room adjoining the kitchen. His touch on a switch lighted a ruby bulb, another snapped on an ordinary white globe. He stood in acrid air, his keen eyes searching the black-painted room for a bottle of cyanide on the shelf of chemicals. There was none.

He turned to a corner where a small but very strong safe stood. "Strange it should be here," Cole murmured and tugged at the handle. It was locked. Stooping, he fingered an iron ring set flush with the floor. He pulled at it and raised a large trap. Cool, damp air gusted into his face as he gazed at a flight of wooden stairs angling downward.

Eyes glittering, he told Kelly: "This dark-room was once an ordinary pantry. Gerard must have converted it after his mother bought the house for him. That's the basement. Keep with me, Brick."

Halfway down the flight, Cole clicked another switch. A cobwebbed bulb spread a yellow glow through the cement-walled cellar. Pipes reached from a furnace like the tentacles of an octopus. Cole went alertly to a door set in the side wall. It opened into a bulkhead. Raising the outer slanting doors, Cole looked into darkness. Across the driveway sat the garage. One of its doors was standing ajar, and the sedan was visible in its stall. He lowered the doors, crossed the basement, climbed the stairs into the dark-room, lowered the trap once more.

Kelly, looking startled, blurted: "He could've slipped out this way, Doc, and come back without Mackler knowin' it!"

Cole's eyes showed dangerous glints. "Last night Gerard, in here, asked Mackler the time at eight minutes of two, again at eleven after. That's an interval of nineteen minutes. Question: could Gerard have gotten out of this place, to his mother's and back again, a distance of twelve miles, in nineteen minutes?"

"And in a polka-dot derby," Kelly prompted.

"Allow him one minute for getting out via the trap and the bulkhead. Estimate five minutes while he was at his mother's place, if he was. Then another minute for getting from the outside of this house back into the dark-room. That's seven minutes to subtract from nineteen, leaving twelve. Twelve minutes, Brick, in which to travel twelve miles."

"That's fast goin'," Kelly opined skeptically.

"He didn't use a car. If he had, Mackler would have heard it. I would have spotted it also, leaving Julia Gerard's place. Besides, I made sure last night, by feeling the radiator of Gerard's sedan, that it hadn't been used—it was cold. Brick, Gerard didn't cover those twelve miles in twelve minutes in an automobile. Nor, I may add, in an airplane."

"I agree with you there, Doc," Kelly said sadly.

"He uses a bicycle to flutter about the countryside on his picture-taking tours. How fast, Brick, do you suppose a man can travel on a bicycle?"

"Twenty, twenty-five miles an hour, at a good clip," Kelly guessed. "That ain't anywhere near a mile a minute."

THE THOUGHTFUL light in Cole's eyes deepened. "Right. New doubt is cast upon Linda Barclay's testimony. If she's wrong about Gerard's being at his mother's place, she may be wrong about the whole episode. That brings up the subject of the polka-dot derby. What about it, Brick?"

"Doc," Kelly pled, "don't you think if you got some sleep you'd feel better?"

"When Gerard stepped into this darkroom," Cole grimly persisted, "he was wearing ordinary clothing. I saw him come out, dressed conventionally. If he actually wore a blue derby with yellow dots while at his mother's home, he had to take time to get into the rig and out again. That might take only a few seconds if it were designed for quick changing—the suit large enough to pull over another, the shirt a dickie, for instance. Next question: at what point did he put on the outfit, then change back?"

"Maybe," Kelly suggested pathetically, "you'd like an aspirin, Doc?"

"Answer: probably right here in this dark-room," Cole went on.

He peered at the safe in the corner. While Kelly stared, he strode into the living-room, took up the telephone, called the Cole Sanitarium. Kelly's eyes widened in alarm as he heard Cole's orders.

"June, Jane, whichever you are, get busy on the telephone and find the best locksmith in New York. I want him to be there when I get back. He must be prepared to open a small and very tough-looking safe."

"Yes, Doctor," Miss Day answered.

Cole disconnected and directed: "Spit on your hands, Brick." He led the amazed handy-man into the dark-room and snapped crisp orders. Together they slid the safe from the corner. Its weight strained their muscles as they tottered out of the dark-room. They staggered from the house, maneuvered along the drive.

"Speakin' of breakin' laws, Doc," Kelly panted, "this ain't doin' us any good!"

"We're committing a felony, Brick. To the car!"

They tottered along the edge of the parkway to the Duesenberg. With an exhausting effort they heaved the safe into the rear section. Kelly ruefully examined his barked knuckles as Cole slid behind the wheel.

When their breathing returned to normal, Cole observed: "Scientific research into the fallibility of eye-witnesses tends to show that, though Linda Barclay may be right about the polka-dot derby, she might be wrong about other details. About seeing Willard Gerard squirting lethal perfume into her grandmother's face, for instance. I deem it wise, Brick, to play two gambles at once."

He started the car while Kelly nodded in inarticulate dismay.

"Assume it was not the profligate son she saw. There is only one other possibility. His name is Leon Fendrick. Fendrick was slinking about the Gerard grounds just after the old lady's strange death. He might have been wearing an orange suit—I got a glimpse of his face only. He had ample time to change back to ordinary clothes. In that case, Brick, there may be a will in existence of which we know nothing—one bequeathing Mr. Fendrick a considerable sum."

Kelly asked hopefully: "Are we goin' back home?"

"We are not," Cole said decisively. "We're paying a visit to Fendrick."

Cole had U-turned the car. As he passed Willard Gerard's place he glanced at his watch, jammed the gas-pedal down hard. The Duesenberg leaped. In new alarm, Brick Kelly held onto his hat and watched the speedometer needle swing higher and higher. Five and a half miles clicked off in rapid succession. Near Julia Gerard's estate Cole pressed the brakes.

Again referring to his watch he observed: "We hit seventy-five. Allowing for acceleration and deceleration, we certainly averaged sixty. Six minutes. A mile a minute. Willard Gerard, if he killed the old lady last night, had to equal that speed, both ways, with no means of locomotion evident."

"All God's chillun got wings, Doc!" Kelly moaned.

"But observe," Cole continued as the car hummed, "the home of Leon Fendrick directly ahead." As he turned into a driveway he added: "In fact, it's just about one mile from his late client's home. In his case there is no time limit for the mile. Do you suppose, Brick, he owns a polka-dot derby?"

"If he does," Kelly protested hopelessly, "it wouldn't be in Gerard's safe, would it?"

COLE'S HEADLIGHTS swung across a garage which sat behind Fendrick's house. Its doors were open disclosing two cars sitting in their stalls. Braking at the front entrance, Cole scanned the quiet grounds. Kelly was at his side when his knock brought a sleepy manservant to the door.

"Mr. Fendrick has returned, but he is busy at the moment. If you'll come in, he'll be with you shortly, Doctor Cole."

The manservant conducted Cole and Kelly into a tastefully furnished living-room and withdrew. Cole listened alertly to the voices of two men in the next room. They stopped when the manservant knocked to announce Cole's presence, then resumed. One sharply insistent, Cole identified as Fendrick's. The other, edged with anger, might be Willard Gerard's. He turned speculative eyes on Kelly.

"Having fractured the Penal Code," he said quietly, "I will now violate the dictates of social nicety."

He strode directly to the closed door. No voices were speaking behind it now. Without a knock, without a word, Cole thrust it open. As he strode into the tobacco-flavored library, Leon Fendrick turned in surprise. Astonishment was mirrored in Cole's eyes, for Fendrick was alone. He went quickly past the attorney to a pair of French doors that were standing open, sending a yellow shaft across the garden. Outside he saw no movement and heard no sound.

"Your visitor," he remarked dryly, "made a rather precipitate departure, didn't he?"

Fendrick, fingering his dainty mustache, asked nervously: "What can I do for you, Doctor Cole?"

"You can tell me the truth about your movements last night," Cole answered promptly. "You know I saw you on the Gerard grounds just after the old lady dropped dead. I haven't yet reported it to the police. Now that they know Julia Gerard was poisoned by hydrocyanic acid, they'll be interested, I'm sure."

Fendrick's face became ashen. He blurted: "You've come here to blackmail me—is that it?"

The humorous light in Cole's piercing eyes became a scornful shine. "My only interest," he said coldly, "is to keep a charming and talented young woman out of an insane asylum for the rest of her life. Perhaps I can begin your story for you, Mr. Fendrick. After Mrs. Gerard telephoned you last night, you went to her home—walking, because it is only a short distance. Now, after you entered the house—"

"I didn't go in until you saw me!" Fendrick protested wildly. "I didn't know Mrs. Gerard was dead until you said so! Good God, I'm not a murderer!"

"Can you prove that," Cole asked implacably, "to the satisfaction of the police?"

Fendrick's face became beet-red, then white. He stepped forward, leaning across the table tensely, to blurt: "I'll tell you the truth of what happened!"

"I came here to hear it," Cole said wryly.

"Yes—I walked to the good lady's place last night after she phoned me. I saw your car. You were standing with your secretary at the door, knocking. I was just entering the drive when I heard the first scream. Not knowing what had happened, I stopped at the gate."

"And," Cole prompted, "you saw—"

"Somebody ran out of the house, through a side door. He crossed the grounds, then went along the hedge. He was heading directly for the spot where I was standing, but he saw me, turned back and disappeared. I heard him go through the hedge at the side of the grounds."

"Did you recognize him?" Cole asked.

Fendrick rushed on, unhearing: "I spent perhaps a minute trying to locate him, but he was gone. I was searching through the hedge when you saw me. I was too upset to know exactly what I was doing, so I kept out of sight. Then, when I had my wits about me again, I went to the door—and you opened it."

Cole persisted: "Did you recognize that man? Did you notice his clothing? Was he wearing an orange suit and a polka-dot derby?"

Fendrick gasped: "I've told you enough to prove I didn't have a hand in—"

Cole's voice rasped: "Did you see enough to verify Linda Barclay's fantastic story? As a lawyer, you know that's vital testimony. Coming from two persons, independently, every incredible detail becomes convincing. You and the girl couldn't have had the same hallucination at the same time. Good God, Fendrick, are you going to let that girl stay in an asylum?"

"Haven't I told you enough?" Fendrick protested. "What reason could I have for killing the old lady, or for—"

"For shielding a murderer? Money, Fendrick, is an excellent reason in your case. The old lady's fat fees are at an end. You have no other practise. The first thought in your mind when I came into this room was blackmail—and you're committing it. Last night you recognized the murderer. You're demanding money from him for your silence. He was here a moment ago. How much did Willard Gerard give you to keep quiet?"

Fendrick licked dry lips, staring.

"It was Gerard you saw escaping the grounds last night," Cole pressed inexorably. "He was wearing an orange suit and a blue derby with yellow dots. You can prove Linda Barclay is telling the truth, can't you, Fendrick?"

AT THE moment Fendrick opened his parched lips to speak, a shattering report crashed into the room. A flash of flame in the darkness spun Carter Cole to the French windows. Brick Kelly gasped "Geez!" as Cole sprang toward them, darted into the night. In the light from another window, he glimpsed the face of a man running.

"Gerard!"

The fleeing figure scurried into black shadows, vanished as Cole sprinted. The black maze of the garden baffled him as he groped along winding paths. Reaching clear lawn, he found the darkness empty. Staring back, he saw, through the open doors, Leon Fendrick sagging against the library table. He raced into the light, snapping at Kelly: "Brick! Call Gerard's home!"

He gasped the number as the astounded Kelly wheeled to the telephone. Cole was hurrying toward Fendrick as the lawyer slumped down. He whipped the man over and saw a black hole, streaming red, in the side of Fendrick's head. Cole took no time to feel the attorney's pulse; he knew at once there would be none.

He reached into Fendrick's inner coat pocket, pulled out a fat wallet and opened it to find a sheaf of bills. He thumbed through ten hundreds and exclaimed: "Blood money—from Gerard!"

Cole peered at his watch, as Kelly blurted from the telephone: "No answer yet, Doc!"

"Drop that and stick with me!"

Carter Cole shouldered a dismayed manservant out of the library door and ordered grimly: "Call the police at once!" He hurried through the entrance with Kelly loping at his heels, slid behind the Duesenberg's wheel, kicked the motor into action and sent the tires crunching over the gravel drive. Swinging into the parkway, he glanced at his watch and pressed the accelerator to the floor-boards.

A cyclone rose around the Duesenberg. Its headlights probed far along the smooth cement and with the speedometer trembling near sixty, Cole stormed past the Julia Gerard estate. The needle was quivering past eighty during the next five miles. It dropped abruptly when, near the gate of Willard Gerard's place, Cole pressed the brakes. He swerved to the house, stopped, bounded out.

Peering at shadows moving on the front windows, Kelly blurted: "I heard you holler Gerard's name, Doc, but it couldn't have been him. He's here now!"

Cole snapped: "Seven miles—we made it in less than six minutes. The man who killed Fendrick had almost two minutes headway. Almost two minutes for seven miles. What're you talking about, Brick? I saw Gerard there!"

"No car beat it away from that place, Doc. You're beginnin' to see things yourself. I told you you ought to take an aspirin and go to bed!"

Grimly Cole knocked. Footfalls sounded at once inside the house. The entrance opened and Willard Gerard stood silhouetted in the light. He smiled slowly into Cole's level gaze and said: "Hello! Won't you step in?"

"Thank you, no," Cole answered tightly. "I am here to ask one simple question, Mr. Gerard. Exactly how long is it since you returned to this house tonight?"

"I'd say ten or fifteen minutes," Gerard answered. "I just came back from a stroll through the woods. I often go out with a camera and flash-bulbs—night effects are quite pictorial. If you won't come in—is there anything else?"

"Yes!" Cole snapped. "How did you cultivate your uncanny ability to be in two places at the same time?" He strode away, while Gerard stared, without waiting for an answer. Kelly climbed with him into the Duesenberg.

CHAPTER FIVE
80 M.P.H. MURDER

C ARTER COLE, M.D., had callers. In his outer office in the Cole Sanitarium Chief Wellsmore of the local police, and Louis Mackler of the Reliance Detective Agency shifted uneasily in their chairs and eyed the clock. The time lacked a few minutes of one A.M.

Cole had had a trying day. Obliged to tell and retell his story of the death of Leon Fendrick, he had found himself in the uncomfortable position of flatly contradicting Willard Gerard's testimony while unassailable facts supported Gerard's stand. The reiterated questions of Chief Wellsmore still rankled in Cole's mind.

"You saw Gerard fleeing from Fendrick's place?"

"I did."

"There is no possibility that you are mistaken?"

"There is not."

"You reached Gerard's home in your car about seven and one half minutes after the shot was fired?"

"I did."

"You found Willard Gerard there?"

"He was there."

"You are saying in effect that Willard Gerard, after killing Fendrick, traversed a distance of seven miles in some seven minutes and thirty seconds?"

"It amounts to that."

"You drove to Gerard's place as fast as possible, but you saw no automobile leaving Fendrick's place, and saw none along the way, so it is certain, assuming the rest of your story to be true, that Mr. Gerard made no use of a car?"

"He did not use a car."

"But you realize that for him to transfer himself otherwise over that distance in that time is impossible?"

"Impossible or not," Cole had retorted, "I assure you he did exactly that."

No one in the chief's office had actually tapped finger to temple, but Cole had seen in their eyes that eloquent incredulity which said, "This man is mad!" In cold anger he had returned to the sanitarium, remembering the taunt of Willard Gerard's scornful smile. He had busied himself with the telephone and made many notes. Now, touching a button, he said to the Day twin who responded: "Jane, get Willard Gerard on the wire, June."

"Yes, Doctor."

The call went through promptly. "Mr. Gerard," Cole said over the wire, "this is your accuser speaking. I hope the little matter of two murders has aroused no hard feelings between us. Perhaps we'd better talk it over—amicably, of course."

"Come along right now if you wish," Gerard answered. "I can't talk long, though, because I want to develop some films. The flashes I took in the woods last night, you know."

"I'll see you soon." Cole disconnected, strode into the outer office. "Gentlemen," he addressed Chief Wellsmore and Mackler, "I am in the most uncomfortable position of my career. You doubt my sanity and think Linda Barclay insane. It revolves upon me to demonstrate that the impossible is true. If I fail, my reputation is irreparably injured, and Miss Barclay's life is wrecked. If I succeed, we'll have a murderer. May I depend on your cooperation?"

The two men looked at each other uncertainly.

"There's no doubt someone killed Julia Gerard and Leon Fendrick, is there?" Cole persisted. "There is only one suspect—Willard Gerard. The circumstantial case against him is conclusive, except for the one vital detail that he has an iron-clad, water-tight, witness-supported alibi. The only way I can establish his guilt is to prove Linda Barclay's incredible story is true down to the last detail, and to substantiate my own. I am determined to make the attempt tonight. Your assistance, gentlemen?"

Chief Wellsmore ventured: "I'll do what I can, Doctor."

Mackler sighed. "You need help for a sweet job like that."

"Wait here, please."

COLE CLIMBED stairs. At the end of a polished corridor he entered a room where a man was squatting intently in front of a small safe. He was not an inmate of the institution, but the cleverest locksmith in New York undertaking Cole's orders. He looked up wearily to say: "She's still got me buffaloed."

Cole followed another shining hallway and in another remote room found Linda Barclay sitting at an easel, under a daylight bulb, touching vivid color to a canvas.

The girl said, as Cole studied the painting: "You see, color is everything in my work. I love to experiment with it. It's in my mind constantly. So I couldn't be mistaken about what I saw that night."

"I most sincerely hope not," Cole said wryly. "Miss Barclay, a question. You have insisted from the beginning that you recognized Willard Gerard in spite of his weird garb and the fact that his back was turned. Why are you so sure?"

The girl answered calmly: "His ears. Have you noticed them? They are peculiarly formed. At the top there is a little blunt point. Perhaps it may seem queer, but I did know him immediately because of that."

Cole was staring. "Queer? Not a particle! Ears, next to fingerprints, are the most characteristic part of the body. No two ears are exactly alike. They remain unaltered from birth until after death. Furthermore, the little tip at the upper helix, which you mention, is a distinctive type known as the Darwinian tubercle."*

He drew the girl from the easel. "Listen carefully. I want you to come with me. I'm determined to set a trap for a murderer, and I must use you as bait. You may well look

---

* Alphonse Bertillon, inventor of anthropometry (the identification of individuals by means of anatomical measurements, which preceded our present fingerprint system) recognized the value of the human ear as a means of identification. The facts stated here by Carter Cole are well known to criminologists.

An actual and interesting case along these lines concerns a woman who, after an attempt at suicide in Berlin, shortly following the World War, declared herself to be the Grand Duchess Anastasia, daughter of the murdered Czar Nicholas of Russia. Her story was that she had escaped the execution of the Czar's family in Ekaterinburg, Siberia, had suffered a loss of memory as a result of a blow on the head, and had reached Berlin after many trying adventures. She closely resembled Anastasia, but the head of the Scientific Police Institute of Lausanne, Switzerland, Professor Marc Bischoff, proved her to be an impostor. A comparison of profile photographs of this woman and of the real Anastasia disclosed that the ear types of the two were distinctly different.—F.C.D.

startled—it's a serious risk. It will endanger your life. I wouldn't ask it of you if there were any other way. Will you take the chance?"

"Of course."

"Good girl. Come along." They went along the gleaming hall, down the stairs, into Cole's office. He stepped to his desk, selected a few notes from a sheaf, tucked them into his pocket. Then he asked the Miss Day who came at his gesture: "Did you make the inquiry? Has Gerard complained to the police that his home was burglarized last night?"

"No, Doctor."

"Excellent!" He went out to Chief Wellsmore and Louis Mackler. "It is now past one. By the time we get set, it will be about two. I've chosen this time so that conditions tonight may duplicate those the night Mrs. Gerard died. Are you ready, gentlemen?"

He maintained a cryptic silence as the girl and the two men followed him out to the Duesenberg. A light roadster was standing behind it, Brick Kelly at the wheel, and it trailed the massive sedan through the gate. Turning onto Rainbow Parkway, Cole drove without speaking. He swung into the Gerard grounds, signaled the girl and Chief Wellsmore, and went to the entrance with them carrying a small suitcase.

When the door opened he directed the decrepit Gerard butler: "Go to your room at once and remain there. The police are in charge."

The butler gulped: "Very good, sir!" Cole conducted the wondering girl into the room where Julia Gerard had died. Linda Barclay looked in anguish at the spot where the old lady had fallen, and shrank back. Cole strode to the French windows at the side of the room—through which the girl claimed to have seen a murderer flee—and partly drew the drapes. He lighted the table lamp, turned out all others, led the girl with gentle firmness to a chair sitting in its glow.

"You are, as I said, the bait in a trap set for a murderer. Chief Wellsmore is here to keep a protective eye on you. In case of a miscarriage of plans, your life will be endangered. That is my responsibility. But it's vital that you stay right here—with this."

COLE OPENED the overnight case. Calmly he lifted from it a blue derby with yellow polka-dots. He removed also a bright red shirt, a brilliant orange suit, and a pair of blue, yellow-dotted shoes to match the hat. Chief Wellsmore, staring from the door, uttered a startled exclamation. Linda Barclay gazed wide-eyed.

Cole reassured her. "No murderer ever wore these garments. They are all mine. With the help of my secretaries, I dyed and painted these things this afternoon. They, like you, Miss Barclay, are bait. They must remain on this table, in plain sight. Watch the clock. In fifteen minutes, call the number of Willard Gerard's home on the telephone. Ask for me. If you hear me saying strange things, pay no attention. You won't forget?"

"No," the girl breathed.

Cole left her peering fascinated at the grotesque raiment as he conducted the amazed Wellsmore out of the house. Making sure the French windows were unfastened, he went with the chief to the nearby garage. He flashed his fountain-pen torch to compare his watch with Wellsmore's.

"Yours is a bit faster than mine. Our watches must be synchronized." And when the adjustment was made, "Watch the windows carefully, Chief. If anyone approaches them, note the exact time. The girl's safety is important, but the time is even more vital. I realize you think you're humoring a madman, but please do exactly as I've said."

He left Wellsmore stationed in the shadow of the garage and circled the mansion to the waiting cars. He directed Brick Kelly: "Leave your car outside Gerard's drive and walk in quietly. Take a position where you can watch both the bulkhead and the garage. If you spot Gerard doing strange things, don't try to hinder him. Note the exact time on your watch and let him go."

Cole set Kelly's dollar timepiece to coincide with his own, then climbed into the Duesenberg. Mackler sat at his side as he drove with Kelly trailing in the roadster. As he turned into Willard Gerard's drive, Kelly eased back. Cole stopped, went with Mackler to the entrance, knocked. While they waited, Kelly slipped into the grounds and vanished.

Inside the house a muffled, far-away voice called: "Come in! Come in!"

Cole and Mackler entered curiously. Another distant, "Come in!" led them toward the lighted kitchen. Mackler said with a grin: "He's in that dark-room again." Cole smiled with satisfaction and rapped on the door. "In there, Gerard?"

Gerard's voice came through the panels: "You were so long, Doctor, I thought you'd decided not to come. I've gone ahead with my films. They're in the developer now and I can't open the door. That needn't keep us from talking."

Cole answered: "I've put myself into a ticklish position, Gerard. The police don't believe I saw you at Fendrick's place last night, you know. They didn't say so, but it's obvious they not only question my sanity but suspect me of the murder."

"That's absurd."

"Nevertheless," Cole insisted, "being suspected of murder, no matter how illogically, is not pleasant. Mr. Kelly can vouch for me, but after all I pay him regularly every week. Fendrick's manservant saw me rushing from the room where his master lay dead. The police consider that my accusing you is a flimsy way of shielding myself. It's an ugly mess, Gerard."

"I'm afraid," Gerard answered, "you've put yourself into it, Doctor, and I can't help you out."

"But perhaps you know a possible reason for Fendrick's murder, or suspect—"

THE TELEPHONE rang. Gerard called through the door: "Answer that for me, will you, Cole?"

"Gladly!" Cole said, and went to the instrument in the living-room. His "Hello?" was answered by Linda Barclay's voice.

"Doctor Cole," the girl said uneasily, "I don't understand what you're doing. It's so strange here—so quiet. I've—"

"Excellent!" Cole interrupted. He knew Willard Gerard, in the dark-room, was listening. "All of it—indeed? You did perfectly right to telephone Chief Wellsmore. Certainly— it's conclusive evidence. Yes, under the circumstances we will."

The girl was plaintively protesting: "But Doctor Cole, I don't understand—" when he hung up.

He strode at once to the door of the dark-room, declared through the panels: "Extraordinary girl, that niece of yours, Gerard! Imagine what she's done. She's actually found the clothing she described—the polka-dot derby and the orange suit and all the rest. It substantiates her story perfectly. She's alone at the other place with it, but she's called Chief Wellsmore, and he's on his way now."

Gerard's voice came tightly. "Where did she find it?"

"She didn't tell me that—but wherever it was, the fact is vitally important. Moreover, there are ways of proving the ownership of the clothing. Microscopic examination— dust, for example. It's going to send the murderer to the chair, Gerard. What do you think of that? Plucky girl! I say, Gerard, what do you think of it?"

Silence in the dark-room. Cole turned tensely. He thrust his watch before the eyes of the startled Mackler and snapped: "Look at that! Note the time exactly! Don't forget it!" Mackler stared bewildered while Cole turned back to the door. He continued to talk—until, suddenly, a quick step sounded on the rear porch.

Brick Kelly thrust his red head in. "Doc! Gerard came out of the bulkhead a minute ago! He's gone out of here like a bat out of hell! Left at ten and a half after! God's sake, I never thought—"

"Pipe down, Brick! Wait!"

Kelly and Mackler stood frozen while Cole stared at his watch. Its ticking became audible in the hush. Four times a second the tiny clicks came, for an eternity. Only a bit more than a minute had passed when Cole whipped about. "Stay here, Brick, in case he comes back! If he does, grab him!" And to Mackler, "You're coming with me!" He thrust the private detective along the hall, out the entrance, to the Duesenberg. Its motor roared.

Cole wheeled into the cement with only the parking lights shining. His thrust at the gas pedal opened the motor wide. Cyclonic wind whipped over Mackler. He grabbed his hat and struggled for breath while Cole peered at the smooth lane of concrete ahead. Miles whizzed past with dizzy speed. At last they skidded on loose gravel into the Gerard drive. Near the house Cole slammed to a stop.

He gripped Mackler's collar, again thrust his watch before the detective's eyes and snapped: "Now look at that!" Chief Wellsmore's name was on his lips as he left the wheel and sped along a garden. A glimpse of a prone figure near the French doors kept him silent. He stopped abruptly, desperately gesturing Mackler back, staring at the man lying sprawled in the grass. It was Wellsmore, scalp gashed, unconscious.

A stifled, fearful cry turned Cole quickly to the open doors. He reached to his arm-pit holster, leveled his Luger. Shifting into the lane of light, he peered narrow-eyed into the Gerard library. He saw Linda Barclay backed to the table on which the fantastic garments lay, one hand raised in terror to her mouth. A man—a towering black shadow—was advancing, shoulders hunched, toward her. She wailed again, went limp in a faint, fell.

The shadow man sprang toward her. She lay helpless as Cole glimpsed a bottle of sparkling amber in the hand of the man who bent over her. Cole sprang forward at the moment a trickle licked to the neck of the open bottle. He snapped: "Get back!" and sent a bullet snapping across the room. Willard Gerard, jerking up, whirled from the girl. With one swift movement he hurled the bottle at Cole. Flashing drops sprayed from it as it spun.

"Look out!" Cole gasped. "Hydrocyanic acid! One breath will kill you!"

FLAME SEARED from the gun in Gerard's hand. He leaped across the room. On the stair landing he paused to blast out another shot. Cole, holding his breath, reached to the unconscious girl. His Luger spat into the report of

Gerard's gun. A numbing shock in his arm jolted him as Gerard sprang higher. Cole felt hot blood flowing to his fingers as he commanded Mackler: "Help get the girl out!"

He lifted her, stumbled into the living-room. Mackler slammed the door shut on air that was growing pungent. Cole pushed into the hall, sprang toward the base of the stairs. Quick footfalls were sounding on the upper floor as he bounded up, three steps at a time. He glimpsed blood spots on the landing, knew his bullet had gone home. He sped to the top of the stairs—and into a storm of combat.

A wild leap hurled Gerard on Cole. An automatic beat at Cole's head as his up-thrown arms parried the blows. He twisted desperately, seizing the gun. On the top landing they writhed in struggle, Gerard's thumbs digging into Cole's throat. Cole's jab brought a gasp from Gerard. Gerard's eyes rolled as he toppled backward. He sprawled down the stairs, slumped into the hall, lay limp.

Cole's left arm trailed blood as he went down. In the living-room he slapped the casement windows open. As clean air breezed over Linda Barclay he ordered Mackler tersely: "In the hall, Mr. Detective. He's our murderer." Mackler went out, gun glittering, while Cole raised the girl's feet on a pillow. He hurried out the front entrance and angled to the open French windows to find Chief Wellsmore tottering up. Then he tugged Wellsmore away, to the front entrance. Blearily, the chief stared at Gerard, Mackler's gun leveled at him. Cole hurried into the kitchen, came back with a basin of water, returned to the girl. His wet handkerchief was cooling on her forehead when he asked: "At what time, Chief, did Gerard arrive at this place?"

"Eighteen minutes past two!"

"At what time, Mackler," Cole went on, "did Brick Kelly announce Gerard's departure from the other house?"

"Ten and a half minutes past two!"

"Interval," Cole calculated, "seven and a half minutes. Distance, six miles. Average speed, approximately sixty miles per hour. In a moment you'll understand."

Linda Barclay's eyelids were fluttering. Cole helped her up.

Wellsmore, stooping over Gerard, clicked a pair of handcuffs in place and declared: "No matter how he got here, he did it—that's enough for me!" Cole led him out the front entrance, and Mackler followed. The beam of Cole's fountainpen torch probed the shadows. He said "Ah!" as the shaft stopped. "There we are!"

Mackler, staring, asked: "Sure—but it's only a bicycle—with a big windshield attached. You're not trying to say Gerard got here that fast on a bicycle!"

It was leaning against the ivy-covered garden wall. And the tin deflector, shaped like the prow of a small boat, which Cole had seen in Gerard's garage, was affixed to the bicycle by its braces. Cole, smiling happily, spoke with a chuckle.

"You probably believe, Chief, like most people, that twenty or twenty-five miles an hour is a good speed for a man on a bicycle. You underestimate the possibilities. The bicycle is one of the most efficient engineering achievements of the ages. This one, besides being equipped with a streamlined windshield, is provided with variable gears. Willard Gerard actually, on three separate occasions, on the last three nights, traveled on that machine at a speed greater than sixty miles an hour." Wellsmore gasped.

"And that," Cole continued, "is well under the speed record established by bicycles. Looking into the matter this afternoon, I found that the latest official bicycle speed record is no less than eighty and a half miles an hour. It was made recently at Los Angeles by Frank Bartell and is attested by the A.A.A. I undertook this murder trap tonight to prove, beyond all doubt, that Willard Gerard could do almost as well on his wheel—and I have."*

WHEN, ALMOST an hour later, Carter Cole entered the Cole Sanitarium with the girl and the bewildered Brick Kelly, one of his twin secretaries hurried from his office. She announced: "The locksmith has just opened the safe, Doctor!" In the upper room Cole found another Day twin looking into the steel box while a mystified locksmith stood by.

He removed a blue, yellow-dotted derby from the safe. He drew out also an orange suit, a weirdly striped tie, a brilliant red shirt, and a pair of shoes to match the hat. Lastly he took up a small decorated atomizer in which an amber fluid twinkled.

"Small wonder Gerard didn't report the theft of this safe. Brick's watching him kept him from destroying these things. He used paints stolen from your box, Miss Barclay, to decorate the derby and the shoes. His purpose was to make the story of any possible eye-witness seem so fantastic as to be downright incredible—and he almost

---

* Until recently the bicycle speed record was held by William Peden, Canadian—76 miles per hour. It was broken by Frank Bartell, 33 years old, a bearded Czech-born six-day bicycle racer, in a test on a concrete boulevard outside Los Angeles. Bartell's record was certified by an A.A.A. official at 80.5 m.p.h. He rode behind an Auburn speedster, which served as a wind-breaker. Two motorcycle policemen, racing behind him, were outdistanced when Bartell hit 85 m.p.h. The bicyclist shot over the finish line at 90 m.p.h. and was hitting 100 before he stopped.—F.C.D.

succeeded. Part of his devilish scheme made use of two identical atomizers—very easy to obtain. While you watched him, his back turned to you, he switched one for the other. The one he left beside the dead woman contained perfume. That he used as an instrument of murder—this one—contains hydrocyanic acid. Keep hands off!"

His gesture cleared the room. He pressed a large banknote into the befuddled locksmith's hand while Linda Barclay gazed profound gratitude at him. Smiling, he directed a Day twin: "Telephone Chief Wellsmore that the case is cracked, complete with polka-dot derby. In the meantime, see that no one enters this room, June."

Miss Day answered: "Yes, Doctor."

Cole stared. "What!" he said. "What! You actually are June and not Jane?"

"Yes, Doctor."

"Wonders," said Carter Cole with a sigh, "will never cease."

THE CASE OF THE SILENT GIANTESS

OVER THAT ANCIENT MANSION
HOVERED A HORROR-SHADOW,
FOR THERE, IN THAT GAS-
LIT HARK-BACK TO THE PAST,
LIVED A DROOLING MONSTER
WHO GUIDED THE LIVES OF ALL
WHO DWELLED WITHIN. WHAT
WAS THE SECRET THE SILENT
GIANTESS HID BEHIND HER
MUMBLING GIBBERISH? WHY
WAS CARTER COLE ALONE ABLE
TO INTERPRET THOSE ANIMAL
SOUNDS THAT SEALED THE
MYSTERY OF THE RABBIT-DOOM?

CHAPTER ONE
DOCTOR'S DILEMMA

STEPPING THROUGH the entrance of the house on Court Road, Carter Cole, M.D.—whose prominence as a psychiatrist was equaled only by his reputation as an investigator of unusual crimes—found himself transported from a hustling modern world into the musty quaintness of the gaslight era.

Incandescent mantles burned with a steady whisper in the bronze brackets along the broad, deep hall. The flat white glow, with its semblance of full moonlight, added to the outmoded somberness of the gingerbread furniture, the faded tapestries, the gloomy oil portraits. Forty-five years of progress seemed to vanish with the closing of the door behind Cole.

Yet there was nothing old-fashioned about the girl who had admitted him. The stained smock she wore only emphasized the smartness of her trim pumps and gossamer stockings; set off vividly the ripe color of her cheeks and full lips.

Cole introduced himself. "I have come," he said, "in response to a call from Mr. Homer Morehouse."

Miss Celia Ashurst gave him her name and a capable hand. "Mr. Morehouse isn't here now, but he'll probably be right back. Do you mind waiting for a few minutes?"

Beyond the sill a weird being was standing.

"Not at all…. It concerns," Cole added, "Mr. Ronald Fairlee, about whom Mr. Morehouse is considerably worried. As I understand it, a mental condition which I am to diagnose and treat."

The girl's poise did not completely conceal her surprised concern. "I am Mr. Fairlee's assistant," she explained. "I've got to go back to the laboratory now. I'm finishing up an important experiment. Won't you come with me and wait there?"

COLE THANKED her and chatting briskly ascended the stairs with Celia Ashurst. "I've heard of Ronald Fairlee's work. He is isolating certain hormones of the endocrine system, isn't he—particularly the pituitary? A most important field—the very frontier of medical research. I never expected to find such an attractive young woman as you, Miss Ashurst, absorbed in the problems of the duct-less glands—nor a splendid laboratory like this in such an antiquated dwelling."

They had reached a large, glittering room equipped with the most modern apparatus for biochemical research—with the striking exception that here too electricity had not penetrated. Welsbach gas mantles illuminated the orderly benches and shelves.

As the girl turned to a retort in which a meaty hash was simmering over the blue flame of a Bunsen burner, she answered with a warm smile. "I love it. Working with Ronald Fairlee is thrilling—scientific pioneering—and we're getting somewhere. Let me return the compliment, Doctor Cole. I've heard of you, as everyone in medicine has, but I pictured you as an officious old man with a stringy white beard."

They laughed together at the absurdity. Cole, glowing with dynamic health, had the tapering physique of an athlete. Humorously piercing eyes looked out of his unusually large head that housed a lightning-quick brain. His achievements in the field of psychopathology, remarkable for one so young, mile-stoned by his classic treatises, had evolved from his experience as director of the famed Cole Sanitarium on Long Island—located not far from the Fairlee home—where he lived among more than a thousand patients representing the full category of mental derangement.

The girl's smile faded as her dark eyes searched Cole's. "Mr. Fairlee is a rather queer man, but we're all a little bit queer, aren't we? Mr. Morehouse—Mr. Fairlee's brother-in-law—has seen much less of him than I have. Mr. Morehouse's concern is unwarranted—it was silly of him to consult you."

"Just what, Miss Ashurst," Cole asked quietly, "is the nature of Mr. Fairlee's idiosyncrasy? Has it something to do with his preference for gaslight over electricity? Has it any connection with this laboratory being located in his home instead of, say, a college building? Might it be related to the mysterious disappearance of Mrs. Fairlee two months ago, and—"

Celia Ashurst's eyes widened with alarm. Cole knew at once that his incisive questions had struck at the roots of some strange dread that haunted her. She was shaking her head in anxious protest when his words stopped— stopped because, suddenly, a peculiar mumbling scream rang through the house.

"Alice!" The girl blurted.

Cole spun, stepped from the lab. He strode toward a branch hallway while Celia Ashurst, her experiment forgotten, hurried frantically after him. "Please!" she begged, catching at his arm. "Please come back!"

Just past the corner he stopped short, not in compliance with the girl's entreaty, but because cold amazement halted him. The gas bracket of the hall angling into the ell was not burning, but white light fanned into the gloom through an opened door. Beyond the sill a weird being was standing—a monstrosity belonging to a nightmare world. It was huge, towering more than seven feet, with an enormous bulbous head, great dangling hands, tremendous feet—a hideous creature—a giantess.

THE MONSTER was whimpering with terror, yet an uncanny stupidity made her face blank. One side of her loose white dress was reddened with flowing blood; the fabric was slashed over a bleeding knife wound. The blade was gripped in the hand of a man who stood facing her—a man of average build, clad in a loose smock, dwarfed by the appalling stature of the giantess.

His back turned to Cole, he sidled from the room in which the wailing giantess stood, too stunned by the attack to retreat. Cole's quick footfalls, Celia Ashurst's voice, had warned him. The grotesque creature in the room vanished as he slapped the door shut. The gloom swallowed him and he twisted the key in the lock, flashing a terrified glance over his shoulder. Cole caught the glitter of eyeglasses, glimpsed a dark blot of blood on the smock as, with a leap, he crossed the hall to the opposite door. Suddenly he disappeared into darkness and a bolt clicked into its socket.

Cole strode to the second door, thrust at it, found it fast. Turning, he saw Celia Ashurst fumbling a key from the pocket of her smock. "Alice—don't be afraid!" she called through the opposite door. The pitiful babbling of the giantess was audible through the panels. Cole stepped to the girl's side, said quietly, "Perhaps I'd better," and was startled when she turned on him in frantic protest.

"Please go! Leave the house!"

"Leaving the house," Cole answered firmly, "won't eliminate me from this affair. I've been witness to a felonious assault, perhaps an attempt at murder. Who was the man who rushed out of this room? Ronald Fairlee?"

The girl inserted the key, looking up hopefully as rapid footfalls sounded on the stairs. A young man hurried into the hall. "What's happened?" he blurted—and Cole realized at once, his concern was for Celia Ashurst.

She answered him breathlessly. "Alice is hurt. I'll take care of her. Show Doctor Cole out, Steve."

The young man's response was immediately to grasp Cole's arm.

Celia Ashurst opened the door, stepped quickly through. Cole again glimpsed the giantess. She had fallen back across a bed. Her tremendous head was lolling on the coverlet and she was crying helplessly with pain. Only the whites of her protruding eyes shone beneath lids not fully closed. The scene ended in a flash with the slap of the door and the click of the bolt.

"Good-night, Doctor Cole."

Cole looked intently at the handsome young man gripping his arm. "Who are you?"

"I'm Steven Vaill, Mr. Fairlee's secretary. You're not wanted here."

Cole peeled Vaill's fingers off. "I haven't the slightest intention of leaving until I see the man who summoned me. I shouldn't advise you to try to eject me forcibly. Where is Mr. Fairlee?"

Vaill's jaw squared. "This is none of your business," he countered. "If you'd rather have Mr. Fairlee himself order you out, all right. He's resting in there." Vaill indicated the door through which Cole had seen the giantess' assailant flee.

Cole's eyebrows arched. "In there?"

"That's his study. He was very tired after dinner and lay down for a nap."

Vaill rapped on the panels with startling violence. "Mr. Fairlee," he explained bitingly, "sleeps very soundly." He pounded again.

Cole looked from one door to the other. Through the first he could hear the whimpering, childish crying of the giantess, the crooning reassurances of Celia Ashurst. From the other came a husky, "Who is it?" and slow footfalls. The knob of Ronald Fairlee's study turned. A drowsy voice said: "That's odd—I don't remember bolting it." A rattle, and the man appeared hooking a pair of rimless eyeglasses to his ears. He was of average stature and wore a smock.

IT WAS Ronald Fairlee, the noted biochemist. "Is anything wrong?" he asked in bewilderment. "This is Doctor Carter Cole, isn't it?"

Cole looked at the side of Fairlee's smock while Vaill explained. The garment of the man who had fled into this room had been spotted with blood. The smock Fairlee wore now was stained by chemical reagents, but on it there was no trace of red.

"But what could have happened to Alice?" Fairlee asked Vaill. "You say you heard her cry out? I must have slept through it—I didn't hear it at all." He strode to the opposite door. "Alice! Is she all right, Celia?"

"I was having dinner downstairs," Vaill added. "I haven't the straight of it yet. Celia said Doctor Cole is to be shown from the house. He refuses to go. It's up to you, Mr. Fairlee."

The door of the giantess' room opened before Fairlee could answer. Celia Ashurst slipped out, challenging Cole with a forbidding glance. Ronald Fairlee went into the room quickly.

The girl said quietly to young Vaill: "Steven, bring the first-aid kit from the lab—quickly. She has a cut in her side, painful but not dangerous. I'm sure I can dress it properly. Doctor Cole's services will not be necessary."

Cole smiled wryly. "I have seldom," he said, "found my presence so undesirable, especially when, in the first place, it was requested. I'll wait, if you don't mind, for Mr. Homer Morehouse—he sent for me, you'll remember."

Steven Vaill had hurried toward the laboratory. He paused, looking down the stairs, at the sound of the opening front door. "Mr. Morehouse has just come in," he said, and went on.

Celia Ashurst stood her ground at the door of the giant-ess' room. She caught Cole's arm, her eyes pleading, as he bowed affably, started away.

"Please forgive me. I'm only acting out of consideration for Mr. Fairlee. He has tried to keep Alice a complete secret—her very existence. It would mean cruel gossip if it became known. Please understand that Steve and I are completely loyal to him."

"Quite," Cole smiled. "Whoever she is and whyever she's here, Alice is an interesting case of marked glandu-lar unbalance—doubly interesting in view of Mr. Fairlee's researches. Please count on my cooperation if you wish it. Goodnight."

He went down the stairs to find a middle-aged, bald man shedding hat and coat in the hall. "Doctor Cole—here in response to your call," he introduced himself, grip-ping Homer Morehouse's fattish hand. "I find myself profoundly interested in Mr. Fairlee's case, whatever his trouble may be. Shall we discuss it privately—and frankly?"

"Yes, yes," Morehouse agreed nervously. "Frankness is vital—vital."

He led Cole into a somber library—lighted, as was every other room in the house, by gas mantles—and blurted out in a husky whisper: "I called you here because I am afraid—afraid Ronald Fairlee is stark mad—afraid, Doctor Cole, that his madness may drive him to murder."

CARTER COLE remained silent as Homer More-house pulled a chair close, eyes narrowed with thought. The bald man spoke at last as if choosing every word with painstaking care.

"Ronald Fairlee's wife Ethel is my sister. You have doubtless read in the newspapers that she disappeared two months ago. It occurred while I was in London on business. I heard of it aboard ship, while I was returning to this country. I am unmarried, and she is my only living relative—if she is still living. I have been staying here the past four weeks. This explains my connection with the case."

Carter Cole nodded.

"I was disturbed first"—Morehouse resumed his systematic recital of facts—"by the strange circumstances surrounding my sister's disappearance. One evening, after dinner, she simply vanished—suddenly and completely, from this house—but Ronald Fairlee did not report it to the police. Day after day passed and she did not return, but he made no move to find her. I think it is most extraordinary."

Cole nodded again.

"The neighbors and the tradesmen missed her. They inquired. Ronald made excuses for her absence—flimsy and unsatisfactory, apparently, for through one of the neighbors the police learned of the matter. When they investigated, Ronald admitted Ethel had been missing three weeks. They began a search at once."

The police, Morehouse's story continued, had brought other unusual circumstances to light. None of Mrs. Fairlee's suitcases or traveling clothes was missing. Even the dress she had worn that evening was found in her bedroom. Evidently she had vanished while preparing to retire. It seemed extremely unlikely she had left the house, but the police were continuing their hunt for her before taking more drastic steps. So far they had been unable to find any trace of the missing woman.

"I have no theories as to what happened," Morehouse concluded. "The police are doing everything possible to find my sister, and with that we must be content. Your profession, Doctor Cole, doesn't involve finding missing persons. I wish your advice on a phase of the matter the police cannot touch. I am afraid something else will happen in this house—something horrible, to any one of us—if Ronald Fairlee is actually, dangerously insane.

"You suggest he's somehow responsible for his wife's disappearance?" Cole said quietly. "I've had only a glimpse of Mr. Fairlee, but he seemed quite rational. What makes you believe him unbalanced?"

Morehouse leaned forward tensely. "He and Ethel were not happy together—but could a normal man care for his wife so little as not even to report her disappearance to the police? Do you know that for three years Ronald Fairlee has scarcely stepped outside this house—that he has never, literally, in all that time, left the grounds? And there is another thing—some weird power, some strange fear that haunts him—something he calls the Dynamo God."

"The Dynamo God?" Cole repeated.

"Have you noticed there is no electricity in this house?" Morehouse asked huskily. "Ronald won't permit it. He mortally fears it. It comes from this dread thing he calls the Dynamo God. The same fear keeps him prisoner here— fear that the Dynamo God, which dominates the outer world, will destroy him. Doctor Cole, you've got to learn what this thing is that's festering in his mind—or it may mean the deaths of those around him."

"Is Mr. Fairlee willing to put himself in my hands?" Cole asked alertly.

"He refuses to explain himself to me, because he insists I couldn't understand, but when I suggested he receive treatment from you, he was eager. Perhaps I'm wrong to think him dangerously irrational, but after all my sister is still missing—and delay may cost innocent lives."

Cole said decisively: "I'll see him at once."

CHAPTER TWO
THE LOCKED DOOR

COLE WAS stepping from the library, with More-house nervously following, when a sharp rap sounded on the entrance. Morehouse admitted two brusque, grave-faced men. Cole knew them both—Wellsmore, chief of police, and Blake, ace plainclothesman of the town in which both the Cole Sanitarium and the Fairlee home were located.

Immediately, anxiously, Morehouse asked them: "Have you found my sister?"

Chief Wellsmore was a grizzled, tough-skinned veteran. His hard lips tightened as he answered with characteristic bluntness: "I have a warrant for the arrest of Ronald Fairlee on suspicion of murder. Where is he?"

Morehouse stood speechless.

As Wellsmore and Blake started for the stairs, Cole fell into step with them. Climbing, he asked: "What makes you believe Mrs. Fairlee has been murdered?"

Wellsmore's explanation was crisp and to the point. "We're convinced she never left this house. Nobody would be keeping her here a prisoner alive. If she'd died a natu-ral death or committed suicide her body wouldn't have vanished. The only conclusion is murder. The circumstances justify the charge."

"I quite agree," Cole answered, "but Fairlee's make-up—a scientist laboring night and day in the most difficult field of medicine to assuage sickness and preserve health—is hardly that of a murderer."

Their quiet exchange had been overheard by Ronald Fairlee. He was standing dismayed in the entrance to the laboratory, staring widely through his rimless eyeglasses. Beyond him, near a work-bench, Celia Ashurst and Steven Vaill were side by side, silent in consternation.

Chief Wellsmore's brass-tacks methods made Cole wince. "Mr. Fairlee," the chief said, "we're determined to get at the bottom of your wife's disappearance. We think it's a case of homicide. Do you care to read this warrant? You're coming with us to headquarters for further questioning."

Fairlee did not glance at the document. "Gentlemen, I've already told you everything I know—everything. I'll answer any questions you wish, gladly—but please ask them here. I implore you not to take me out of this house."

"Why not?" Wellsmore asked bluntly. "Is there something here you're afraid to leave? Something you think might be discovered because you're absent? I can't agree to that. Come along."

"No—no, it isn't that," Fairlee answered tautly. "Anything you like, here, but don't—I beg of you, don't take me away." His lips trembled with fear, his face was drawn. "I can't explain but—I can't leave my home."

"We let you get away with that before, but not this time. You're going to headquarters and you're going to stay there until you come clean. Get into your hat and coat."

WELLSMORE GRIPPED Fairlee's left arm, Blake the other. He tried to tear away from them, but they pulled him protesting to the stairs, forced him down step by step. As Fairlee approached the entrance his attempts to escape became desperate.

"Don't! Don't take me out! Let me stay here! You don't understand what you're doing to me! I can't leave this house—I can't!"

But they maneuvered him out the entrance while he resisted with all his strength. Morehouse, watching in the hall, muttered: "It's pitiful—brutal!"

Cole, eyes compassionate, was descending when Celia Ashurst hurried to his side. She seized his hand and exclaimed: "Doctor, I don't know any better than anyone else why Mr. Fairlee dreads to leave the house—but it's torture. I know he hasn't done anything wrong—they're making him suffer unjustly. Please help him—please try to get him back."

Cole turned, a question on his lips. "Do you agree, Mr. Vaill—" he began, but he didn't ask it. The expression of horror on Vaill's face silenced him. An ashen pallor surrounded the young man's eyes. Stark fear shone out of them. Astounded, sensing a strange emotional storm breaking within the man, Cole waited for him to speak. But he didn't say a word. Instead he turned abruptly, strode into the laboratory and slammed the door.

Vaill's consternation communicated itself subtly to the girl. She hurried anxiously after him. Quietly thoughtful, Cole went down to the entrance. Morehouse, wheezing with agitation, blurted, "I'm going with them," and rushed out. Cole slid into his coat, donned his Homburg and took up his stick. He reached his parked Duesenberg, just in time to witness an astonishing scene.

Chief Wellsmore and Detective Blake were literally dragging Ronald Fairlee to the police car sitting in the drive. The chemist was fighting madly to escape. He dug his heels into the gravel, braced against the running-board, blurted incoherent protests. Wellsmore answered with a puffing, "Cut it out—put you in a straight-jacket!" A powerful heave slammed Fairlee to the seat. Instantly Blake dove upon him, pinning him down.

Cole watched silently as Wellsmore sent the car rolling toward Court Road. Morehouse, intent on following, hurried to a coupé standing at the side of the house. Cole ducked into the Duesenberg.

The squat, bull-necked, rusty-haired young man at the wheel of the powerful car said abruptly: "Geez, Doc, you're gettin' into another one of these screwy cases!"

"Follow them, Brick," Cole directed.

Brick Kelly, Cole's strong-arm assistant and handyman, promptly weaved the massive vehicle down the drive and onto the cement, turned after the police car with a frown. "You know me, Doc," he said expansively. "I think you're the swellest guy alive. I don't know how you can keep your nut, livin' night and day in that loony-bin of yours—"

"Watch that car!" Cole blurted.

The police sedan had been, until that moment, traveling at a good clip over the straight-away concrete. Abruptly it began to waver. Its body rocked like a boat in a swell as it shuttled from curb to curb. One of its rear doors burst open and a man scrambled onto the running-board, wild with desperation—Ronald Fairlee. While the car was still swerving dangerously, Fairlee leaped. He sprawled violently on the pavement in the shafts of the Duesenberg's headlamps, sprang up, plunged into the darkness.

Kelly toed the Duesenberg's brakes as the police sedan slapped to a stop. Chief Wellsmore wrenched out of it, his collar torn, tie askew, a police positive glittering in one fist. Blake heaved after him, his jaw bruised, a cut over one eye.

Cole, hurrying from the Duesenberg, heard Wellsmore blast: "Choked me! Where'd he go? He can't get away! I'll have every cop on Long Island after him!"

Pointing, Blake blurted: "He beat it over there. Better flash the alarm, Chief. He won't get away from me next time—he'll be out cold!"

"Gentlemen." Carter Cole put a restraining hand on Blake's arm, stepped in front of Wellsmore. "There's no need to call out the militia. Locating Ronald Fairlee is not going to be a difficult task. I think you'll find he only wants to get back home."

Wellsmore snapped: "If that's so, he'll be damned sorry for it! Cole, you don't know what you're talking about. He's heading for the tall timber—because he's guilty of murder. Out of my way!"

"Watch back there by Fairlee's driveway," Cole directed firmly. "I think he's keeping in the shadows and working back to it. Yes—there he is!"

A dark form fluttered between the gateposts at the entrance of the Fairlee grounds. Before Wellsmore could bring up his gun it disappeared swiftly. Cole, running to the Duesenberg, snapped orders to Brick Kelly to reverse it. The motor surged with power and accelerated toward the drive. Across rolling, gloomy grounds Cole spotted a running man. In a minute Ronald Fairlee shouldered desperately at the front door of the house, thrust in, and vanished.

KELLY PULLED over to let the police car whizz by, plunge between the posts, wind up the drive and buck to a stop at the entrance. Wellsmore and Blake charged in together, guns in their hands. When Cole's car stopped, he sighed, opened his silver case, said: "Have a cigarette, Brick."

"Thanks, Doc!" Kelly exclaimed. "Looks like them two's all set to commit mayhem. Ain't you goin' to do anythin' to save him from the majesty of the law?"

"The law resents interference, Brick," Cole observed, "as much as I resent stupidity in psychopathic problems. Wellsmore and Blake are ready to tear this house apart in order to capture a man who is no more guilty of murder than they are."

"What makes you think he isn't, Doc?"

"A man," Cole answered cryptically, "wearing a blood-stained smock and eyeglasses rushes out of a room in which he has knifed an unfortunate girl more than seven feet tall, and ducks into another room across the hall. In a moment he reappears, wearing a smock which is not stained, putting his eyeglasses on as though he had just awakened from a nap. Either it's a trick or he's not guilty of the attack. If he's guilty it doesn't make sense. Until I find a sound psychological reason for believing—"

A loud, hammering sound, issuing from the house, broke into Cole's words. A husky voice bawled: "Open that door! Open it or we'll break it down!" Another snapped: "Look out, Chief, he's liable to shoot through!"

Cole reluctantly tamped his cigarette. "The stag is at bay," he remarked to Kelly. "Wait here, Brick." He went into the house quietly, climbed the stairs, saw the reason for the turmoil.

Wellsmore and Blake were shouldering at the door of the giantess' room. They crashed against it, drew back red-faced. Celia Ashurst and Steven Vaill were watching them, speechless with dismay. Cole heard whimpering cries of pain which meant that the giantess was still inside.

Wellsmore, stabbing a forefinger at Celia Ashurst, burst out: "We know he's in there! We heard his voice. Somebody must have a key to that door. If you don't unlock it, we'll break it down!"

"In that case," the girl answered in a cold rage, "go ahead and break."

Cole smiled his admiration while Wellsmore and Blake gathered themselves for another assault on the door. They paused in surprise as Ronald Fairlee's voice sounded through it. The scientist was speaking breathlessly, entreatingly. "Alice! Don't you understand, Alice? You saw the man who did it. Tell me who it was. Alice, you've got to tell me! Alice…! Alice…!" But his only answer was the pained, mumbling whine of the inarticulate giantess.

COLE WENT quietly into Fairlee's study. He closed the door, bolted it. Diagonally across the room another door stood, he noted, opening into the main hall. It was unlocked. Cole shot the bolt, began a swift examination.

He looked first in a closet, exclaimed "Ah!" when he saw a smock hanging on a hook, inspected it intently. It was burned by acids, tinted by aniline dyes—and colored with the crimson of human blood. That it was the blood of the giantess, Cole could not doubt. He replaced it, concern shining in his eyes, to turn to a desk. While he probed thoroughly into the drawers, crashing sounds in the hall marked Wellsmore's determined attack on the door.

Cole stiffened with dismay. He had lifted a sheet of stationery to find an encarnadined weapon. It was a long-bladed, keen-edged kitchen knife, still redly wet. Cole did not touch it but closed the drawer, turned, looked at the studio couch on the opposite side of the room. It bore the impression left by a resting body; the pillow showed the indentation of a head. Cole was attempting to add up his findings when a violent smashing noise indicated the achievement of Wellsmore's purpose.

Stepping from the study, Cole saw the chief and Blake standing stock-still just inside the other room. They had torn out the socket of the lock, had lurched in after their man—but now they were staring, frozen with horror, at the apparition rearing at the foot of the bed.

The giantess was bleating her fear, cowering back from the broken door, her protruding eyes staring blankly in the shadow of her bulging forehead. A flowing night-gown now concealed the dressed wound in her side. Her gigantic hands dangled from its sleeves, her enormous bare feet were visible beneath its hem. She was a thing out of a distorted dream, yet she was a living, breathing being whose grotesque proportions made the men in the room seem puny.

Ronald Fairlee said piteously: "She's only fourteen. She is my daughter."

Cole stepped back to allow Celia Ashurst to enter. Fairlee's assistant appeared even smaller beside the gargantuan Alice, her beauty even more striking in comparison with the ghastly abnormality of the giantess' features. She took one of Alice's massive hands, spoke as if to an infant.

"Don't be frightened. They won't harm you. You know I'm your friend. You must tell me now—now, before it's too late. It wasn't your father who did it to you, was it, Alice? Do you hear? Tell me, Alice—please."

The touch of Celia Ashurst's small hands on her own mammoth ones brought a pathetic peacefulness to the face of the giantess, but it could not wipe away the blankness of her expression. Her protruding eyes remained vacant as she turned her heavy head slowly to blink at Ronald Fairlee. Her loose, wet lips made mumbling noises, unintelligible to Cole, yet they brought shining relief to Celia Ashurst's eyes. The girl interpreted in a whisper.

"She said no—no."

Carter Cole gently took Ronald Fairlee's arm. He gestured Wellsmore and Blake out, led the chemist after them as they went dazedly into the hall. Leaving the giant-ess alone in the room, he closed the door. He smiled at the chief's horrified expression, spoke quietly.

"That unfortunate girl, gentlemen, is a victim of one of nature's crudest tricks, an example of what might have happened to any of us if the balance of our ductless glands had somehow been upset. She is human as you are—at birth she probably was not deformed at all. Basically she differs from the normal—from you, gentlemen—only in the slightest degree."

Wellsmore and Blake listened in bewilderment.

"In a bony cup beneath the brain, gentlemen, lies the pituitary gland, one of a number of ductless organs which control our destinies. It is no larger than the kernel of a hazelnut, and it weighs only one-fiftieth of an ounce, yet it secretes at least eleven powerful hormones. One of these determines our stature. An antipituitary defect causes enlarged hands and feet and head, as well as extreme height, as you have seen. It is most unfortunate but easily explained, thanks to Mr. Fairlee and others who are making such admirable progress in the field of endocrinology."*

---

* Research proceeding apace in the subject of endocrinology (the study of the system of ductless glands in the human body) reveals that these strange organs hold the key to most of the mysteries

Wellsmore and Blake were silent.

"Those not familiar with this phenomenon," Cole went on quietly, "may reach grievously wrong conclusions. Mr. Fairlee has confessed himself the father of this unfortunate girl, but that indicates nothing. The layman might assume her condition points to an abnormality in her father or mother—not at all. Most certainly it has no connection with Mr. Fairlee's mental condition. It is very important, gentlemen, that you understand this clearly."

Wellsmore flushed. "I'll take your word on it, Cole, but a jury will have the final say in this case. I'm surer than before that Fairlee's behind his wife's disappearance. I'm going to get a confession and I'm going to find the body. What's more, Fairlee's going to headquarters with us and he's going to take a grilling."

Fairlee recoiled in dismay. "Don't take me away again! Don't force me to leave this house! I beg of you—"

"You're coming with us this time, all the way!"

Cole's eyes narrowed. "Chief," he said quietly, "I am interested principally in psychological truths. If murder has been done, I am as eager as you to see the guilty person punished, but you're making a regrettable mistake. You're

---

of life and death. They produce sideshow freaks, fanatics, neurasthenics, loafers, executives whose energies seem to have no limit. Abnormalities of the ductless glands may produce geniuses or morons. Their imperfect functioning cause such afflictions as diabetes, goiter, Addison's, Graves' and Simmonds' diseases. Space does not permit even a bare outline of the various glands and their known functions, but even with the wealth of material at hand, science has not yet advanced beyond the kindergarten stage in its knowledge of them. It is certain, however, that the hormones poured into the body by the ductless glands are its high explosives.—F.C.D.

not in the mood to listen to any further explanations—so I'm obliged to promise you, you're going to find me right in the middle of this case until it's cracked wide open."

"Mistake?" Wellsmore barked. "If you think Fairlee's innocent of this job, you're making a bigger one!"

Cole smiled. "In the interest of justice, Chief, allow me to give you some vital information. A short time ago the girl Alice was attacked with a knife, perhaps with intent to kill. Miss Ashurst and I are witness to the fact that the assailant escaped into Mr. Fairlee's study. In that room you will find a bloody knife and a bloodstained smock. They are evidence pointing to Mr. Fairlee as the attacker of his daughter. If Mr. Fairlee is guilty of one crime commit- ted in this house, he may logically be presumed guilty of another—possibly the murder of his wife.

"But, gentlemen," Carter Cole added firmly, "I'm convinced Ronald Fairlee is absolutely innocent, and I stake my professional reputation on a promise to prove it. Good-night."

He stepped past the stricken Fairlee, the dumfounded Wellsmore. Celia Ashurst's haggard eyes followed him as he passed Homer Morehouse, who was standing in the branch hall. Looking back, Cole saw again, on the face of Steven Vaill, that expression of numb fear. He went out, climbed into his Duesenberg with a sigh.

"Home, Brick," he ordered.

CHAPTER THREE
THE INVISIBLE PRISON

THE COLE SANITARIUM sat amid spacious grounds bordered by a high fence topped with barbed wire, a retreat peopled by more than a thousand mental patients. Some toiled in the gardens, rolled the gravel walks, basked in the sun living vegetable existences. Others shrieked with ecstasy or moaned with stark despair or sang or preached—a cacophonous chorus of the demented that never ended. While he strove to cure their derangements, Carter Cole, M.D., reigned supreme over their destinies.

The sprawling building was a labyrinth of hallways, along which, by day, blank-faced men and women interminably pushed heavy blocks based with felt, a mechanical routine which eased their minds while it burnished the floors. Along one of these bright corridors Carter Cole strode, having returned from the Fairlee home, to his offices. As soon as he appeared, two pretty and efficient nurse-secretaries came alertly to his desk.

"June, Jane," he addressed the Misses Day, "I need accurate information quickly. You've a big night's work ahead of you. A man's life may depend on what you find."

"Yes, Doctor," said June Day. And "Yes, Doctor," said Jane.

They were perfectly alike—identical in every detail of their pert faces, their slender figures, their quiet voices, their trim uniforms. If they had family, friends, sweethearts, Carter Cole had never gleaned a hint of them. He knew only that the twins were ideal, tireless secretaries, whom nothing ever ruffled, who could perform any bizarre task with efficient dispatch. And—a confusion which he often thought might some day make him a patient in his own institution—that he was forever calling them by their wrong names.

"To begin with, June, some first-class snooping must be done. Fairlee's neighbors will be only too eager to oblige, I think. Is Miss Celia Ashurst in love with Ronald Fairlee or with Steven Vaill? Is Mr. Fairlee in love with Miss Ashurst? As to whether Mr. Vaill is in love with the girl I need no information—he is. Before you leave, June, please bring from the files the newspaper clippings concerning the recent disappearance of Mrs. Fairlee."

The girl he was looking at said: "Yes, Doctor—but I'm Jane."

"Ah, yes," Cole sighed. "You always are. June, information also on Fairlee's brother-in-law, Homer Morehouse. Particularly, was he actually in Europe at the time his sister disappeared, and on the high seas, returning from London, when he heard of it? How much does the missing woman mean to him? Also what does Fairlee stand to gain, if anything, by his wife's death? On your way."

Jane Day promptly brought Cole a folder of newspaper clippings and left him alone at his desk. The twins would not rest, he knew, until they had placed in his hands the complete answers to his questions. Now he glanced over black headlines announcing the startling disappearance of the chemist's wife, and singled out a few paragraphs.

Mrs. Fairlee's probable movements, just prior to her disappearance, were evidently her usual routine. She prepared herself a stew, dined alone, tidied the kitchen, then retired to her bedroom. No one witnessed these movements but, following the discovery of her disappearance next day by her husband, indications were found, he related, pointing to these actions.

The police investigation revealed the situation in the Fairlee home to be an unusual one. Though Mr. and Mrs. Fairlee lived under the same roof, they were estranged. During the course of several days the wife might see nothing of her husband, since his laboratory research work absorbed him completely. While she prepared her own meals in the large kitchen downstairs, Ronald Fairlee and his assistants ate at irregular hours, their meals being prepared by Celia Ashurst, the chemist's assistant, in a kitchen adjoining the laboratory. Fairlee's waking moments were confined to the laboratory and his study, while his wife occupied a separate bedroom and made use of the rest of the house. This situation was generally known to the neighbors. Mrs. Fairlee was said to have been preparing an action for a legal separation at the time of her disappearance.

The missing woman is Fairlee's second wife. Fairlee's first marriage occurred in 1921, to Marie Ostend, of New York. A few months after the birth of a daughter, Alice, in 1922, the first Mrs. Fairlee obtained a divorce in Nevada on the grounds of mental cruelty. She remained in New York with her daughter until her death three years ago. Mr. Fairlee remarried in 1930 to Ethel Morehouse, also of New York, the missing woman.

The telephone interrupted. A strained, anxious voice came from the receiver—Homer Morehouse's. Cole listened alertly to a rushing message.

"For God's sake, Doctor Cole, come to police headquarters at once. They have Ronald here. He's behaving as though he's lost his last vestige of sanity. They're trying to force him to talk—it's frightful. Somehow you've got to help him—or anything may happen."

"I'm on my way," Cole answered promptly.

He touched two pearl buttons. One would summon Brick Kelly to the entrance with the Duesenberg. The other brought a remarkably personable young woman to his desk. She was Doctor Mary Grafton, his first assistant, whom he had met in one of his most amazing cases and literally saved from the electric chair. In a moment she was in hat and coat, ready to leave with him.

"A case, Mary," he told her, "which needs your understanding and sympathy. Notebook and pencil for a statement. Let's hurry."

UNDER BRICK KELLY'S masterly handling, the Duesenberg whirred along the broad cement road which led to the trim police-headquarters building. With Doctor Grafton, Cole went into Chief Wellsmore's outer office. Through a connecting door he heard the chief's flat voice, Blake's growling tones. They were shooting out questions at machine-gun speed.

"Why didn't you report your wife's disappearance?"

"Where have you hidden her body?"

"Why are you afraid to leave the house?"

"Where did you hide her after you killed her?"

"What are you afraid of now if you're innocent?"

"Where did you hide your wife's body?"

"What are you afraid of?"

An answer came, blurted and husky, in Ronald Fairlee's voice. "The Dynamo God—the Dynamo God!"

Cole's lips tightened as he stepped into the inner office. Fairlee was slumped in a chair in the corner. Two pairs of handcuffs shackled his wrists to its arms. He was staring wildly, possessed by an uncontrollable fear. Wellsmore and Blake were leveling accusing forefingers in his face. Cole went toward them quietly as the grim question rasped again.

"Where did you hide your wife's body?"

"Gentlemen." Wellsmore and Blake turned impatiently. "You are laboring under a cruel misunderstanding. You are mistaking Mr. Fairlee's agitation for guilty knowledge. The truth is, he is beside himself because he is a victim of a distance phobia."

Wellsmore growled: "Doctor, I think you'd better keep out of this. If he's insane, it's all the more reason for thinking he killed his wife."

"Another error," Cole said calmly. "Mr. Fairlee is not insane. We all have phobias in some degree, some very slight, some marked. Many women are afraid of thunder— that's called astraphobia. Others are afraid of blood— hematophobia. A great many persons are afraid of high places—acrophobia. Mr. Fairlee's happens to be an acute fear of being away from home. An awful thing to him— but it is not insanity." *

---

*   At birth infants possess only a few inherited fears—fear of falling, of loud noises, of restriction of movement. Some fears are learned by children from others—as, for instance nyctophobia, or fear of the dark—others are acquired through emotional shock. A mild phobia may manifest itself as shyness (fear of ridicule) as a "New England conscience"; in an extreme case the phobia may become a constant dread powerful enough to determine the whole course of life. Fear of disease accounts for the publication of health columns in newspapers and fear of loss accounts for the institution of insurance. There is—weak or strong—some form of phobia in the make-up of everyone.—F.C.D.

"Yes—yes, that's true," Fairlee murmured. "At home I am safe. Here—the Dynamo God—" He closed his eyes convulsively and was silent.

"Suppose," Cole went on, "Mrs. Fairlee is found dead—murdered. Unless Ronald Fairlee is cured, by having the roots of his fear pulled out of his mind by a skilled psychiatrist, he will behave in just this same way if he is forced to appear in a courtroom—merely because it is far from his home. The jury, totally unversed in the lore of the mind, will believe Mr. Fairlee a raving maniac. It will inevitably mean the chair for him."

"If my hunch is right, he'll deserve it!" Wellsmore countered.

"But if you're wrong, you'll have an innocent man's death on your conscience," Cole firmly pointed out. "Listen, Chief. Questioning Fairlee like this will get you absolutely nowhere. He can't think straight here. Suppose you turn him over to me. I promise you it will mean progress in the case."

The chief scowled. "What do you want to do with him?"

"Take him back home," Cole said.

Wellsmore's jaw squared. "All right, go ahead. We'll make it a party. I'll bet a million Mrs. Fairlee's body is hidden somewhere in that house. While you're trying to find out about this thing he calls the Dynamo God, I'll be tearing the place apart. Go ahead—Fairlee's in your hands, and you're responsible."

Pathetic relief shone in Fairlee's eyes. Cole gently unlocked the handcuffs, took his arm. With Doctor Mary Grafton, they went out to the Duesenberg. Brick Kelly's eyes widened with alarm at sight of the wildly staring Fairlee. The car whirred back to the broad cement. Cole said nothing, but watched the chemist. While he stared out the windows, seeking familiar landmarks, Fairlee's tension eased.

"Thank God you understand, Doctor Cole!" he said fervently. "I can leave the house, and go to the edge of the grounds, without feeling this horrible fear. If I go a few yards beyond the gate, it begins to burn in my mind. A few steps more and I tremble. It is absolutely impossible for me to go beyond a certain point, of my own volition. For years—for an eternity—I've lived in an invisible prison."

KELLY SHOT the car into the Fairlee drive. The instant the gate posts were behind him, a vast sigh of relief came from the chemist's lips. When he stepped from the Duesenberg he was quite composed. Once beyond the entrance he was completely unafraid. Cole chuckled and slapped his shoulder reassuringly.

"Doctor Grafton," he said, "will talk with you awhile in the library. I feel sure we're going to demolish the walls of your invisible prison. Forget everything else—be at ease. Have I ever told you I'm deathly afraid of crowds. That's called ochlophobia. Go along, now."

Ronald Fairlee, smiling, went into the library with Doctor Grafton. Cole turned back to the entrance. A police car had drawn up behind the Duesenberg. Wellsmore, Blake and two other men were piling out of it, carrying shovels, picks, crowbars. They trooped in with the tools, determination grimly pictured on their faces.

"Get at it," Wellsmore directed. "Start with the cellar. Dig it up. If we don't find a woman's dead body tonight I'll call in a wrecking crew."

They marched along the hallway with their implements, opened a door at the rear of the house, went down into the darkness of the cellar. Cole, climbing the stairs, met Homer Morehouse. Morehouse made an agitated gesture.

"They ordered me out of headquarters after I phoned you. I was only trying to help Ronald. Even though he may be guilty of everything they say, I couldn't let them torture him that way. What is this thing he keeps calling the Dynamo God? Doctor Cole—is he mad?"

"You'll soon be satisfied on that point," Cole answered and went into the laboratory. Among the glittering apparatus he found Celia Ashurst and Steven Vaill. They eyed him uneasily, the flat gaslight heightening the pallor of their features.

Cole said with startling abruptness: "Vaill, you're concealing something."

Vaill stiffened, but said nothing. Celia Ashurst's eyes searched his anxiously.

Cole went on: "I don't believe Ronald Fairlee attacked Alice tonight. It was another person, wearing one of his smocks and his eyeglasses. When it happened he was asleep in his study. If you'll come with me, I'll show you exactly what I mean."

They followed him wonderingly as he strode into the branch hall. Out of the corner of his eye Cole saw Vaill restraining a torturous anxiety. Suddenly Vaill stopped short. The girl paused at his side, startled by the gasp of dismay which broke from his lips. They listened to irregular thumping sounds echoing dully through the house. The noises of heavy blows were issuing from somewhere below.

Celia Ashurst asked tightly: "What's that?"

"I believe," Cole answered, "it's Wellsmore digging in the cellar—hunting for the dead body of Mrs. Fairlee."

A single word broke past Vaill's numb lips. "God!"

Cole searched Vaill's face intently, then abruptly turned away. He opened the door of Fairlee's study, pointed across it to the other door connecting with the main hall.

He explained quietly: "The person who attacked Alice rushed into this room, bolted the door, put the bloody knife in the desk, hung the stained smock in the closet, left the eyeglasses, then went out the other door around the corner of the hall, slipping away without being seen. All the while Fairlee, a heavy sleeper, lay there on the couch. It's reasonable to suppose, isn't it, that if Fairlee had made the attack, he wouldn't have put the knife and the smock where they'd be so easily found. The guilty person left them to fasten suspicion on Fairlee."

"But why?" Celia Ashurst asked the question tensely while Steven Vaill remained white-faced and silent, listening. "Why should anyone want to make Ronald Fairlee appear guilty of trying to kill that unfortunate girl?"

Cole gave the answer. "That person's purpose was to make Fairlee seem dangerously insane. Perhaps the police investigation was proceeding too slowly and this act was calculated to hasten it. With his insanity apparently established, Fairlee becomes suspect of any other crime which may have been committed—for instance, murdering and concealing the body of his wife."

FROM BELOW, the noise of chuffing shovels and driving picks continued. The irregular rhythm lent a ghastly undertone to the aura of horror hovering over the house— it seemed like the hand of doom knocking at the door.

Cole, eyes sharp, said to Celia Ashurst quietly: "There is a bond between you and Alice. She trusts you, and you can understand her. Because she is mentally an infant, because she is inarticulate, she can never take the stand as a witness in her father's defense—yet she knows the simple truth. She has already told you Ronald Fairlee is not the man who wounded her. It remains now for you to induce her to tell you who actually is guilty."

Celia Ashurst moved at once to the door of the giantess' room. She had no need to use a key because Wellsmore's attack had broken the lock. She stepped in and stopped short, struck with dismay. The grotesquely long bed was empty. The girl was not in the room.

"Alice!"

Alarm quickened Carter Cole's movements. He jerked open two closets in which huge dresses were hanging, looked into the adjoining bath. There was no sign of the giantess. He turned to Celia Ashurst.

"She slipped out—probably she's hidden herself in the house somewhere because she's frightened. It's a perfectly natural impulse. She's vital to the cause of proving her father innocent because she knows and can tell who actually knifed her. We've got to find her quickly—before anything happens to her."

Cole allowed the girl to lead him on the search. Celia Ashurst repeatedly called "Alice!" as they went into room after room. Determined to overlook no possible place where the giantess might hide, they climbed into the cobwebbed attic—but she was not there. The lower floor yielded no clue to the girl's whereabouts. Cole avoided the cellar because the thumping of picks and shovels told him Wellsmore's men were still busy at their ghoul's work.

He stepped out the rear entrance. "Possibly somewhere on the grounds," he suggested, shrewdly eying Steven Vaill. "Look everywhere." He started off at the side of Celia Ashurst.

The gardens were a gloomy baffling maze of shadows. A path led to a shed in the rear against which a covered outdoor pen was built. Cole paused, hearing a gentle hopping sound, vaguely saw small bushy animals rearing curiously on their hind legs.

"Rabbits," he said. "Why rabbits?"

"Homer Morehouse sent them," Celia Ashurst answered, scarcely aware in her anxiety of what she was saying. "At the time, he left for London—Mrs. Fairlee liked them for dinner. He sent eight and there are six left. Nobody's touched them since Mrs. Fairlee disappeared.... Doctor Cole! Do you think something has happened to Alice?"

"There is the fact," Cole answered tightly, "that the man who attacked her knows she can identify him."

They went on, circling the grounds. The fruitless hunt brought them back to the rear entrance. They were entering when quick footfalls sounded on the cellar stairs. Chief Wellsmore, face streaked with cobwebs, stepped into the light, grinning grimly. His eyes shone with triumph as he bluntly announced: "We've found her."

Celia Ashurst's hand rose in terror to her lips. Steven Vaill, just entering the rear door, stood transfixed. Cole looked sharply at them both, shouldered past Wellsmore. He went down gritty wooden steps into a dank, musty underground room buttressed by ancient beams. Picks and shovels had ripped up half its flagstone floor. Three men were turning the beams of their flashlights upon a wall.

The walls of the cellar were large stone blocks. One of the blocks had been torn from its bed. The light of the torches was shining into a cavity. Rich black dirt had crumbled away, exposing a bed of white. "Quick-lime," one of the men murmured as Cole stared. Framed in the hollow was a shrunken, waxy face. Like a rough-hewn statue in process of excavation the dead woman stood upright in the shroud of lime—the missing wife of Ronald Fairlee.

CHAPTER FOUR
DEATH TO RATS

CARTER COLE said quietly: "I am surer than ever, gentlemen, that Ronald Fairlee is not guilty of murder."

The detective snorted at him. He turned as Chief Wellsmore trudged down the stairs. The chief announced: "Leave her just like that until the photographer shoots the whole layout. Everybody upstairs." He squinted at Cole. "Well, Doctor? What did I tell you. He killed her with rat poison."

"What!"

Wellsmore pointed to a tin container embedded in the lime near the dead woman's head. He lifted it from its socket. It had rusted and most of the printed label had become illegible, but the trade name of *Ratex* remained and a line promising *Sure Death to Rats*. Wellsmore shook the can and a liquid sloshed inside it. As he replaced it in the hollow Cole looked impatient.

"Have you stopped to wonder, Chief," Cole asked dryly, "why Fairlee, a chemist, should make use of rat exterminator for murder purposes when he has a number of far subtler poisons in his laboratory, some of which are almost impossible to detect?"

"I'm satisfied with this case. You've certainly missed fire this time, Cole. Blake, be sure the back door's bolted.

Everybody out of the cellar. The rest of this is just routine. I've got Fairlee cold."

"I consider," Cole observed quietly, "my professional reputation is still intact."

Celia Ashurst and Steven Vaill had been standing on the mouldy stairs, peering at the corpse. They hurried up. Cole, waiting while the headquarters men filed into the hall, watched Wellsmore lock the cellar entrance. He saw Doctor Mary Grafton leaving the library with Ronald Fairlee.

Wellsmore strode grimly to the chemist, bluntly announced the discovery of the woman's body. Stunned, speechless, Fairlee sank into a chair. Doctor Grafton passed her notebook to Cole. He read three pages of terse stenographic observations and nodded his satisfaction. He went at once to Wellsmore.

"This," he said, "explains Ronald Fairlee's phobia. First, an unforgettable nervous shock suffered in early childhood—a violent scare caused by the explosion of a generator in an electrical power house. That didn't cause the phobia, but planted the seed. Second, another shattering experience later in life—the discovery that his only child, whom he hadn't seen since she was a few months old, was a horrible monstrosity. The two forged a mental chain binding him to his home. I will gladly supply you a copy of this report, Chief."*

---

* Carter Cole has kindly furnished me with a full report of the case of Ronald Fairlee, of which the following are excerpts offered so that the reader may grasp a clear understanding of his phobia. "My father was an electrical engineer. As a boy I often went to the power house where he worked because I was fascinated by the huge switches, fuses and meters. I was particularly interested in the

"That doesn't matter now," Wellsmore answered. "Sane or not, we're nailing him on a murder charge."

"May I," Cole asked with a sigh, "ask a privilege in the interests of justice? Please allow me to go to the cellar, say with Miss Ashurst, for a brief inspection of my own. My word of honor for good behavior. I think it's vital."

Wellsmore grunted. "You know the seriousness of concealing or removing evidence, Cole. But— Sure, go ahead."

Cole removed his coat, turned at once to Fairlee's laboratory assistant. "We have not yet located Alice," he reminded

————————

whirring dynamos which sent their magic power out into the city... One day, while I was standing near a huge dynamo, something went wrong. Sparks like lightning flashed out of it. It seemed to explode with a terrific thunderclap. I was so struck with fright that I obeyed my first impulse... I ran home, as fast as I could, for dear life—home because it meant safety.

"I forgot the incident in time, except that its effect was to make me afraid of everything concerned with electricity.

"An emotional shock equally violent was when I saw my daughter Alice for the first time since separating from my first wife. I had not seen her, even a picture of her, since she was a baby. My first wife had concealed her deformity from me, probably through consideration for my feelings. When Alice's mother died, Alice was brought to my home by distant relatives. My first glimpse of her was an overwhelming experience that tortured my whole being. It was then I began strongly to experience fear of leaving my home. My duty to Alice demanded that I care for her constantly—a duty I would have gladly evaded though I could not—and the world outside the house became, in my mind, a domain dominated by electricity—the Dynamo God—into which I dared not venture."—F.C.D.

the girl. "Keep hunting for her outside, will you, Vaill? Miss Ashurst, bring a test tube from the lab, and a cork. Hurry!"

STEVEN VAILL hastened out the entrance as the girl ran up the stairs. Wellsmore unlocked the cellar door for Cole. He took an electric torch from Blake as Celia Ashurst came to him with a glittering tube in her hand. Her face whitened as she went down the swaying stairs with Cole. He paused at the opened wall, the beam shining in the dead woman's face.

He looked up. Bracketed to the beams above the hollow was a wooden shelf loaded with old cans of paint, bottles of turpentine and oil. "The rat poison," he observed, "might easily have fallen off, been walled in by the murderer without his knowing it." Cole wedged his torch in a niche in the wall. Carefully he lifted the rusted can from the bed of lime and pried the lid off, poured the test-tube full of the poison.

"Listen!" Celia Ashurst blurted, backing instinctively to the barred window.

A faint, scraping sound came out of the gloom. Cole turned quickly to the opposite wall. It rose head high to an air-space between leveled ground and the floor joists. The light probed far back into the flat space, reaching the brick base of a chimney. Something was crawling from the shadow behind the column—a huge being with bulbous head, great hands clawing to drag itself forward.

"Alice!" Celia gasped.

The giantess' face was smeared with grime. She made a whimpering, pleading sound in answer to Celia Ashurst's soft call. She had, Cole conjectured, retreated to the cellar to escape the fear of things unintelligible to her undeveloped mind and at the approach of Wellsmore's men, had dragged herself into deeper security. The instinctive sympathy she felt for Celia Ashurst was drawing her from her hiding place. Slowly, laboriously, she crawled to the edge of the wall.

"Poor Alice—come to me. There's nothing to be afraid of. You know we're your friends. Come—come."

The giantess crawled down, stood with lips lax, eyes vacant, yet somehow evincing gratefulness. Celia Ashurst spoke to her crooningly.

"Alice—do you remember the man? The man who hurt you—you remember? He made the blood come and ran away. Tell us who he is, Alice."

The answer came, not in the slavering mumble of the giantess, but with the sharp, lethal crack of a gun plus the sound of shattering glass.

Cole, who had been watching the hesitant approach of the giantess, whirled, the poison still in his hand, to see an arm encircling Celia Ashurst's throat through the bars of the window. In the same split second the arm was withdrawn and Cole caught the gleam reflected from a disappearing gun. A man took a running step past the broken pane and was gone.

Cole jerked back as an animal moan broke from the lips of the giantess. She was swaying forward, her lids drooping over her protruding eyes. A black hole with a tangent of red marked the center of her bulging forehead.

Cole corked the test-tube, slid it into his pocket and whirled as Celia groped to break the fall of the giantess. He bounded to the rear entrance of the cellar, fought the rusty bolt. He slapped out of a bulkhead, sprang past the low window. Bringing his 9mm Luger into his hand, he ran along shadow-matted gardens. Suddenly he stopped in the glow from a window, staring at a young man moving toward him—Steven Vaill.

"What happened?" Vaill exclaimed. "I heard a shot. Is Celia all right?"

Cole said grimly: "Through no fault of yours."

Vaill started, broke past. Cole let him go and followed along the path. When he reached the front of the house he saw two headquarters men skirmishing out, alarmed by the report. "In the cellar!" he snapped at them. He heard an outbreak of action in the rear of the house while he circled the grounds. He caught no other sound, saw no movement while he searched. Entering the dwelling at the front, he went rapidly along the gaslighted hall, paused when he saw Celia Ashurst hurry from the cellar.

The girl whispered: "She's dead."

"I expected that," said Cole.

He looked into the library. Ronald Fairlee was standing uncertainly beside the table, too overwhelmed by mental confusion to move. Homer Morehouse was grasping one of his arms, saying: "Keep hold of yourself, Ronald."

Cole turned back, stepped to the side of Doctor Mary Grafton with, "Wait for me in the car." He was striding toward the cellar entrance when Chief Wellsmore stepped up.

"Doctor, did you see the man who killed that poor girl?"

"Unfortunately, I did not," Cole answered. "Nor did Miss Ashurst. He got away across the grounds. I think it best, Chief, that I retire until your official furor subsides. You can always find me at the sanitarium. I only have one statement to make tonight—that the man who shot Alice is the man who knifed her and the man who murdered Mrs. Fairlee. And one question: Where was Ronald Fairlee when the shot was fired?"

"He was with me," Chief Wellsmore answered confusedly, "in the library."

Cole smiled wryly as he went out.

CHAPTER FIVE
MURDER FEAST

THE MANIFOLD duties of directing the Cole Sanitarium kept Cole in his office until long past dawn. Once routine matters were dispatched, he took up the terse, typewritten reports prepared for him on the Fairlee case.

The life of Ethel Fairlee was insured for $100,000, half of this payable to her husband in the event of her death, half to her brother.

Mr. Fairlee's financial condition is strained. He is desperately in need of funds to carry on his researches.

Mr. Morehouse's relationship with his sister was quite casual until he learned she was not happy with Fairlee, at which time he began writing her letters and sending her gifts, in a brotherly attempt to cheer her.

Mr. Fairlee's domestic unhappiness was definitely due to his phobia and to the presence of his monster daughter.

Mr. Morehouse was attempting to close an important contract in London, England, at the time of his sister's disappearance. He failed his purpose, which placed him in an even more pressing financial situation than that which had forced him to make the trip. He immediately booked his return. The captain of the *S. S. Ultima* confirms his presence on the ship, en route from London to New York, at the time his sister's disappearance was reported to the press. He went immediately to the Fairlee home.

JD

The ringing telephone drew Cole's hand. The voice of Chief Wellsmore reached Cole with a triumphant chuckle. "News, Doctor," the official said, "which will interest you. An autopsy has been performed on Mrs. Fairlee. Reinsch's test shows arsenic. Practically everybody knows some rat poisons are mostly arsenic."

"But," Cole inquired, "is arsenic present in the particular rat poison you found in the woman's grave? And, furthermore, did you find any in Fairlee's lab?"

Wellsmore growled: "None in his lab, but that doesn't prove there wasn't some there two months ago when his wife died. I'm turning a sample of the rat poison over to another chemist for checking. Why did Fairlee bury the poison with her if he didn't use it to kill her? I tell you, we've cracked us a case."

Cole disconnected, sat musing. He rose, climbed to the spacious laboratory on the upper floor. He took from his pocket the tube he had filled with rat poison at Mrs. Fairlee's lime-packed grave and began a systematic qualitative analysis. When he reached a positive indication he murmured: "The digitalis, sea onion type."

He returned to his desk, touched a button, smiled when Doctor Grafton appeared. "Mary," he said, "can you cook?"

"I've cooked for myself," she answered, "and survived."

"Good. First, please telephone everybody connected with the Fairlee case and invite them to have dinner with me at eight o'clock at the Fairlee home. Allow none of them to refuse. Later, I'll personally make arrangements with Chief Wellsmore so that Fairlee will himself be present—with a certain article of evidence. Once you're assured everyone is coming, hie yourself to the Fairlee home and make ready. I'll telephone you the menu later."

"Something plain and simple?" Doctor Grafton asked.

"Tonight," Cole answered, "we shall all partake of a very special dish."

Mary Grafton left wondering. Cole again took up the reports prepared by the Day twins. He was reading a note concerning Steven Vaill when one of his personable secretaries appeared to announce that Mr. Vaill was calling. "So?" Cole said. "Show him in, June."

Reaching for the bookcase, he moaned with despair when Miss Day answered: "Yes, Doctor—but I'm Jane." He tugged down a copy of *Webster's Toxicology* and another volume entitled *Tolerances and Their Relationship to the Endocrine System.* He looked up to find Steven Vaill, pale and anxious, staring across his desk.

Vaill began without preliminaries: "You know I'm hiding something. I admit it. I've got to. I can't stand it any longer. You think I murdered Mrs. Fairlee—but it isn't true. I—I—"

Cole said quietly: "Sit down, Mr. Vaill."

VAILL PERCHED on a chair. "It's all got to come out sooner or later," he resumed, "and I want to clear myself in your eyes because you insist Ronald Fairlee is innocent. I'll probably go to prison—it was a mad impulse—but I did it for Celia's sake."

"What," Cole asked, "did you do?"

"Mrs. Fairlee," Vaill hurried on, "was a nagging, spiteful, suspicious woman. She thought Celia and Ronald were in love with each other. She accused him of an affair with her more than once. It wasn't true. Celia was going—was going to marry me. Ronald's is a paternal affection for Celia—but his wife put the worst possible construction on it."

Cole asked: " 'Was'?"

"This will make marriage for Celia and me impossible—if I'm made to suffer for what I did. I was desperate to avoid a scandal—to keep Celia's career from being ruined—to keep her name from being dirtied in the papers and the courts—but now it's all gone for nothing. You can't realize how I felt when I found Mrs. Fairlee in her bedroom—dead."

Cole sat up. "You found her?"

"Dead," Vaill repeated huskily. "That night Ronald and Celia were working late in the lab. I went downstairs for a bite to eat. Passing Mrs. Fairlee's bedroom, I saw her door open. She was lying on the floor. She'd been in robust health—there wasn't any wound—I knew immediately she'd been poisoned."

"Acute arsenical poisoning," Cole observed, "leaves no visible symptoms."

"But I knew it!" Vaill insisted. "Can you realize what it meant? Someone in the house had killed her. I hadn't. I swear I hadn't. I had no reason for it. But the gossip going about—suspicion would point either to Celia or Ronald. One or the other of them getting rid of the wife in order to be free for each other. There was nothing to it—nothing—but I knew it wouldn't be looked at in any other way. It would ruin them both."

"Yes?"

"I hid her body in the cellar wall."

Cole jerked up. *"You?"*

"Hoping they'd never find her, praying it would never come out. It was a crazy thing to do—but Celia and Ronald both mean so much to me. I waited until Celia had gone home, until Ronald was asleep—he sleeps heavily, you know. There was some construction work going on next door. I stole several bags of lime to help destroy the body. God! You don't know what it's been, living and working there in that house, knowing a dead woman was buried in the cellar."

"Do you think," Cole asked quietly, "Roland Fairlee poisoned her? Do you think Celia Ashurst did it? And—have you told me the whole truth?"

"Celia—certainly not! Ronald—what else is there to think? Yes—I've told you everything!"

Cole frowned. "Young men in love," he observed, "are truly addicted to regrettably foolish acts. I advise you to say nothing of this to anyone else. Let that phase of the case remain forever unsolved—it's your only hope of escaping a prison sentence, at the very least, for disposing of a dead body. You might, you know, find yourself up for murder."

"But I tell you—" Vaill blurted it, jerked up, began again. "I tell you I didn't—"

"I know, definitely and beyond all doubt who the murderer is," Cole interrupted him. "I have a special reason for withholding the information a little while. I plan to announce the murderer's identity at a little dinner party I'm giving tonight at the Fairlee home. You'll be present of course. I hope you'll excuse me. I have a great deal of reading to do."

Vaill stared. "What are you talking about?"

"You'll find the dinner, I think, most intriguing," Cole said as he began to read.

He was completely absorbed in the weighty treatises when Vaill went baffled from his office.

IN THE dining-room of the Fairlee home gaslight gleamed on silver and crystal and china. Immaculate linen shone on a table set for eight. In the kitchen Doctor Mary Grafton, assisted by several women brought from the sanitarium, was preparing the repast. In the library the guests were waiting, silent and mystified. The appointed hour was at hand but their host, Carter Cole, M.D., was absent.

The silken hum of the Duesenberg announced his arrival. Stepping from the massive black car he directed Brick Kelly: "Wait here, Brick, and keep a wary eye on that door." He strode into the house, followed by the twin Misses Day in smart tailored dresses exactly alike. Smilingly entering the library, he affably greeted his waiting guests.

"Sorry. So sorry. Important researches delayed me. Gracious of you to permit me this privilege, Mr. Fairlee. Good evening, Mr. Morehouse. Miss Ashurst, Mr. Vaill, you look fresh as daisies. Why the scowl, Mr. Blake? Ah, Chief—you've brought the bit of evidence I mentioned. I'd like to have it now, if you don't mind."

Chief Wellsmore, uneasy in a new suit, opened his briefcase and handed Cole the corroded can of rat poison found in the murdered woman's secret grave. Cole sloshed its contents cheerfully. "Cocktails, my good people?" he inquired. Even as he spoke a uniformed maid appeared, bearing a tray. Cole waited until all his guests were served, then took up his own glass—empty.

"You will be glad, I'm sure, to learn," he said, "that we have reached the root of the trouble which has kept Mr. Fairlee imprisoned in this house for years. Half the cure is his realizing the cause of the phobia. The treatment is simple—merely short trips, farther away each day until he becomes sure the outside world holds no terrors for him. A toast, good people? Let us say—Here's to crime."

They stared, but they sipped. They stopped sipping when Cole pried open the can of rat poison. Quite deliberately he poured his cocktail glass full of the stuff. Holding it jauntily, he resumed: "You will also be happy to learn—all but one of you, that is—that it is equally simple to prove Mr. Fairlee innocent of murder. The dead body found in this house was, as you know, packed in quicklime. Quicklime was used for the purpose of destroying the corpse. Many murderers have learned, much to their regret, that the action of quick-lime on a body isn't destructive at all. Quite the contrary. It's preservative. Mr. Fairlee, being an eminent scientist, knows that—but the murderer didn't.

"You aren't drinking," Cole chided his guests. "Come, let's get on with it. Here, again, is to crime."

He was raising the glass of rat poison to his lips when Wellsmore blurted in dismay: "Cole, for God's sake, that stuff'll kill you!"

Cole's hand paused. "Interesting mixture," he observed. "It is composed of digitalis, the juice of the sea onion or sea lily, and other aromatic substances added to attract its victims—but no arsenic, Chief. When rats get it into their systems it paralyzes their respiratory apparatus, drives them into the open for water, and soon makes an end of them. Deadly indeed—to rats."

While seven people stared aghast, too stunned to speak, Carter Cole raised the glass of poison to his lips and drained it.

"But not," he went on, "to humans. I assure you the last thing I wish to do is to die. I promise you I will suffer not the slightest ill effects. You, Chief, a layman, weren't aware of the interesting properties of this stuff. To Mr. Fairlee and me, men of science, it is not at all surprising. It is one more point in the proof that he did not use this stuff to poison his wife. He'd have known it couldn't kill a human."

Chief Wellsmore grumbled: "Well I'll be damned—but if you fall over dead any minute, Cole, I won't be surprised."

"Don't worry," Cole assured him. "I hope, Chief, you're still not wondering why Mr. Fairlee didn't report his wife's disappearance. Since she was planning on a separation, he probably thought she'd merely left him. Perhaps he hesitated because of his unusual mental condition, wanting to avoid having it paraded in the newspapers. He is a highly intelligent, sensitive man and naturally—"

Fairlee blurted: "I dread—dread that people will think me mad—capable of any irrational act!"

"Naturally," Cole agreed. "Shall we go in to dinner?"

COLE LED the way into the dining-room. His guests were ill at ease but he was affability itself. He made sure each was comfortably seated. The blaze crackling in the fireplace lent a warm cheer.

The tension was beginning to ease when Cole, pausing at his own chair, laconically remarked: "I believe it was directly below his room that the body of Mrs. Fairlee was found hidden in the wall, wasn't it?"

Cole's guests winced. He smacked his hands zestfully when Doctor Grafton appeared carrying a huge, steaming tureen of stew. Deftly serving it in the topmost of the stack of dishes placed before him he explained: "This evening we will sample a rather unusual dish. Finding six rabbits penned behind the house, I asked and received Mr. Fairlee's permission to make use of them. This, ladies and gentlemen, is rabbit stew. I hope you like it, because I'm going to give you generous portions. Mr. Fairlee?"

The murder suspect accepted his plate silently. Cole began filling another.

"A most interesting animal, the rabbit," he went on. "Having decided upon this dish, I took the trouble to learn something about them. The rabbit—*Oryctolagus cuniculus*, of the family *Leporidae*—is, you may be surprised to learn, a rodent, which is distinguished by its peculiar incisor teeth. It is a first cousin to the rat, the gopher, the porcupine, the beaver, the hauty muskrat, the elegant chinchilla and the unfortunate guinea pig.... Miss Ashurst?"

Cole passed a plate to Fairlee's laboratory assistant and went on: "I was surprised to learn that the rabbit is found in a greater number of variations than any other mammal on earth except the dog. On the one hand there is the old English lop-eared rabbit which has ears six inches in width and measures twenty-three inches from tip to tip—truly a considerable amount of ears.... June?"

"Thank you, doctor," Miss Day said, taking her plate. "I'm Jane."

Cole went on blithely: "Inevitably, you are.... There is, on the other hand, the Pica rabbit, which is quite small and has no tail. There is also the Angora, prized especially for its fur, the Albino, and the Flemish, which is the biggest of all rabbits. Jane—I mean June?"

The second Miss Day took her helping of rabbit stew and Cole continued: "The rabbit must not be confused with the hare. It is distinguished from the hare by its smaller size, its shorter ears and feet, the absence of black on the ears, its gray color, the fact that its young are born naked and blind, and also because it lives in burrows.... Mr. Vaill, please.

"Very prolific, the rabbit. It begins to breed at the age of six months, breeds from four to eight times a year, each time producing three to eight young, and lives seven or eight years. Each rabbit therefore, in the course of its life-time, becomes approximately two hundred rabbits, barring accidents, such as this dinner... Yours, Mr. Morehouse."

IN SPITE of themselves, the guests were listening to Cole's happy discourse with rapt attention.

"Being so prolific," Cole went on, "it was practically inevitable that the rabbit, which originally inhabited the western half of the Mediterranean, should soon spread over the entire globe. Besides being made into stew, as at present, the rabbit may also be roasted, curried, and jugged—one variety of the jugged rabbit being *hassenphef-fer*. Rabbits, furthermore, ladies and gentlemen, are not only eaten but worn.... Chief Wellsmore?"

The chief took his plate with an expression of complete wonderment.

"Rabbit fur is the most popular low-priced fur. Furriers call it cony, but it is known under literally several hundred names. You can buy any one of a long list of furs, and still get rabbit. I was amazed to learn how many rabbits we humans consume in the form of adornment. From Australia alone some seventy million rabbit skins are shipped annually.... Mr. Blake? Now for myself. I can hardly wait."

Homer Morehouse asked slowly: "Did you say this stew was made from the rabbits kept in this back yard?"

"Why not?" Cole asked. "If something weren't done with them the place would soon be simply flooded with bunnies." He was filling his own plate. "You are proba-bly now aware, gentlemen, that your felt hats are made of rabbit fur—also your derbies. Forty or fifty skins make a dozen hats. Well, enough of talking about rabbits. Let's eat them."

Hesitancy was evident on the part of the guests, but Cole went at his plate with zest. "Delicious!" he exclaimed. Looking around the table, he asked eagerly: "What do you think of it, Miss Ashurst? June, Jane, whichever you are, or both of you, do you like it? Very tender, don't you think, Mr. Fairlee? Delightful for a change, Chief, wouldn't you say? Marvelous flavor, eh, Mr. Vaill?"

"It—it is good," Celia Ashurst answered.

"Very nice, Doctor," said Jane Day.

"Very nice," June Day echoed.

Fairlee observed: "I—I'm not very hungry, I'm afraid."

"Never," Wellsmore opined, "tasted rabbit before. Not bad."

"A little," said Steven Vaill, "like chicken."

Cole said: "Delicious! I didn't dream Doctor Grafton was such a talented cook. Mr. Morehouse, you're not eating."

Morehouse jerked up. "Don't! For God's sake, don't touch this stuff! It will kill you!"

Cole calmly spooned a generous helping into his mouth. "What in the world are you alarmed about, Mr. Morehouse? You sent these rabbits to your sister as a gift, and for eating purposes. It doesn't taste deadly at all."

Morehouse stifled a dismayed shout. He rushed to the window. He peered across the grounds, at the rabbit cage. Cole said calmly: "Don't you believe me? It's empty, isn't it? Really delicious stew." Morehouse jerked back. No one but Cole was eating now, but Cole was eating ravenously. Morehouse shouted in a frenzy: "It's poison! It's certain death! Doctor Cole, for God's sake, stop!"

Cole put down his spoon. "What Mr. Morehouse really means, Chief," he said calmly to the staring Wellsmore,

THE CASE OF THE SILENT GIANTESS 239

"is that Ronald Fairlee is not guilty of murdering his wife, but Homer Morehouse is guilty of murdering his sister in order to acquire the tidy sum of fifty thousand dollars."

Wellsmore sprang up to blurt: "By God, if that's so—"

MOREHOUSE KICKED his chair away. He stumbled around the table, lurched out of the room. He was running crazily along the hall when Cole sprinted after him. Morehouse slammed out the entrance, kept running. Cole shouted: "Stop him, Brick!" Kelly was already away from the Duesenberg's wheel, diving after the fleeing man.

Morehouse glimpsed him, desperately swerved away. Cole sprang, dropped directly into Morehouse's path. Morehouse struck out wildly, blindly. Cole took a stiff jolt on the jaw, poised on toe-tips, slammed a left, then a right, between Morehouse's eyes. Morehouse sprawled down. Glittering gunmetal twinkled. Cole grabbed at a whisking revolver.

He lunged on Morehouse. A frantic struggle rustled the grass. The gun whipped out, then down between Cole's and Morehouse's bodies. Abruptly a muffled explosion sounded. A smell of scorched clothing wafted into the air. Wellsmore, Blake, Kelly stared appalled. Neither Morehouse nor Cole was moving. It was Cole who pulled up.

"Anybody hit?" he asked. "Morehouse wasn't. I'm glad of that. He deserves the chair."

Suddenly Wellsmore and Blake were gripping Morehouse's arms, dragging him. Cole extended the revolver to the chief, saying: "You'll want that. He must have used it to kill Alice." He went in first into the house, entering the library.

Ronald Fairlee had hurried from the dining-room, was staring incredulously. Celia Ashurst and Steven Vaill had a hysterical, hopeful look in their eyes. The Misses Day were unperturbed. Cole stood by while Wellsmore and Blake maneuvered the sobbing Morehouse into the room. They forced Morehouse into a chair—he slumped.

"You'll get a confession, I'm sure," Cole told them. "In case any of you ate any of the stew, let me reassure you. The rabbits formerly in the pen—those sent to his sister by Morehouse—are now at my sanitarium. Those dedicated to the stew were purchased today and are quite innocuous. Mrs. Fairlee—"

"Wait a minute!" Wellsmore blurted. "Morehouse was in Europe at the time his sister died. How can he be responsible for her death?"

"He murdered her as surely as though he had shot her in the heart," Cole answered. "The logic is simple. Fairlee didn't murder his wife—I've been sure of that from the start. No one else in the house had a motive. Therefore, someone outside the house. The only possibility was Morehouse. Morehouse didn't commit the crime personally, so he did it indirectly. His agent must have been one of his gifts—gifts that began coming probably when he first determined on his plan, to prepare the way for the rabbits. Living rabbits, Chief, are the instruments of murder."

Wellsmore snarled: "How the hell could they be?"

"There is one more interesting fact about rabbits," Cole went on. "Morehouse knew it long ago, somehow, and I learned it today because logic forced me to the answer. Just as rats succumb to certain poisons to which man is immune, rabbits are immune to a poison which is deadly to man—arsenic.

"Sprinkle generous quantities of arsenic on lettuce. Feed it to rabbits. The rabbits eat it, but do not die. The arsenic remains in their systems, impregnating their flesh. Made into stew, they become a deadly dish. The fact is simple to prove. By killing the rabbits remaining from the shipment Mr. Morehouse admittedly sent, and analyzing their tissues, we'll find arsenic. You have your man, Chief—and I'm still hungry."

Cole reached for his coat, hat and stick. "Chief you and Blake are going to be busy with Mr. Morehouse, aren't you? Mr. Fairlee, there is an excellent inn a short way down the road—I'm sure you'll enjoy having dinner there. June, Jane, Celia, Steve, Mary—it's still a party, and it's waiting for us."

Cole smiled as, steering Fairlee to the door, he noted a new confidence in the chemist's eyes. "We shall all have," Cole said with a chuckle, "a toothsome vegetable plate."

THE CASE OF THE QUEEN'S HEADSMAN

ONE BY ONE THEY DISAPPEARED,
ONLY TO TURN UP DECAPITATED
CORPSES GARBED IN THE RUFFLED
VELVETS OF ELIZABETHAN
ENGLAND. WHAT WAS THE WEIRD
SECRET LURKING IN THE STONE
CORRIDORS OF WHITEHALL,
THAT DANK REPLICA OF THE
TUDOR COURT? WHAT MAD
MURDER SCHEME HAD HATCHED
ITSELF IN THE WARPED BRAIN OF
THE WOMAN WHO INSISTED SHE
WAS THE LIVING ELIZABETH THE
QUEEN?

CHAPTER ONE
HEADS SHALL FALL

DOCTOR CARTER COLE, striding across the luxurious library, paused abruptly. The humorous twinkle left his piercing eyes, his head lifted with a start, his tapered body stiffened. As a psychiatrist of vast experience, he had long ago become inured to biological and mental horrors, but his first glimpse of the two ghastly objects on the mantelpiece caught him unprepared.

"Good Lord!" he said softly.

Two human heads rested there, side by side, on the cleanly severed stumps of their necks. Their horrified eyes were staring at Cole, their white faces twisted into fixed expressions of suffering—two bodyless beings whose features preserved the agony of death by decapitation.

Cole glanced reprovingly at the agitated young man at his side. When he had been summoned from the complex duties of directing his famous Long Island sanitarium by young Metcalfe's urgent telephonic plea, "A matter of life and death!" to this ground-floor apartment on East Fifty-seventh Street, Manhattan, Cole had scarcely expected to be greeted by two severed human heads staring implacably from the mantelpiece.

"Is this why," he now asked Herbert Metcalfe quietly, "you asked me to come here? And if it is," he added, "what does it mean? I think an explanation is in order."

There on the bed lay the body—
and the head had vanished!

Metcalfe answered nervously: "It is startling, isn't it? Horrible. But the heads are wax, Doctor Cole. That's all. Wax."

COLE STUDIED them. The head on the right was that of a middle-aged man, partly bald, of aristocratic mein—a man, obviously, of breeding, talent and integrity. That on the left was the head of a pretty girl in her early twenties. At first glance they had seemed dismayingly real. Stepping closer, with intent scrutiny, Cole saw that both were indeed artfully fashioned models. A dry smile playing upon his lips, he took them into his hands. Metcalfe's breath caught, his eyes closed revulsively.

From the corner of the library came a tinkle of glass, as a second man poured himself a generous shot of brandy. Cole had been introduced to him at the door—Doctor Jerome Lanne, whose home this was. Lanne swallowed the liquor with a gasp. Metcalfe took a deep, steadying breath. Cole, replacing the heads on the mantel, observed: "Excellent pieces of work. Most lifelike—or deathlike. Well?"

Jerome Lanne strode close. His strained eyes twitched in his thin, haggard face. He said breathlessly: "This—this devilish thing has unnerved us. Surely you can understand that. The man's head was delivered by messenger yesterday. No word—no explanation. Just the head, in a box."

"Surprising, at least," Cole remarked.

"The second came this evening. Whoever sent them"— Lanne's thin hands wagged bewilderment—"and why"— another baffled gesture—"we don't know what it means. Herb telephoned you at my suggestion, Doctor Cole. Of course we both know of you by reputation, and this seems to be a case demanding—" Lanne became inarticulate.

Herbert Metcalfe explained. "I am a protege of Doctor Lanne; he is sending me through medical school. I still have a year to go. I live here. There is a special—a very special reason why I am consulting you, Doctor Cole. The whole ghastly thing—"

Because Metcalfe joined Lanne's abject silence, Cole asked quietly: "Why should these two heads affect you so? Are the faces familiar?"

Lanne blurted: "The man's head—it's Doctor Lewis Rutledge. He and I shared a fine practise. He lived here— had his office here, as I have. He was a friend of many years standing. The girl—Doris Lyon, his secretary. You know, Doctor Cole—surely, you read in the newspaper—the horrible way they died."

Cole's fine eyebrows arched. He was indeed familiar with all the published details of the case. They had provided the dailies with banner headlines and the police with a baffling puzzle.

The body of Doctor Rutledge had been discovered in a pile of melting snow on South Street, a wide thoroughfare flanking the East River near the point of Manhattan. Doris Lyon's remains had come to light two mornings later on a slope of Riverside Park, overlooking the Hudson. In both cases the severed heads lay nearby; both bodies had been found clad in costumes of the Elizabethan period.

"The police," Cole answered, "thought Doctor Rutledge and the girl had been attending a masquerade party or taking part in a theatrical performance, but a thorough check exploded that theory. There hadn't been any masquerade party, public or private, in New York or anywhere near it, and no play of the period had been presented. Strange, those Elizabethan costumes. These waxen heads are even stranger. You have informed the police?"

"No!" Young Metcalfe looked terrified. "Doctor Cole, you've investigated a number of strange cases, but I've not called you here to solve a mystery. I want your advice as a psychiatrist—your advice, that's all. Do you understand?"

"Not quite," Cole answered.

Metcalfe's gaze grew intense. "The question of *who* sent these heads to us, Doctor Cole, and why, is beside the point. We don't know whether they were intended for Doctor Lanne or myself, because there was no name on the packages, only the address and the apartment number. But that doesn't matter either. Let the police find the murderer— that's their business, not ours, nor yours, Doctor Cole. I want you to answer a question for me—a vital question."

"Yes?"

Metcalfe forced it out, his eyes glinting with anxiety. "Does the fact that somebody sent us these wax heads— somebody, no matter who it is—show that person is insane?"

"Go on."

"And if it does, Doctor Cole"—Metcalfe was making a desperate effort to control himself—"if it does, is that type of madness inheritable?"

"Is that all?"

Metcalfe swallowed in agony. "I've got to know the truth—the stark truth. It means everything to me. My whole life depends on it. For God's sake, tell me the facts!"

"You know, then," Cole said quietly, "who sent you these heads of the dead."

"No!" Metcalfe shot out.

"What?" Cole protested. "You don't know?"

"No!"

"Then why," Cole asked gently, "are you so anxious concerning the mental condition of the person who sent them?"

Metcalfe's lips stiffened. Doctor Lanne made a dismayed gesture. Into the tense hush broke the clatter of the telephone bell. Lanne strode to the instrument in the corner. Cole kept a silent, reproving scrutiny on Metcalfe, until, striding back, Lanne said: "An emergency call. I—I hope you'll give Herb the full benefit of your wide experience, Doctor Cole. The uncertainty is more than he can endure. I'm sorry but I must go." Lanne thrust into coat and hat, hurried out.

SILENCE RETURNED to the library as Metcalfe shrank under the stare of the two waxen heads on the mantelpiece. Cole answered the pleading of his blinking eyes with: "I can't possibly answer your questions, can't undertake a diagnosis with so little information. If you want the truth there is only one way to find it—a careful mental examination of the patient. But you say you do not know who sent the heads."

Cole's lips curved wryly. "I never accept a case on such an unsatisfactory basis. I must have complete confidence. Under the circumstances, there's nothing I can do—except give you a friendly warning."

"I beg of you—"

"The police," Cole interrupted firmly, "are completely at a loss to account for the deaths of Doctor Rutledge and Miss Lyon. These heads are important evidence. If you withhold what you know about them, Mr. Metcalfe, it may bring about disastrous complications. I might sympathize with you, if I knew more of the circumstances, but as matters stand—"

"But—it must mean something—the sending of the heads!" Metcalfe implored. "They might be a warning—a warning that either Doctor Lanne or myself is marked to die the same death as Doctor Rutledge and his secretary. *Is* it an insane act? I tell you, if I don't learn the truth, I'll—"

"But," Cole pressed, "you don't know who sent the heads. Yet you are beside yourself with worry for that person—"

"No, I—don't know."

Cole bowed. "Perhaps another psychiatrist will advise you. Good-night."

He left Herbert Metcalfe swallowing. In the vestibule he slipped into his Chesterfield, tilted his black Homburg to a jaunty angle. He had his hand on the doorknob when a buzzer sounded. Cole opened the door to find a uniformed attendant proffering a brown parcel.

The dimensions of the wrapped package aroused Cole's curiosity. "I'll take it," he said. "Who brought it?" As he sensed its weight he noticed it bore no name—merely the street address and apartment number.

"Telegraph messenger, sir," the attendant answered. "If you want the boy back, I'm afraid he's gone."

COLE CLOSED the door, stepped back into the library in time to meet Metcalfe on his way to answer the door. At sight of the package, Metcalfe's face went white. He took a recoiling step as Cole placed it on a table. Cole snapped the cord, peeled off paper, pried the cover from a box. Removing wadded tissue, he saw the head.

He took it up slowly, while the two others on the mantelpiece seemed to watch with mocking smiles. This was the head of a man. The hair was grizzled, the features firm, the brown eyes staring, tortured. The mouth was twisted with pain, the stump of the neck a clean, crimson cut. Carefully Cole placed it on the mantel with the others. A choking cry broke from Metcalfe's lips as Cole turned back.

"Who," Cole asked, "is the third victim?"

"Chamberlin—Mark Chamberlin," Metcalfe mouthed. "God! Only tonight—a few hours ago—I was speaking to him on the phone. He can't—he can't be—"

Carter Cole became briskly impatient. "Look here, Metcalfe. Whether or not you choose to inform the police is your affair. If you want to risk ruining your career, of going to prison for concealing evidence, of making yourself an accessory after the fact of murder, very well. But, as you say, these heads may be a warning sent you by a homicidal maniac."

Metcalfe stood stricken. Cole murmured, "Your telephone, if I may," and went to the instrument in the corner. While Metcalfe continued to stare aghast at the three heads on the mantel, Cole dialed the number of his sanitarium. The cool, efficient voice of one of his twin secretaries responded.

Quietly, so young Metcalfe could not hear, Cole said: "June, I want all the information you can get concerning one Herbert Metcalfe, medical student, protégé of Doctor Jerome Lanne of East Fifty-seventh Street. I'll call back later."

"Yes, Doctor," Miss Day answered, "but I'm Jane."

"You're always the other one," Cole sighed, "but it no longer seems to matter. If I keep trying to tell you apart I'll soon be an inmate of my own institution. In any case, Jane or June, I want that information quickly."

"Yes, Doctor."

Cole hung up and immediately dialed another number, that of the famous, eccentric, medical examiner of New York City, Doctor Morse.

"What is it now, old boy?" Morse's gruff growl demanded when he came on the line.

"When and where was the third decapitated body found, Doctor," Cole asked, "clad, I presume, as the others were, in Elizabethan costume?"

"The third, old boy? There isn't any third," Morse answered. "Just two, you know."

Cole's eyes sharpened. "In that case you'd best hold yourself ready for a hurry-up call. The third beheaded corpse will certainly be found soon. Don't say I didn't warn you. Good-night." He heard an astonished gasp as the connection broke.

Metcalfe started and whirled as Cole crossed and touched his arm. His breath beat uncontrollably as Cole remarked: "If you still don't know who sent the heads, I'll be going." The other's numb lips seemed unable to manage an answer. Cole bowed, repeated "Good-night," and strode to the entrance.

THE APARTMENT was located at the rear of a court. In the driveway circling from the street sat Cole's massive Duesenberg. He slipped into the front seat beside the stocky, red-headed young man at the wheel. Brick Kelly was the handyman at the sanitarium, Cole's strong-arm assistant when engaged upon investigations of matters mysterious.

"I wonder how it feels to be beheaded, Brick," Cole said casually.

Kelly's eyes bugged out.

"Let's," Cole suggested, "go back home and wait until a certain gentleman turns up with his head neatly and permanently sliced from his body."

"When you talk like that," Kelly said earnestly, "home sounds good to me. I can see you're all ready to mix into another one of those screwy cases." He sighed and swung the Duesenberg through an archway, turned twice, mounted the Queensboro Bridge. After a brief struggle through congested traffic on the Brooklyn side, he opened up on the broad cement turnpike which led past the sanitarium, home of his employer's more than a thousand deranged patients.

Cole sat silent, musing over the waxen heads, until the sanitarium gate cut a pattern in the headlamp shafts. Kelly kicked the brakes, leaned forward tensely and said, "Geez!"

"What the devil is it, Brick?"

Kelly swallowed audibly. The gate was a high, formidable barrier, securely locked, never opened except on signal. It was part of the high spiked fence strung with barbed wire which completely enclosed the sanitarium grounds and made prisoners of its inmates. Now Kelly had slammed to a stop ten feet short of it. Tightening muscles lifted him as he moaned: "Home don't look so good to me after all, Doc!"

The strained horror in Kelly's tone urged Cole from the car. In a moment he was stooping, with astonished exasperation, over a body which lay directly in front of the gate. It was clad in the silken, beruffled garb of another day—an Elizabethan court costume. Turned toward Cole was its glistening, crimson stump of a neck. The head lay only a few feet away. No tortured grimace marred its expression; the eyes were closed as though in sleep for this was no sculptor's replica but a thing of flesh—and blood. And its features were that of the third waxen head.

"The name," Cole murmured grimly, "is Chamberlin."

CHAPTER TWO
THE MAKER OF
THE HEADS

TWO HOURS later Carter Cole stepped into the office of Inspector Brackett in police headquarters in Center Street. He found the quizzical, vandyked medical examiner, Doctor Morse, here before him.

"I've been waiting to see you, old boy," Morse greeted him. "I haven't spilled the beans yet, but how did you know beforehand that the third body was going to turn up? Very curious."

"May I impose upon our long-standing friendship," Cole countered, "and withhold that information until a little later?"

"This beheading bee," Morse parried, "isn't the work of one of your inmates, is it?"

"Certainly not! I admit that finding the third body at my gate might lead one to think so, but the body was outside, so none of my patients could have managed it. Anyway, it would be a bit unusual for even a homicidal maniac to drag the body of his victim back home with him as a cat drags a dead mouse. Furthermore, all my patients are nice people. Look here, Doctor. Do me a further favor. Don't mention to anyone, until later, that I knew a third body was about to turn up."

"Might become rather embarrassing," Morse rumbled, "but I'll risk it for a pal." He smiled at Cole sardonically as he ambled out.

Cole picked up the inspector's telephone and called the sanitarium, asked briefly of the Day twin who answered: "Have you the report on Herbert Metcalfe?"

"Yes, Doctor." It came with characteristic efficiency. "The Physician's Exchange gave me the name of Doctor Lanne's hospital; the hospital knew Metcalfe's medical school; Doctor Hartman of the faculty told me something about him; and I learned the rest through your friends, Mr. Falk of the credit association and Mr. Gregory, the investigator for the Rocky Mountain Insurance Company."

"Let's have it!"

Miss Day went on to say that Doctor Lanne had known Metcalfe from the latter's boyhood. Metcalfe, who had been fatherless and motherless for ten years, might have been penniless without Lanne's generous assistance. Lanne was devoted to the cause of giving Metcalfe a medical education, and the young man had proved himself to be an ambitious student with fine possibilities. "He is engaged, against the wishes of her father," Miss Day continued, "to Miss Lyda Sutherland, a young sculptress. She is estranged from her parents, who live on Fifth Avenue at—"

"Sculptress!" Cole exclaimed. "I want her address." He jotted it down—a number on East Ninth Street—and added that of her parents. "To you, Jane," he said heartily, "my compliments."

"Thank you, Doctor," the girl said, "but—"

"You're June," Cole put in. "I don't know why the devil I don't call you both Beulah and be done with it."

HE LEFT headquarters, returned to his seat beside Brick Kelly in the waiting Duesenberg, and directed him to drive to the address of Miss Lyda Sutherland.

"I shouldn't like to be on the homicide squad at a time like this, Brick," Cole mused, as Kelly navigated the car northward with skilful despatch. "Trying to find a clue to the car that dumped that body at my gate is worse than useless. Further complications arise from the fact that two police forces are now at odds on the case. That may give me a little time before I'm caught between Long Island Scylla and the Center Street Charybdis.

"Inspector Brackett is losing his hair trying to trace the Elizabethan costumes worn by the decapitated cadavers. He's getting nowhere with a great celerity. There's only one lead. Chamberlin was a lawyer and a close friend of the first victim, Rutledge. And Brackett keeps saying over and over again, 'Whoever is behind this is nuts'."

"I wish," Kelly moaned, "you'd stay out of it, Doc. I don't want you to find out how it feels to get your conk carved off."

"I'm told," Cole observed, "it isn't at all bad—in fact, quite painless. In the old days, in merry England, Brick, it was a distinguished manner in which to die."*

———————————

*   Beheading as a mode of capital punishment is believed to have been introduced into England from Normandy by William the Conqueror. Waltheof, Earl of Northumberland, was the first to suffer this method of inflicting the death penalty, in 1076. Decapitation was a punishment usually reserved for offenders of high rank, and from the Fifteenth Century onward the victims of the ax include some of the highest personages in the kingdom. An ancient block and ax, upon which many nobles died, are preserved in the armory of the Tower of London.—F.C.D.

In a few minutes the car was in front of the Ninth Street address. Cole got out and went into the lobby to find a mosaic of mail boxes there, including one bearing the name of Lyda Sutherland. Cole did not touch her call button, but pushed another. A deluded tenant obligingly tripped the electric lock for him and he went in, climbing three flights of stairs, until he heard raised voices ringing out of the girl's apartment. One was feminine and tearful, the other, Metcalfe's, strained and anxious.

"I won't tell you!" the girl was protesting. "Not even you… Don't look at me so strangely. You make me afraid."

"I am afraid—for you," Metcalfe retorted "I'm thinking only of you, Lyda. I don't understand why you don't trust me. If you'd only—"

"I'm not going to tell anyone," the girl interrupted. "Not anyone! You've asked me again and again—it's more than I can stand. If you do it once more I'll go mad!"

A strained silence was broken by quick footfalls and Cole bounded up the next flight, was out of sight on the fourth-floor landing when a door snapped open. He toed down silently, watching Herbert Metcalfe's angrily rapid descent. In her room the girl was sobbing. Cole waited until the house-entrance catch clicked, then he went to the apartment door Metcalfe had left open, and quietly stepped through.

THE GIRL had flung herself on a couch, pressing a handkerchief to her eyes. The studio, Cole saw, was tastefully furnished, colorful. On a pedestal near the north window sat a half-completed bust. Other examples of the girl's work stood on the sills, hung on the walls. Cole found them excellent. One, on a smaller stand, was covered by a linen cloth. Seeing the outline of a head through the fabric,

Cole moved toward it. At the sound of his footsteps the girl looked up, stopped him with a glance.

"Oh!" she said. She drew herself up—a very pretty, very intelligent-looking young woman, Cole saw. "What are you doing here? What do you want?"

"I'm Doctor Carter Cole."

"Well? Look at me." Her eyes flashed scornfully. "Give me your shrewdest, most professional once over, Doctor Cole. It's perfectly absurd that Herb should have called you—but here I am. Just how mad am I?"

"Offhand," Cole answered gravely, "I should say not at all." He smiled. "Don't be too hard on him because he's so solicitous. After all, it's because he's deeply in love with you. And he doesn't understand about—the heads."

The girl went rigid. "You'd better go."

"I'm not," Cole said quietly, "an officer of the law. My professional standing grants me certain ethical privileges. Confidences to me may remain inviolate even on the witness stand. Since I had a headless body spilled almost into my lap this evening, I feel rather involved. I suggest you tell me—"

"I'll tell you nothing! If you don't leave immediately I'll—"

"You have," Cole observed, looking around, "a rare talent. I should regret your getting into serious difficulties with the law. It might ruin your entire career."

CARTER COLE'S hand had strayed to the linen cloth covering the head. He was lifting it gently when the girl flung herself upon him with a choking cry of fury. She struck his arm down, thrust him back—but not before Cole caught a brief glimpse of the head. He saw, in that split-second look, that it was a colored waxen image, its features twisted with torment. He recognized the face of Doctor Jerome Lanne.

"Get out!" The girl's small fists pounded on his chest. "Get out, get out!" Her frantic attack drove him back. "If you don't get out I'll call the police!"

"I shouldn't advise that, Miss Sutherland," Cole said quietly. "Not until you rid yourself somehow, of that head. But perhaps you were just about to send it to Doctor Lanne's apartment?" Cole smiled affably, bowed, backed into the hall.

He had left the girl standing transfixed with terror, no sound came from the studio while he went down the stairs. When he got in the car beside Brick Kelly he halted the red-head's thrust at the starter pedal. "Not yet," Cole said quietly. "No woman who is as worked up as Lyda Sutherland can keep from raising hell. Let's wait."

He kept his eyes on the apartment-house entrance. "Is it news to you, Brick," he asked after a moment's interval, "that women are insane in their complete irresponsibility toward society and the law? True, I assure you. Because a woman's mind is completely subservient to her emotions. Legal right and wrong mean nothing to her; but her loves and loyalties mean everything. When a woman puts a bullet in her husband, harbors her public-enemy lover from the police, lies herself black in the face on the witness stand to defend her son, she is doing what she considers to be utterly right, law or no law. When you stop to think of it, it's rather terrifying."

"I keep away from women," Kelly said.

"In the light of that observation," Cole suggested, "you may profitably study Miss Lyda Sutherland." The apartment door had opened. The girl emerged warily, clutching a bundle under her arm. "It contains," Cole murmured, "a head—the waxen likeness of a man in whose shoes I should not care to be."

The girl gave the Duesenberg a searching scrutiny but its darkness shielded Cole. She started toward the taxi station at the corner. When she was beside the car, Cole slipped out. Startled, the girl stopped.

"Miss Sutherland," Cole said gently, "if you take a taxi, I shall be able to follow you with no difficulty whatever. I shall learn in that way where you're going, and once you're there I shall probably bully my way in. You see, I'm involved in the case because the third corpse was dumped at my very front door. I'm determined to learn more about the waxen heads. Suppose we both go about our purposes in a forthright manner. May I offer you my car?"

"Oh!"

"It's really the only sensible thing to do, isn't it? It'll save time and the inconvenience of playing hound and rabbit. You'll find my car quite comfortable."

The girl hesitated; then, with a defiant lift of her chin, she entered the Duesenberg. Kelly looked back expectantly. She hesitated again, then gave him the Fifth Avenue address which Cole already knew. Kelly angled expertly into the Avenue, drove north briskly.

THE OPEN darkness of Central Park lay on the left, massive apartment houses towered on the right. Not even after Kelly braked at the proper number did Lyda Sutherland speak. She simply got out.

Cole followed her into a cavernous, somber foyer furnished with the faded, dust-catching appurtenances of a generation ago. They entered an automatic elevator which, Cole surmised, was private. It drifted upward a long time; at last halted. Cole accompanied the girl into

an ominously murky vestibule lighted by tapers burning
in a standing candelabrum. Its furnishings were the heavy
royal gilt and plush of the Elizabethan period. Cole felt
he had been transported backward through centuries to
Tudor England.

Two men's voices were faintly audible through heavy
drapes hanging in one corner.

The girl said: "You may wait here, Doctor Cole."

She disappeared through the drapes. Cole caught a
glimpse of a long corridor which might have been part of
an ancient castle. He stood in silence, waiting. The hush
was broken by the girl's voice, raised and tense. Cole heard
her urge frantically: "Take it—take it away! I didn't know
what I was doing. I didn't realize until tonight, when Herb
told me, who they were for. It's an insane thing. I think
you're all mad!"

A man's weary tones protested. "Be quiet, Lyda, your
mother might hear. What is it? What are you saying?
Dane, what does she mean?"

A younger man's voice snapped: "I'll not forgive you
for this, Lyda—saying that here. He doesn't know. He's
ill—don't you realize that? You're exciting him. You had
no right to come here."

"No right!" the girl cried. "No right, when—"

The voices ceased. Cole realized that during the past hour
Lyda Sutherland had been fighting down an emotional
storm. Now, after its first burst, she remembered his presence. Footfalls were approaching along the corridor. The
drapes whisked aside and a young man stepped into the
vestibule. At sight of him Cole took a deep breath.

He was wearing a resplendent costume of the Elizabethan period, all colorful silk and ruffles, complete with a
gleaming court sword.

"Doctor Cole, my sister should not have permitted you to come here," this apparition volunteered. "She's distraught—she doesn't know what she's doing. We don't wish anyone to intrude upon our privacy. Anyone!" With one lace-cuffed hand he gestured to the open elevator. "Good-night, Doctor Cole."

He turned at once, with a rattle of his sword, a swish of his cape, and vanished through the drapes. Cole listened a moment to the click of his heels, then with wry determination he stepped into the corridor.

Candles in wall-sconces lighted it. The doors were ponderous slabs, strap-bound, set into deep stone frames. One of them was standing open, emitting a flickering gleam. The amazingly costumed young man marched through it. Cole strode ahead as an animated conversation began in the lighted room. His appearance in the arched doorway halted the beginning of an altercation.

He looked into a room with patterned ceiling, hung with tapestries, lighted by candelabra. It was royally rich but chill as a dungeon cell. The girl was standing beside a huge carved bed, apprehensively silent. An emaciated man was lying beneath silken spreads, his eyes shining with alarm. The younger man turned to face Cole. In his hands he held the bundle the girl had brought—the wrapped head Cole knew to be a likeness of Doctor Jerome Lanne. Startled, he thrust it out of sight behind his cape. For a moment Cole was the focus of startled stares.

"I beg pardon for the further intrusion," he said firmly. "Regardless of the social niceties, I have no intention of leaving just yet. Forgive me, but I must insist on seeing this through."

The girl said automatically: "This is Doctor Carter Cole. My father, Hugh Sutherland—and my brother, Dane."

THEIR ONLY acknowledgments were continued stares. Dane Sutherland stood rigid. Hugh Sutherland lay breathing hard, the veins in his neck pulsing rapidly. The girl's eyes were pleading.

"This matter involves me considerably—and deliberately," Cole went on. "Tonight a costumed, decapitated body was left at my sanitarium gate for no other reason than to entangle me in the case. Whoever placed it there, wishing me to meddle, is going to be thoroughly satisfied. After all, this is murder—"

Hugh Sutherland, his breath coming in a rush, elbowed up on the bed. "Murder? Dane, what does he mean? Lyda, what is it? Are you quite sure your mother can't hear?"

Neither answered his questions. The girl was speechless with anxiety; the eyes of the costumed young man were a blazing challenge. "What is there to explain, Doctor Cole?" Dane Sutherland retorted.

Cole looked amazed. "Let's not bluff. The wax heads, including the one you are now holding behind your back, must be explained. Your costume, very similar to those in which the bodies were found, must be explained. This whole amazing layout"—he indicated the ancient room with a sweeping gesture—"must be explained. If you refuse to tell your story to me, then I must inform the police and they—"

"Don't do that!" Dane Sutherland blurted. "In God's name, don't! We had nothing to do with it. You can't drag us—"

"Stop!" his father broke in anxiously from the bed. "I told you she would hear. She's coming!"

Carter Cole heard footfalls in the hallway, light and gentle, yet approaching with a certain commanding deliberation. A musical rustle of silk accompanied them.

The sound obviously agitated Hugh Sutherland. His son looked around with quick anxiety. The girl caught Cole's hand firmly, tugged him away through the heavy drapes of a connecting doorway.

Looking back, Cole saw the son concealing the wrapped head under the heavy silken spread of the bed. The curtains dropped back, enveloping him and the girl in thick darkness. Lyda Sutherland stood motionless, her hand tight and cold on Cole's, her breath caught.

Past the edge of the curtain, Cole glimpsed the woman who appeared in the next room. She was tall, her eyes dark in a thin alabaster face that was cruel yet somehow compassionate. She too was garbed in regal garments of the Tudor period. She spoke in a low, throaty, commanding tone.

"God's death! Is the wish of your Queen not to be heeded? There has been unwonted talk here, disturbing the good Burghley. It frets me not a little that you do not remember he is sore ill. Let those who make him restless not forget I hold their lives in my hands. Away!"

"Be not too hard on them, Your Majesty," the man on the bed whispered. "I feel my strength returning hour by hour."

"Faugh!" the woman answered. "All my physicians have done you no benefit. My Lord. I am at the end of my patience. They will pay for it with their heads. Sleep now, Burghley. Let the room be darkened while you rest."

"As you wish, Your Majesty," Dane Sutherland murmured in a quavering tone.

Cole listened in amazement. Lyda Sutherland was tugging her hand from his. He brought his lips close to her ear, whispered: "Who in the world is that woman—what does this mean?"

A bitter answer came through the gloom. "She is Elizabeth, the Queen!" Then, suddenly, the girl snatched herself away.

A DOOR opened and closed quickly upon the candle-lighted hallway. Cole eased out, glimpsed the girl hurrying into a stairway in its depths. He followed rapidly down the stone flight, found himself in yet another cold passage that branched bewilderingly. As he passed a broad open archway he paused in astonishment. In the great, vaulted, taper-lighted room beyond, a score of men and women clad in Elizabethan costumes were waiting near an empty throne!

Cole hurried on. Stepping into a small room, he heard a faint whirring sound coming through a closed panel. It told him that an elevator was carrying the girl down. He was punching the button impatiently when quick steps sounded behind him. Dane Sutherland appeared, face anguished, eyes gleaming. He grimly seized Cole's arm.

"That's right—get out of here. Get out, and don't come back! If you tell the police about this, you'll destroy a good woman's life, expose her to ridicule before the whole world. If you do that, I'll make you pay for it! Get out!"

"A speech scarcely in keeping with the dignity of Queen Elizabeth's court," Cole murmured.

The young man tramped away, his sword clattering. Immediately the elevator appeared and Cole stepped in. It transported him in less than two minutes through more than three hundred years—from a period steeped in the must of the Renaissance to the brisk air of a modern street.

When he slid in beside Brick Kelly he asked quickly: "The girl—where did she go?"

"She hopped a cab, Doc. It went into the side-street. Not much chance of finding it now."

"Back to Doctor Lanne's place, Brick, and step on it."

Kelly made short work of the crosstown trip. When Cole left the Duesenberg on Fifty-seventh Street, his manner was impatient, tense. His ring at Lanne's apartment brought the doctor to the door and Cole strode into the library, pausing only to fix Herbert Metcalfe with a piercing gaze. He noted, without glancing at the mantel, that the three waxen heads were no longer there.

"Look here," he said bluntly. "I'm in what is technically known as a spot. Very soon the police are going to put me in a corner and ask me questions. They'll want to know how I knew beforehand that Mark Chamberlin's beheaded body was going to turn up. I have no patience with those who don't trust me. I'll tell them the truth and wash my hands of the whole bizarre business unless you come clean."

Metcalfe's face flushed. He turned to a desk, flapped open a checkbook, scribbled, tore off a leaf and proffered it to Cole. "There is your fee. I hope it's sufficient. As your client, I'm entitled to your confidence. I forbid you to divulge anything you've seen or heard. Professional ethics bind you. Now, Doctor Cole, that's all."

Cole nodded slowly. "I see. I'm being paid and dismissed."

"Exactly. Good-night."

"Please make allowances, Doctor," Lanne put in solicitously. "He's unreasonably anxious to protect someone very dear to him. He has excellent reason to believe she—that person—must be unbalanced. If the police should learn the truth, it will mean tragedy, but I know he must be mistaken and in spite of it all he needs your help. Please remain on the case and—"

"Miss Lyda Sutherland is not mad," Cole broke in, "but she appears to have implicated herself in murder." Lanne's jaw sagged. "You, Doctor, perhaps remember that in old

London citizens used to protect themselves from garroters lurking in the pea-soup fogs by wearing iron collars beneath their lace. I suggest you find a good blacksmith and have such a collar forged for yourself. Miss Sutherland has made an excellent wax likeness of you."

Cole smiled tartly into Lanne's and Metcalfe's stares. Very deliberately he tore the check across, then across again. He dropped the flakes into the wastebasket. Eyeing Metcalfe grimly, he said: "If you think for a moment I'm abandoning this case, you're sadly mistaken. I'm going to see it through, no matter whom it hurts. When I've finished, somebody will be going to the electric chair for three ruthless murders—that's a promise. Good-night to you, Mr. Metcalfe."

CHAPTER THREE
THE QUEEN'S SECRET

I N THE lobby of the Fifth Avenue apartment house, Cole spoke tartly over the house telephone. "Is that Mr. Dane Sutherland?"

"It is."

"This is Doctor Carter Cole. I am coming directly up. I suggest that you resign yourself to it. Please instruct the attendants down here to allow it."

His imperative manner obtained results.

Dane Sutherland spoke over the wire to an attendant and in a minute the elevator was lifting Cole to the fourteenth floor. He entered the vestibule to find the young man waiting, still clad in the resplendent court costume, and scowling forbiddingly.

"What do you want?" he challenged.

"Satisfaction, and lots of it," Cole retorted. "Specifically, a talk with your father. Let me remind you, you're in a decidedly ticklish position—as the present holder of the waxen image of a man apparently marked for death. Resisting me will only make the water hotter. Well?"

Dane Sutherland's jaw-muscles tightened. He turned without speaking, led Cole along the gloomy corridor. The room in which Hugh Sutherland lay was dark now and the son closed the heavy oaken door, began lighting the tapers. As the flickering gleam brightened, the man on the bed aroused from a restless doze. His haggard eyes fixed on Cole who drew up a chair and sat beside the bed.

A strained silence held until Dane Sutherland said resignedly: "I think—I think we'd better tell Doctor Cole about Mother."

Hugh Sutherland nodded slowly. "Yes—it's best. There's no man living better able to understand this strange situation than you, Doctor Cole. We've kept up this tragic pretense for years. I've pledged myself never to abandon it as long as my poor wife lives. It's her whole life—her happiness."

"She believes," Cole said gently, "that she is Queen Elizabeth?"

"Yes. Utterly and completely. Did you see her, Doctor—did you recognize her? When she was younger, she was one of the finest actresses the world has ever known. She became famous by playing the title role in *Elizabeth Regina* year after year. Surely you have heard of her—Adele Dane. A marvelous woman, Doctor Cole, who fought against the hardest adversity, who struggled every inch of the way for her career, until she became a figure of world renown."

"I remember seeing Adele Dane play Elizabeth when I was a boy," Cole answered. "An experience I shall never forget."

"Of course! I counted myself the most fortunate man in the world when she consented to marry me, Doctor. It wasn't until years later that her mind began to fail. The delusion began to grow slowly at first—that she was the woman she had so often portrayed on the stage. At last she became, in her own belief, the identical person of Queen Elizabeth. I knew it was madness, but in that madness she found happiness, and I was determined not to destroy it."

"A clear-cut case of paranoia," * Cole diagnosed. "And yours was a unique and courageous decision."

HUGH SUTHERLAND sighed. "I'm glad to hear you say that, because your life is devoted to curing mental ailments. My friends told me 'She is insane, she should be sent to an institution,' but I knew that would only tear down the imaginary world she'd built up for herself, make her infinitely less happy. My marriage pledge, Doctor Cole, was to love and cherish my wife until death do us part. I have done my utmost, by means of this elaborate, heart-rending pretense, to cherish the woman she became."

Cole nodded sympathetically.

---

* Paranoia is a type of mental derangement classified under schizophrenia (formerly called dementia praecox) which results from a splitting of the personality through an unsuccessful attempt of the individual to make adjustments necessary to his wellbeing. True paranoia is sometimes characterized, as in the present case, by fixed delusions of a grandiose type. It is believed the condition results from an inborn schizoid constitution, and possibly from over-protection of a child by its parents during the formative period. In lesser degree, it afflicts thousands—indeed, there are more paranoiacs, mildly afflicted, outside institutions for the insane than inside. The reader may find among his acquaintances certain persons who are extremely suspicious, cranky, unreasonable, over-poweringly ambitious, rather ruthless in gaining their ends, head-strong or hard to get along with, and always active. Paranoia may be indicated. Many paranoiacs have become great men, and have improved the world, while others have left only a trail of tragedy behind them. In every case the extreme paranoiac—indeed, almost every insane person—is seeking release and happiness and often, as again in the present case, has found it in his delusions which to him are completely real and satisfying.—F.C.D.

"I am a rich man. I've gladly spent hundreds of thousands of dollars in order to carry through Adele's illusion. I rebuilt these apartments to reproduce, as nearly as possible, Whitehall and some of the London state-buildings of the time, including the Tower. There are actors and actresses in constant attendance, portraying personages of the time. They speak in the Elizabethan manner, their costumes are perfectly made by my own tailors, every detail of everything is accurate. You were hurried from this room when Her Majesty entered, Doctor Cole, because we've never allowed the slightest suggestion of the modern world to intrude.

"My wife is Queen Elizabeth, this is her palace, we *are* her court."

"She spoke of you as Lord Burghley," Cole prompted.

"Yes. I am her Principal Minister, her Lord High Treasurer, her right hand. All the notable figures of Elizabeth's time are present. One of our dear friends who understands, frequently comes to portray Robert Dudley, the Earl of Leicester, Master of Ordnance and Master of the Horse. Another becomes Lord Howard, the Queen's uncle and Lord of the Privy Seal. Another is Sir Thomas Smith, Principal Secretary of State. Another is Christopher Hatton, Captain of Her Majesty's Guard. My wife is living the life of Elizabeth as she herself wills it in every particular."

"Even—" Cole checked himself. He had been about to ask: "Even to the extent of warranting the deaths of those she considers traitorous to the Queen?" He inquired instead: "You knew Doctor Lewis Rutledge and his secretary, Miss Doris Lyon?"

Dane Sutherland's breath caught, but the father answered without hesitation. "Yes. Both of them aided me in this tragic pretense. Doctor Rutledge, who attended me some time ago as a physician, portrayed Thomas, Duke of Norfolk—"

"What!"

"Miss Lyon generously gave much of her time to act the part of Mary, Queen of Scots—"

"What!" Cole stared while Sutherland was silent. Then, forcing himself to seem casual he commented: "The Duke of Norfolk and Mary were both beheaded for high crimes against the true Elizabeth's state."*

A hard hand gripped Cole's shoulder. He straightened to confront Dane Sutherland. The son, eyes blazing, burst out: "I know what you're thinking—but it's not true. Mother had nothing to do with it. She's completely consumed by her delusion, yes—but she's a sweet, kindly woman, not a homicidal maniac. It's what I was afraid you would think— what everyone might think—that she's responsible, but I tell you it's not true!"

The outburst left the young man breathless. His conviction possessed him with an unreasoning fury. He stood. Cole noted with a chill, with one hand gripping the wire-bound hilt of his small-sword—a weapon which might, with one sharp slash, sever a human head from its body. Dane Sutherland realized his posture, jerked out of it.

---

* Thomas, Duke of Norfolk, was beheaded on June 2, 1572, for treason against Queen Elizabeth. His subversive activities were connected with Mary, Queen of Scots, who herself suffered the same penalty for the same crime on February 8, 1587. Elizabeth's duty to her state compelled her to sign the death warrant for another treasonist who stood high in her personal favor—Robert Devereaux, Earl of Essex, who died on the block February 25, 1601.—F.C.D.

Cole asked him quietly: "And Mark Chamberlin—what part did he play in the Queen's court?"

The young man smiled triumphantly. "The part of Sir Walter Raleigh—and Raleigh, you must remember, Doctor Cole, did not die on the block until after the true Elizabeth was in her grave."

"True," Cole mused, "quite true. Yet your father said a moment ago, 'My wife is living the life of Elizabeth as she herself wills it.' And you are desperately anxious to defend her. Why?"

The young man answered tightly: "Because she is innocent. Someone has done all this to make her appear guilty. The use of the block—the costumes—everything. Why, I don't know, but if the police find the connection it will destroy everything we've built up for her. She'll be ridiculed by the newspapers, she'll be thrown into an asylum for the insane. We've devoted our lives to making her happy, and now she's in danger of losing it all, but— God, I'll do anything to stop it!"

DANE SUTHERLAND stood trembling and again his right hand gripped hard on the hilt of his sword. Cole heard the door open and when he turned, amazement widened his eyes. The man, clad in colorful court attire, who had paused upon the point of entering the room was Doctor Jerome Lanne.

"For your sake, for her sake, I hope you're right," Cole told Dane Sutherland tersely. He stepped to the door, took Lanne's arm and closed the door after him. They went along the cold candle-lighted hallway into another room walled with plastered designs of heraldry.

Cole said tersely: "You heard all that. You're part of this world of make believe. You know the woman who believes she is Queen Elizabeth. I want the truth, Doctor. Is she capable of carrying her enactment of the character so far as to take the lives of her subjects—to kill the counterparts of those whom the real Elizabeth killed?"

Lanne paled. "As a Queen, she wouldn't wield the ax with her own hands. Would others do it for her, knowing it is all pretense? Of course not—impossible! Yet in her own mind, she's the absolute monarch. I've heard her say again and again, from the throne, 'Being a Queen and a Prince Sovereign, I am answerable to none for my actions but to Almighty God'—words once uttered by Elizabeth herself!"

" 'What the laws cannot do to his head'," Cole quoted, " 'my authority will do.' Elizabeth also said that."

Lanne shuddered, straightening. "But I don't believe it, Doctor Cole. How she might fare in the hands of the law, considering the evidence, I don't know, but I don't believe it. Yet, I must admit, I—I am afraid. Since Sutherland—Lord Burghley—took ill, she's several times promised the block to his physicians if they don't cure him. Though it's not my part in history, I'm one of them. Rutledge was another."

"What is Sutherland's ailment?"

"Auricular fillibration.* Incurable, as you know. Rutledge and I did everything possible, and since his death I've done

---

* In auricular fillibration, the auricle chambers of the heart do not function with their normal rhythmic contractions because they are subject to a barrage of irregular stimuli, as a result of which the heart is in a constant state of incoördination, beating at a rate of from 120 to 180 times per minute. It is a dangerous condition, producing great disability, and brings about the death of the victim within ten to twenty years at the most, though the condition can be controlled somewhat by treatment with digitalis and by quiet living.—F.C.D.

my best, but Her Majesty frequently flies into a fury at me because 'Burghley' doesn't improve."

"And," Cole persisted, "was Rutledge particularly in the Queen's disfavor?"

Lanne's silken shoulders squared. "She promised him the worst punishments. It had nothing to do with what happened to him—I'm sure of it, but it was a serious matter."

"I think," Cole urged, "we'd best bring it to light."

Lanne hesitated a moment. "It was only a few days before Rutledge—died. I came here one evening to find him working frantically over Hugh Sutherland. Sutherland was on the point of death. He'd been having a siege of insomnia, due to his heart trouble, and he'd begged Rutledge for a sedative. Rutledge—it was his failing—was drunk. He gave Sutherland an overdose of phenobarbital and didn't realize it until too late."*

Cole nodded. "Serious. Treating a patient while under the influence of liquor is criminal malpractise."

"Understand, this must remain confidential between us. Sutherland would have died if I hadn't happened in at the right time, but we succeeded in reviving him. His condition

---

* Phenobarbital is the most commonly used sedative and anti-convulsive. It is a white crystalline powder given in solution. An overdose causes a toxic condition like that of heavy alcoholic intoxication, with a characteristic rash. The victim sinks into a deep coma marked by dangerous depression of the heart and lungs. Death is usually due to respiratory paralysis. Clinical records are not conclusive as to the amount of a fatal dose. Treatment consists of the use of a stomach pump, giving cardiac and vascular stimulants, infusing normal saline with Fischer's solution, colonic irrigation and artificial respiration.—F.C.D.

was serious for several days afterward. Her Majesty—it's become a habit to speak of her like this—blamed Rutledge for it, rightly, of course. She denounced him before the whole court, swore to have his head. That means nothing—I insist it doesn't—but Rutledge's act of criminal malpractise might have sent him to prison if wind of it had gotten out."

"Still," Cole said quietly, "the Queen threatened Rutledge—Lord Norfolk—with losing his head. History says Norfolk died on the block—and Rutledge was decapitated."

"Cole! Even if Her Majesty had condemned him, no one would have carried out the sentence—I insist on that!"

Cole indicated the candle-lighted doorway. "In there," he said, "are two men who have devoted their lives and a huge fortune to preserving Adele Dane's delusion. Perhaps they—especially her son—would go that far if circumstances demanded it."

Lanne swallowed painfully. From Sutherland's room a feeble call came—"Essex! Essex!" Immediately Lanne turned, hurried back.

In cold dismay, Cole followed. At the oaken door he caught the physician's arm. "One moment. In this world of pretense you are—"

"Robert Devereaux, Earl of Essex."

Lanne stepped into the chill room, closed the door. Cole turned away in deep thought. In the vestibule he pressed the call-button, waited for the elevator. He was thinking intensely of the fourth waxen head—the head he had seen in the girl's studio, fashioned so artfully in the likeness of Doctor Jerome Lanne.

Half aloud Cole murmured: "In Sixteen One—if I remember rightly—Robert Devereaux, Earl of Essex, was beheaded for treason by warrant of Elizabeth the Queen."

CHAPTER FOUR
BLOOD ON THE BLOCK

COLE DISMISSED Kelly and entered the huge rambling building where his thousand deranged patients lived their unnatural existences. His executive offices were located far in the depths of a maze of labyrinthine hallways. The corridor floors were brightly polished for by day irrational men and women pushed huge wooden blocks, based with felt, from end to end of them interminably, the task easing their warped minds while burnishing the wood.

Tonight, as always, the quiet was disturbed by mournful moans and ecstatic shrieks from the maze of wards. Cole scarcely heard them nor did they disturb the poise of the two secretaries who were awaiting him.

The Misses Day, exactly alike in appearance, equally lovely and efficient, worked at Cole's side the remainder of the night. The manifold duties of directing the institution absorbed him. He paused only for hot coffee prepared by his assistant, Doctor Mary Grafton. But even while he worked, his mind was constantly busy with the strange aspects of the decapitation cases. Dawn was approaching when a call flickered in through the switchboard.

"Mr. Dane Sutherland, Doctor."

The son of the fancied Queen Elizabeth spoke rushingly over the wire. "Doctor Cole, you were right from the beginning. We should keep no secrets from you. You're able to understand this as no one else can, and we need your help. Please forgive me. Can you come back to Whitehall at once?"

"What's up?"

"I can't explain everything on the phone, but please remember always that my one thought has been to preserve my mother's happiness. Someone has been trying to destroy her. I've been fighting that person secretly. He's the one who is really guilty. I've no proof, only a suspicion. I've been trying to force a confession—and that's why I sent the wax heads."

"*You* sent them?"

"Yes, but—listen! The man I think guilty will be here tonight. We're facing a showdown and the truth must come out. No matter what happens, Doctor Cole, you must believe that the murders are in no way connected with her—with my mother. I need you, as a witness. I'll be waiting, Doctor."

"Coming!" Cole snapped. And as he rose, "I'm damned!" He crackled orders to the Misses Day. A minute later he was striding out the entrance of the sanitarium. The Duesenberg whirled out of the darkness and Cole climbed in beside Kelly, who was still buttoning his shirt. In a moment the heavy car was through the spiked gate, on the cement lane, heading once more toward Manhattan.

Oppressive darkness lay over New York. When they reached upper Fifth Avenue, Central Park was a vast murky hollow among towers in which few lights gleamed. The hush of the coming dawn enveloped the metropolis.

COLE HURRIED through the somber foyer, into the elevator. Upstairs in the vestibule the tapers in the candelabra were guttering low. The only door, leading into the corridor, was a formidable oaken barrier—bolted. Cole knuckled it. His repeated rap echoed hollowly in the depths beyond. Again and again he knocked, but no response came.

"Open up!" he called, and a click answered at last and the portal swung wide under the quavering hand of Hugh Sutherland.

The old man was clad in a long robe of royal scarlet velvet. He sagged against the wall, palsied, his eyes mirroring terror, his breath beating. The intensity of his agitation gave Cole pause.

"What the devil's the matter? Your son called me here. Where is he?"

"I've been asleep—under a sedative," Sutherland muttered. "I—I scarcely know what I'm doing. Doctor Cole, for God's sake, what can we do?"

"Where's Dane?"

Acute distress held the stricken man silent. Cole pushed impatiently past him. He looked into one after another of the rooms along the passage. All were dark; some were empty; in others men and women were asleep—the players hired by Sutherland to enact the parts of Elizabeth's court functionaries. Cole followed the curving stone stairway to the next lower floor. It was dark except for a few flickering tapers. The throne-room was deserted.

A swishing, rippling sound came up another curving flight; a scrubbing noise followed. Cole descended toward it. Only one gleam shone along the dark corridor, beneath the edge of a closed oaken door. The rhythmic brushing sound issued from beyond it. Cole released the latch, stepped through—and stopped short.

It was a deep room, chill and dank, completely bare except for the grisly object which sat in the center of its stone floor—a beheading block. Against the block a huge ax was leaning. Its six-foot handle was ornamented with rows of burnished brass nails. Its gleaming blade was almost two feet high, ten inches wide—and stained. Glistening crimson was blotted over it. Cole's thought flashed a chill through him: that this was a dungeon in the Tower of London where a sentence of death by beheading had just been executed.

The one man in the room froze at Cole's entrance. He was garbed in black. A heavy leather apron was tied about his thick waist. He was, Cole realized, the reincarnation of an Elizabethan headsman. His ancient broom, the pan of water, the floor and the block, were all encarnadined. Cole caught the scent of blood and he surmised that it was human.

He went down three curving stone steps, confronted the aproned man. "Who are you?" he demanded. "And do you realize what you're doing?"

"My name's Tom Grady. I just work here. I got to follow orders, ain't I? What if I go home some night and the missus finds out I ain't got this goodpayin' job any more?"

"The 'missus' won't like it much either," Cole answered laconically, "if the police drag you up for removing evidence. Fortunately for you, blood is indelible. Whose orders?"

"Why, Mr. Sutherland's."

COLE CLIMBED out of the dungeon. Bounding up the broad flight at the rear of the corridor, he heard faltering steps descending. Hugh Sutherland, velvet robe swishing, was venturing down. Cole stopped, tight-muscled facing him. "What happened?"

"I scarcely know. I was sleeping—sleeping heavily, because of the sedative. Something awakened me—it sounded like a struggle. I called for Dane, but there wasn't any answer. I was too weak to get up for a long time. When I went hunting for Dane—"

"Yes? Go on."

"All of Whitehall was silent. Something drew me to the Tower Room. I saw it—the blood. And—and—" Sutherland choked. "My only thought was to try to undo it, some-how—so Her Majesty would not know. I ordered the block cleaned—the whole room washed. Doctor Cole, in God's name—"

"Where is your son?"

"Here." The word was a mere breath. Sutherland stumbled down the flight, to an oaken door. He pushed it wide, quaking with anguish. Cole looked into the light of low-burning candles, at a still form lying on a huge ornate bed. The silken coverlet was stained by a flow that had poured from the stump of a beheaded man's neck.

Cole recognized the beruffled costume of the victim of the block, though it was ripped and torn almost off the headless body.

"Where is his head?"

"It's gone," the old man whispered huskily.

Carter Cole led him from the room, closed the door. He took Hugh Sutherland's shoulders firmly. "You must have a suspicion of who did it. Someone who slipped in while everyone was asleep, or someone who was waiting inside. You alone heard the sounds of a struggle. That man must still be here, or he stole out at once. You've got to tell me everything you know."

"But I know—only what I've already told you."

Cole straightened. "You have a telephone?"

Sutherland led him away. In a remote room on the highest floor he opened a period cupboard. Cole took out the modern instrument inside. Before he spun the dial, he said: "The police can no longer be kept out of this, but I'll do my utmost to hush it up. I've enough influence to manage that, I think, for a little while, but—I'll have only a few hours to attempt to nail the guilty man." The dial whirred under his flicking finger. "I'm calling Doctor Morse, the medical examiner."

CARTER COLE, emerging into a black-shrouded Fifth Avenue, drew a deep breath of crisp air. He had waited for the arrival of Doctor Morse, had explained matters with professional terseness, and elicited a promise of cooperation. Now he slid to Kelly's side, saying: "The girl's apartment, Brick—I phoned her, and she knows we're coming." He maintained an intense silence while the Duesenberg sped south along the deserted thoroughfare.

"Strange," he thought to himself, "that Hugh Sutherland has been completely unaware of the deaths of the Queen's subjects. Unless I can prove, and prove quickly, that Elizabeth had nothing whatever to do with the murders, her whole life will be tragically ruined, as well as her husband's—and the girl's—

He got out at Lyda Sutherland's apartment and his touch on her call button brought an immediate responsive clicking of the electric lock. He ran up the three flights, found her waiting in the open door. She was wearing a thin negligee over pajamas and looked worn with sleeplessness. Cole eased her into a chair, gave her a cigarette.

"The truth must come out now," he said quietly. "You made the waxen heads. Your brother sent them. Tonight, speaking to me on the phone, he suggested his reason. I must know the whole story."

The girl answered wearily: "First you must understand I'm estranged from Father. I disapproved strongly of his surrounding Mother with such elaborate pretense. We broke over it. Dane is as determined as Father to carry it through, for Mother's sake, but he's more understanding. He never held it against me because I refused to cooperate. I'm very fond of him. So when he came to me—"

"Go on."

"He told his theory about the deaths of Doctor Rutledge and Doris Lyon. He was convinced the murders had nothing to do with Mother. The costumes found on the bodies had been stolen from the wardrobe at Whitehall. It was all part of an elaborate plan of someone to shield himself by incriminating Mother—a woman unable to save herself. Dane was desperate."

"He knew," Cole agreed, "that once the law laid hands on his mother, she could find no escape. She would certainly be torn out of her make-believe world and thrown into a prison institution."

"Yes. He suspected a certain person but he had no proof whatever. He knew nothing could save Mother but a confession by the real murderer. He asked me to model heads of Doctor Rutledge and Doris Lyon, saying he was going to use them to try to break the nerve of the man he suspected and force a confession—but he begged me not to ask him who the suspect was. He was so in earnest I couldn't refuse him, especially because he said there was no one else he could turn to. He gave me photographs, told me exactly how he wanted the heads to look—and I made them."

"Thoroughly understandable."

"But later," the girl continued, "when he asked me to make the heads of Mr. Chamberlin and Doctor Lanne, I refused to do it until he told me more."

"Both," Cole pointed out, "men who had not yet felt the ax."

THE GIRL continued, growing more distressed every minute. "Yes—that was what upset me so. But Dane explained it. He had been reasoning out his theory logically. Tracing the personal connections of the two persons who had already died, he decided someone else would soon die the same way. He believed it was Rutledge's friend Chamberlin who was next in danger, or Doctor Lanne because Lanne was associated with Rutledge. This time he wanted to use the heads to warn them both."

"But still," Cole asked, "he didn't tell you the name of the suspect?"

"Nothing I could say would induce him to tell me. Before I finished the heads he became worried, because he was more and more convinced the murderer would strike again. He didn't wait, but went to see both men. Lanne was greatly alarmed. Chamberlin was close-mouthed, unwilling to take action on nothing more than a suspicion, but he promised to investigate independently."

"Yes?"

"Dane's plan," the girl continued, "was evidently not accomplishing its purpose. The murderer didn't succumb. Instead, he must have known almost at once who was sending the heads and why, because—"

Cole urged her on with intent silence.

"The third head—that of Mark Chamberlin—was stolen from Whitehall early today, before he was killed. Yet it was delivered the same as the others. That proves

Dane was sending them to the wrong person—that his suspicions were unfounded—that he was utterly mistaken. Because the murderer himself must have sent Chamberlin's head to—"

"Your brother," Cole said incisively, "believed that Herbert Metcalfe was guilty?"

The girl straightened in terror. "I tell you—he was wrong! It's someone connected with Whitehall—the third head proves it—but Dane was making a tragic mistake. I'm sure of it."

"You want with all your heart to think that," Cole said quietly, "because you love Metcalfe."

Lyda Sutherland jerked to her feet. "He isn't guilty! I know it's not true! Herb isn't capable of such a thing—he'd have no reason for it. Doctor Cole, I told you this because I thought you would believe me, would help me, but—" She began to sob. "I won't tell you anything more—not anything. Please go."

"You do know more," Cole urged. "I suspect you've deliberately garbled the truth. Unless you tell me the straight of it now—"

She whirled on him in tense fury. "No! I've told you all I'm going to. Now go!"

She ran into the adjoining bedroom; the door slammed. Carter Cole stood motionless a moment, baffled. Then he turned quietly and left the studio.

CHAPTER FIVE
THE CLUE IN THE CORPSE

KELLY SWUNG the Duesenberg to the curb in front of the city morgue on First Avenue. The growing light of dawn, blending into the chasms of the city, did not detract from the grisly dankness of the building. In and out of it passed a constant parade of the lifeless—unknown corpses, those dead by violence. Its scientific genius and official prober into the secrets of those deaths, was the eccentric Doctor Morse.

The attendant whom Cole accosted answered his question with, "The doc's inside, performing an autopsy."

Cole stepped into a small odorous room. Doctor Morse, white-capped, aproned, his hands clad in rubber gloves, was working with glinting instruments over the nude and headless body which lay on the slab. His grizzled vandyke wagged Cole a greeting as the keen edges made clean incisions. His manner was competent, undisturbed, cheerful.

"Perfunctory, old boy," he said. "There's no doubt how he died, but the law demands a thorough looking into him. Something on your mind?"

Cole smiled, admiring Morse's skilled technique. "A great deal, old-timer. No murderer can decapitate three men and a girl without leaving some loophole. You've been in this case from the beginning. What do you know?"

Morse continued delving while he spoke. "No loopholes that the boys have been able to find. This lad was killed, of course, in that apartment. The only possible witness is the lobby attendant and, so far as I could learn, he was too sleepy at that hour of the morning to remember who went up and came down, if anyone did. All around, a neat job."

"Chamberlin?" Cole asked.

"He was cut down inside his home, when no one else was there. The same with Rutledge and the girl. Both of them died in Rutledge's study. The murderer took time, mind you, to clean up the place afterward. It hasn't been published that we found traces of blood on the rug, two different types, one the doctor's and the other the girl's. The bodies must have been taken out the back way, in the early hours of the morning, when no one was about. And after slicing off Rutledge's head, the murderer took the machete with him."

"The machete?"

"That hasn't been published, either." Morse was working industriously. "Yes, the weapon of murder. It belonged to Rutledge. He brought it back several years ago from South America as a souvenir and kept it hanging on the wall beside his desk. Ugly thing—sharp and heavy enough to whack off a man's head at one blow. The murderer took it along."

"Why?"

"Perhaps," Morse answered, "through fear. Better than trying to remove fingerprints—taking the whole weapon. Perhaps, because he knew he'd need it again—if he'd left it, the police would have seized it."

"And perhaps," Cole opined, "his taking the machete was only a blind. Perhaps he used some other weapon—such as a sharp sword."

"Possible." Casually Morse was probing into the incised stomach of Dane Sutherland. "It's a veritable train of murder, old boy, one leading to the other—must be. Keeping this last one quiet is devilish ticklish business. The commissioner will howl down all his wrath on my old head. Maybe he'll order it chopped off, eh? If you don't produce a murderer for him in the meantime, we'll both be in hot water... Hello!"

"What's that?" Cole asked quickly.

MORSE HELD it up in the light, eyes sharpened. "Hello!" he said again. "Notice first that this lad wasn't killed without a stiff fight. Clothing was almost torn off him. Scratches and bruises on his body, not sharply defined because he died too soon afterward. But he fought his utmost, depend on that, old boy. Fought so desperately he bit off a joint of his assailant's forefinger."

Cole said quietly: "I see."

Morse continued, his voice quickening: "The first joint of the right index. Flesh raw and bone crushed. Bitten off—there's no other way to explain it. Neither of this lad's fingers is missing. This one evidently belongs to the man who beheaded him. A bit the worse for wear because of the action of the digestive juices, but damning evidence."*

Cole took the grisly object onto his palm. It was stained, and the ridges were partially obliterated, but the nail was neatly trimmed. Insane fury had empowered Dane Sutherland's teeth to clip this fingertip from the hand of a well groomed man. With a smile Cole replaced it in the dish.

---

* The fact that digestion continues for twenty-four hours after life ceases is sometimes helpful to the medical examiner in determining the time of death.—F.C.D.

"Interesting," Morse mused, "to speculate on just how the murderer's fingertip descended into his victim's stomach. In the fury of the fight the poor lad probably didn't even know he was sinking his teeth in a finger. Suppose, when he was biting on it powerfully, the murderer used his free hand to deliver a terrific blow to the boy's face or body. If to the jaw, the blow might have finished clipping the finger. If to the body, the backward jolt was enough to tear it off."

"The rest," Cole surmised, "purely involuntary reflex. Swallowing is easier than spitting out. Under intense emotional or physical strain, one gasps. The boy couldn't have deliberately swallowed the fingertip to provide us with a clue—it just went down in an instinctive gulp—but there it is. Perfect, conclusive evidence. It's going to send our murderer to the chair," Cole added quietly.

COLE SWUNG the Duesenberg into the court of the Fifty-seventh Street apartment house. His hand was lifting to the call button when the entrance opened. Herbert Metcalfe appeared, wearing topcoat, hat and gloves. He retreated warily. Cole stepped past him without speaking. Metcalfe followed into the library, eyes defiant.

Cole, gazing at the young man's gloved hands, asked: "Where is Doctor Rutledge's study?"

Metcalfe silently led him along a hallway. Cole opened the door of a warmly furnished consulting-room walled with bookcases loaded with technical tomes, containing two desks. His eyes rose at once to an unshelved space between two windows looking out the rear of the building.

Two hooks were embedded in it. Faded wallpaper outlined the object which had hung there—a knife eighteen inches long, with a blade an inch and a half across.

Cole opened another door, looked into a rear court overshadowed by surrounding buildings, then returned to the library.

He observed to Metcalfe: "I'm becoming convinced the murders have no connection with Mrs. Sutherland, except that someone deliberately wished to direct suspicion toward her."

Metcalfe remained silent.

"Whether the murderer's plan was built up before or after Doctor Rutledge's death," Cole continued, "doesn't matter. The fact that Rutledge played the Duke of Norfolk in the court of Queen Elizabeth, and his secretary played Mary, Queen of Scots, fitted into the picture perfectly. Their deaths were not the command of a demented woman. A stronger motive lies behind them all."

Metcalfe's lips pressed.

"Motives," Cole went on, "are fundamentally few. Murderers kill for financial gain, or to escape something, or out of revenge, or because they are insane. In this case, insanity is only apparently the motive, masking the real one. To judge from what I've heard of Doctor Rutledge, he had no enemies. No one, so far as we know, gained financially by his death. One possibility remains. He was killed because the murderer was desperate to escape some danger with which Rutledge was threatening him.

"Let us," Cole suggested, "follow the idea through. Rutledge possessed knowledge of a purpose which would destroy the man who murdered him. In her capacity as his secretary Miss Lyon must have learned of it. Perhaps it was through a letter dictated by Rutledge, addressed to his friend Chamberlin, an attorney. An easy supposition which quite fully explains the connection between the deaths. The murderer silenced those whose knowledge menaced him. Of course, he immediately destroyed the letter and its carbon."

Metcalfe braced himself.

"The death of Dane Sutherland," Cole went on—Metcalfe's eyes widened at the news—"was again motivated by escape. The young man suspected the murderer. The murderer knew it, silenced him. Perhaps, now, the cycle of beheadings is at an end. The murderer may no longer face exposure, except by the police, or by me. You, Metcalfe, are no doubt finding yourself in a very trying position."

Metcalfe at last spoke, one explosive word. "Why?"

"You have no funds of your own. You are wholly dependent for your daily living, as well as your entire future career, on the generosity of Doctor Lanne. But it's possible for you now to come into a great deal of money. In this way, Metcalfe. If Mrs. Sutherland is judged guilty of murder, if Hugh Sutherland dies soon as he surely will, there will be only one person left to inherit his fortune now that Dane Sutherland is dead—Lyda, the girl you are engaged to marry."

Metcalfe tensed as if to spring. "You dare say—"

"I dare say," Cole interrupted quietly, "you could wish, at the moment, for a more comfortable situation." His gaze lowered speculatively to Metcalfe's gloved hands.

Metcalfe stepped forward grimly. "Meaning exactly what?"

COLE TOLD him bluntly. "Dane Sutherland sent the wax heads to this apartment. He suspected either you or Doctor Lanne guilty of the murders. He was trying to break one or the other of you. His plan was disrupted, but his suspicion is still to be reckoned with. How do you answer that?"

Metcalfe's eyes blazed. "You may believe me guilty if you wish, Doctor Cole, but I won't tolerate anyone's suspecting Doctor Lanne. He has been wholeheartedly generous to me. I insist upon his name being cleared as soon as possible. I suggest that you place all your information in the hands of the police without further delay."

Cole's eyebrows arched. "So?"

"Precisely. Let the law proceed as far as the facts merit. Doctor Lanne may even be brought to trial, but I'm positive he can never be convicted. His acquittal will prove his innocence. Anything, even newspaper sensationalism, will be better than whispered innuendos about him."

Cole asked quietly: "Are you really so earnest about clearing Doctor Lanne's name—or are you trying to cover yourself at his expense?"

Metcalfe tensed to strike. At that moment a key clicked in the entrance. Cole waited for the blow, but Metcalfe tightly withheld it. Footfalls came along the hallway and Doctor Lanne strode into the library. His pace slowed when he found Cole and Metcalfe belligerently confronting each other. He tossed aside his hat, ceased tugging at his gloves as he stepped close.

"What the devil's up?"

"Have you anything further to say?" Cole asked Metcalfe.

"Nothing!"

"Doctor Lanne," Cole inquired, "are you able to throw any light on the murder situation?"

"I scarcely know what to answer. I'm more than willing—"

Cole's impatience was at the breaking point. "Never," he said, "have I met a more reticent lot of people. Nobody is telling the whole truth. Everybody is holding something back. The whole thing is assuming the character of a problem in silence. I'm determined to do something drastic about it."

"Perhaps you're right," Metcalfe retorted, "but after all you're not an official investigator."

Cole smiled. "Gentlemen," he remarked, "I have no authority to oblige you to do anything. You may refuse any request of mine and be fully within your rights. I hope, though, you will humor me by coming to the Sutherland home within the hour. Time presses—the situation is urgent. May I expect you?"

"Certainly," Lanne answered.

"Yes," Metcalfe forced out.

Cole bowed. He was slipping into his Chesterfield and Homburg when the entrance buzzer sounded. Lanne strode past him. Cole stood near the opening door and heard the starter outside say: "A package, Doctor." A slow breath sucked into Lanne's lungs. Cole eyed the brown-wrapped box resting in the physician's trembling hands, and saw the fact which Lanne expressed in a burst.

"It's like the others!"

Lanne strode feverishly into the library, placed the box on the table. Metcalfe eyed it haggardly. Cole strode alertly to the physician's side. He said briskly: "I've already told you a wax head has been fashioned in your image, Doctor. You were right at the beginning—they were partly in the nature of warnings. Now the murderer is still desperately trying to cover himself. Another reason, of course, for wasting no time about getting on with the matter."

Lanne nodded tensely as Cole broke the cords, stripped off the stiff paper, thumbed the box lid up. With a quick snatch he tore out the packing of tissue. He stood rigid, peering at the head.

Its pallid features were turned upward. The mouth was lax, the cheeks impassive, the eyes closed as if in sleep. Cole immediately recognized the face.

Through the corners of his eyes he watched Herbert Metcalfe. Then he said quietly into the hush: "This head, gentlemen, is not wax. It is flesh and blood. It was cleaved from the body of Dane Sutherland by the headsman's ax, in London Tower, this morning.... I will meet you there, gentlemen, in exactly one hour."

CHAPTER SIX
THE QUEEN'S HEADSMAN

CARTER COLE stepped, in company with Brick Kelly, into the vestibule of the establishment called Whitehall. The passage was stirring with sounds of activity filtering from the rooms of the court attendants. Signaling Kelly to wait, Cole passed through an oaken door, paused at the side of the huge ornate bed on which Hugh Sutherland lay.

"My thanks," he said quietly, "for granting me a free hand. I promise I'll do my utmost not to disturb Her Majesty. I hope, sincerely, you'll not regret it."

"Anything, anything, to end this torture, to free us of suspicion," Sutherland murmured.

Cole quietly withdrew. With Kelly at his heels he entered an unoccupied room near the head of the stone stairs. They heaved up a weighty, long Tudor refectory table. Cole added a silken pillow to it. They carried it out, down the curving flight.

Whitehall was awakening. The royal day was beginning early. A few costumed men and women were moving in and out of the doors along the passages. Careful that the Queen herself should not glimpse them, Cole hurried Kelly down the second flight with the table teetering between them. They went into the room reproduced from the Tower of London, where Dane Sutherland's head had dropped.

Cole noted that it had been thoroughly scrubbed and cleaned, that the murderous ax had been removed. He placed the table beside the block, noting two doors at the sides of the chamber. He looked through one, along a dim passage, then crossed to the other. It opened into a longer corridor flanked by oaken portals. Cole's signal brought the bewildered Kelly to his side.

"Fade into one of those rooms," he said. "Remember instructions. It's a ticklish job, Brick—if we fail we'll never forget it. In fact, if you muff it, my friend, I'll have your head."

Cole watched him walk into the branched passage, try a door, ease out of sight behind it, leaving it slightly ajar. Cole closed the block room and, smiling with satisfaction, climbed to the top floor.

A familiar voice drew him back to Hugh Sutherland's bed. Lyda Sutherland was there, and she met Cole's gaze squarely.

"When I spoke to you on phone," he reminded her, "you promised to cooperate with me. You needn't speak unless you wish to, but please follow my suggestions. Your whole world is at stake. You may soon find it crashing around you, but there is no other chance of saving it. If anything should happen which you might not think well of, I beg you beforehand to forgive me."

"What do you mean?" she asked in alarm.

"I can't explain now. Come with me."

He led her along the passage, down both stone flights and opened the door to the Tower Room. The girl hesitated, then entered, repressing a shudder. He took her hat and coat, escorted her to the table, then helped her to a sitting position on it.

"I've chosen this room," he said, "not only for psychological reasons, but because in it we are the least likely to be disturbed. Don't be afraid. You're overwrought—if you don't get some rest, you might collapse. This will help you relax."

He brought a silver case from his pocket. From it he removed a hypodermic syringe. To the syringe he affixed a glittering needle. He filled the barrel with the contents of an ampule, swabbed the girl's arm with a ball of cotton wet with iodine. She offered no resistance. He plunged the needle home, discharged the barrel, cleaned the stain away with alcohol.

"I'm going to stay with you a while," he said. "Stretch out on the table. Rest your head on the pillow." He helped her lie at full length. "Please reconsider your decision while you relax. Are you still determined to tell me no more of what you know?"

"I'll never tell."

"Very well. Are you beginning to feel drowsy?"

"Yes."

"Yield to it. Your nerves demand it. You'll be sound asleep soon. You've done everything now I had in mind to ask you. You needn't utter another word unless you wish."

"You can't make me—tell."

"I know."

COLE GLANCED again and again at his strap watch as the girl lay still. Her breathing became slower, deeper. Her heavy lids closed. At the end of fifteen minutes Cole deftly repeated the injection. Even when he administered the third dose of the drug the girl did not succumb completely to sleep, merely seemed to lie resting in deep repose. He pocketed the syringe case, pressed her hand.

"You'll feel much better soon."

He went quietly to the door, stepped out, remained a moment listening. Quickly he climbed the two stone flights. Around the throne-room, he noticed as he passed, more and more of the colorful Elizabethan personages were gathering. He found Sutherland still in bed, both arms hidden under the covers.

"I'm feeling stronger, Doctor Cole. Can I be of help—before I answer the summons to appear before the throne?"

"Merely wait."

Cole walked along the passage into the vestibule. He glanced at his watch impatiently as he waited. Soon a whirring noise throbbed through the panel, signifying the ascent of the elevator. The door slid open to disclose Herbert Metcalfe and Doctor Lanne. Cole took Lanne's arm, remarked to Metcalfe: "I wish to see the doctor alone a moment. Wait here, if you will."

He led Lanne to the end of the corridor, into the room from which he had removed the table. He said, "One moment," and went out. He returned to Sutherland's room, then to Lanne's carrying a brown-wrapped bundle. Once the door was closed behind him, he peeled the paper away from before the physician's startled eyes. A colored, waxen likeness remarkably resembling the nervous man who stared at it was revealed. Cole placed it on a small stand.

"This," Cole said, quietly, "might already have been sent to your apartment if Dane Sutherland had not died so suddenly. He, of course, would have sent it. His sister insists he was acting upon mistaken suspicions. I am giving it over to you because, as you already know it, it was meant to be a warning."

Lanne, staring at the head, licked dry lips. "What am I to do?"

"I want you on hand. I am sure that very soon I shall have positive results. Miss Sutherland is in the Tower Room now, passing under the influence of scopolamin."*

Lanne's eyes widened.

"You're familiar with the action of the drug?" Cole asked. "It will, I'm sure, induce her to reveal information nothing else could ever bring to light. Soon I will ask her questions, and she'll tell me the truth because she'll be unable to hold it back any longer. An absolute necessity, Doctor, believe me. And, at the same time, a risk. Please stand ready to aid me in case the drug should have a toxic effect upon her."

"Of course!" Lanne blurted. "I'll do everything possible."

Cole nodded. "Good. In the meantime, it's best she stay alone a while."

He stepped from the room. Lanne, looking again at the waxen head, shuddered, tossed his hat aside, shrugged to remove his overcoat. Cole closed the door, went back to the vestibule, found Metcalfe nervously waiting. He took Metcalfe's arm, descended another staircase to the floor,

---

* Scopolamin, called "truth serum," a drug made from henbane, has the strange property of rendering inoperative certain inhibitory centers of the brain, but at the same time it leaves unaffected the memory, hearing and power of speech. The part of the mind affected is that used in fabricating falsehoods. A person under the influence of the drug is therefore in possession of his normal faculties except that he cannot lie! Besides, scopolamin has the power of salvaging information out of the subconscious which the patient is no longer aware he knows. The drug is, however, a dangerous one to use and an overdose may prove fatal. Properly administered, it is amazingly effective, though evidence produced in this way is still, due to traditional procedure, inadmissible in court.—F.C.D.

where the Tower Room was located, steered the young man behind the door of a small chamber, closed it.

Head cocked as if listening, he said: "Lyda is protecting you—of that there's no doubt. She's ready to suffer any consequences rather than see you harmed. She's completely in love with you, and nothing means more to her than your wellbeing. Surely you feel the same about her; you'll do as much for her. Now is the time for you to speak—the last chance you'll have before the police take charge."

Metcalfe said stiffly: "I have nothing to say. I don't know what the devil you're driving at, Cole, but—you'll get nothing out of me. Is Lyda here?"

"She is, yes. You're to remain in this room until I come back for you—understand that strictly. I hope you realize that already your position is precarious enough."

COLE STEPPED out, closed the door. He listened a moment, then strode to the entrance of the Tower Room. He looked through a crack. The stone chamber was silent. Even the slow, steady breathing of the girl lying on the table was soundless. Avoiding, as much as possible, the gathering attendants of the living Queen Elizabeth, Cole again climbed the two flights to the room of Hugh Sutherland.

Alarm shone in Sutherland's eyes as Cole softly said: "I suggest that you join Her Majesty. In case of an unavoidable disturbance, please do everything possible to keep it from upsetting her. I hope, in a few moments to have information which will keep her safe from all danger."

Cole glanced at his watch, went out. At the door of the Tower Room he again paused to listen. The bustle filling Whitehall was a muted murmur here. Hidden behind walls decorated with heraldry, the maze of branch passages absorbed the sounds whispering from above. The awakening of a living day out of dead history made Cole feel strangely like an unworldly intruder. He was starting away from the Tower Room when a sound—a sharp click—stopped him.

With quick, soundless movements he opened the heavy door a crack. The chill chamber was still empty, save for the girl lying inert on the table. He drew back, closing the portal. Eyes glittering with sudden suspicion, he turned toward the small room in which he had left Herbert Metcalfe. When he opened it an astonished burst of breath passed his lips.

It was empty. Metcalfe had left.

Cole hurried back to the Tower Room. Again he heard—and this time more distinctly—a metallic click. It echoed within the closed stone cavern. With the utmost care Cole released the latch, eased the oaken door open merely a line. He peered through it, diagonally across the chamber where the headsman's block sat and the semi-conscious girl lay. The door at the far side was slowly opening.

Abruptly it swung wide. A horrifying figure appeared. It was a tall man, clad in close-fitting black. A leather apron was bound around his waist. A black mask, shielding his features, enhanced the evil glitter of his eyes. In his hands, gloved in bulky leather, he was gripping the brass-studded shaft of the heavy headsman's ax. He glanced around once, swiftly, then heaved the blade high.

Carter Cole's right hand sped to his arm-pit holster. With swift dexterity he slipped his 9mm Luger into his palm. It poked through the crack of the oaken door as the black-masked headsman's muscles strained to drive the gleaming ax upon the throat of the unsuspecting girl.

Cole thrust the door wide. The Luger cracked twice, swiftly. Rattling echoes mingled with Cole's sharp call— "Brick!" Then he bounded in, narrowed eyes searching for the effect of his bullets.

One second the masked headsman stood poised—but with the shaft of the ax splintered above his head. One of Cole's slugs had drilled through it. The blade was wavering on a thin stem of wood. Bright red, pouring from a gash in one black sleeve, was trickling off the right elbow of the headsman.

"Close in on him, Brick!"

The headsman lurched back. He made a desperate, convulsive effort to slash the ax to the girl's neck. The snapping action cracked the thin wood supporting the blade. The weapon which whipped downward was merely a stick with a splintered end. The heavy steel head clanged to the floor. With a gasp the masked headsman whirled to leap out.

In the passage Brick Kelly snapped: "Come ahead—try it!"

THE HEADSMAN spun. He bounded across the Tower Room—into the arms of Carter Cole. Cole thrust him back, squared, drove out a straight left. His knuckles smashed against soft leather. The headsman whirled, dove. Brick Kelly leaped, crunched down on the squirming black body, poised a revolver to strike.

"Be good!" he warned.

Cole was aware that the corridor door was opening, that someone was coming in, but his concern was for the girl. She still lay on the table. Her only response to the gun reports was the slow opening of her eyes. Cole crossed to her, took her hand. He whispered: "Don't be afraid. It's all over. Now you may tell us. You know whom your brother suspected."

Her answer was scarcely audible: "Yes."

"Why did you withhold it?"

"Because Herb's whole future was at stake—his whole life—with me or without me."

"Dane even knew why the murders were committed, though he couldn't prove it?"

"Yes—because he was here the night Father almost died."

"The murderer was desperately trying to save himself from the consequences of—what?"

"Criminal—malpractise."

Cole straightened. He stepped to Kelly's side. Kelly was pinioning the masked headsman. Cole took the black-clad man's right, gloved hand. He pulled the glove away, peered at the closely bandaged index finger. He stripped the gauze off, briefly inspected the stump from which the first joint had been bitten. Smiling tightly, Cole thumbed under the headsman's mask, tore it down.

"You played your part well," he said quietly, "from beginning to end. Sending the third wax head to yourself, then the real one to divert suspicion. Deliberately carrying out Dane Sutherland's plan because it suited your first purpose, to make the murders seem the work of an insane person. We've evidence against you now you simply can't escape. You were guilty of the act you blamed Doctor Rutledge for."

Jerome Lanne sagged against the floor. "Why— why should I deny it now? Yes, I was the one who gave Hugh Sutherland the overdose of phenobarbital. I was drunk. Rutledge was outraged—determined to remove me from practise. He wrote Chamberlin about what had happened—they were going to have my license revoked, make a criminal charge against me. Either way, it was my life—and murder was a better chance."

Cole looked around. Hugh Sutherland, in scarlet robe, had hurried into the Tower Room with Herbert Metcalfe. The medical student was bending over the girl on the table. "Lyda!" he was saying. "I've been trying to find you—looking everywhere."

Cole went to his side, bent low. Understanding shone in the girl's eyes as he said: "Don't worry. Herb's career need no longer depend on Doctor Lanne. After this there'll be another man sponsoring him, until he has a practise of his own. His new patron is named Cole."

Cole looked up as Hugh Sutherland hurried from the Tower Room. He followed into the corridor. Brick Kelly kept Lanne pinned down. Metcalfe hovered over Lyda Sutherland, murmuring reassurances. As Lanne strove to rise, Kelly vociferously snarled him into submission.

At that moment Carter Cole reappeared in the door. "Quiet," he urged. "Quiet, if you please, Brick. Queen Elizabeth is holding court."